WHERE THE
WATERS
TURN
BLACK

BENEDICT PATRICK

Where the Waters Turn Black
Copyright 2016 Benedict Patrick
All rights reserved.

www.benedictpatrick.com

Cover design by Jenny Zemanek
www.seedlingsonline.com

Published by One More Page Publishing

ISBN: 1539624579
ISBN-13: 978-1539624578

CONTENTS

ACKNOWLEDGEMENTS

Okay, here we go…

A huge thanks to my original supporters who have continued to grace me with their time for my second book:
My continuing adoration and love to Adele, clearly one of my 'better' readers.
Thanks to Kat, for the level of detail, enthusiasm, and your ongoing love of spiders.
Tip of the hat to Craig, for persevering despite the lack of swords.
To Graham, for spreading the word.
To Mark, for finishing.
To the men who went unnamed last time, who certainly should have been: Aaron, Brian, Elvis and Jeff - shooting the breeze with you guys continues to be inspirational.

Also, a thanks to the newcomers to the team, who each have had a hand in shaping this book:
Ash, for going above and beyond, and for convincing me this was a story worth reading.
Ágnes, for applying your superhuman Knack for finding mistakes that everyone else misses.
To Sean, Rory, Jacinta (my second mum), Mum (my actual mum), Dad, and Helen, for supporting me and helping get this one past the final hurdles.

To the readers of *They Mostly Come Out At Night* who got in touch with me to tell me what they thought, told others what they thought, or left reviews of my book. We didn't always get to speak directly, but every one of you brought a smile to my face and kept me going.

To the amazing community of fantasy authors I am now discovering, especially the SPFBO crew. I love you all for the mutual support and camaraderie, I hate you all so very, very much for your overflowing wellsprings of talent.

And finally, a huge thanks to my brother, Connor, for reading my book despite getting laughed at for doing so. That means more to me than you know.

CHAPTER ONE

"There's a monster in the village."

Kaimana raised her eyebrows at the toddler's words. "No, don't worry. There's no taniwha here."

The young girl was not convinced. She stuck out her bottom lip, kicked up some of the sand at her feet and stared at Kaimana. "No, there is. In the cave in the hills where the stream comes to life. My uncle went to catch it, and he never came back."

Kaimana had been visiting the village's banana grove to gather food for her troupe when the toddler had tugged at her dress and started to chat. Kaimana smiled at the girl's stubbornness. In many ways, it reminded her of herself at that age. She turned to look up at the mountain that rose above the small fishing village, recalling memories of her own childhood, and was surprised at how sad those memories made her feel. "Don't fear. I used to live here. I spent most of my life exploring those hills and I know the cave you speak of. It's always been empty. There are no monsters."

The little girl shook her head again. "I know you. You left. The taniwha is new, it came two months ago. We have a taniwha now."

Kaimana looked about the small village, at the woven huts and the sandy paths that had been formed by generations of fishing folk - her family and former friends - going about their daily lives.

She frowned. *Why would a small child say such things? Has an older brother been telling stories to frighten her at night? Nothing as interesting as a taniwha appearing has ever happened on Pukotala.*

Pukotala was the only settlement on the small island, although some individuals had chosen to erect their own huts in other remote parts of the small patch of green. The island itself was not large. You could walk around it within a couple of hours, as Kaimana often had as a child. However, if a taniwha wanted to make its home here then there would be plenty of nooks and crannies it could crawl into. The island was ringed by yellow sandy beaches, but inland the ground quickly rose to a peak, forming the hills and green mountain that Kaimana knew so well. Kaimana had visited islands with taniwha before, but they had been either well-known and well-avoided threats, or they were dealt with quickly by the war god and his warriors. Some were even seen as blessings, protectors of their islands. Those taniwha, however, tended not to eat people.

"What kind of taniwha is it?" Kaimana asked, her curiosity piqued. "Who's seen it?"

The girl shrugged. "It's big. The chief's man has seen it, and a few of our farmers. It's big enough to eat people. It ate my uncle, and two others."

Kaimana looked about, shaking her head. The rest of the village were preparing for the festival, carrying food and drink to the beach for the feast. None of them seemed particularly concerned for their lives.

No, no monster here. Why then, is this child so certain? Who's been telling her these tales?

"Are we safe here?"

"Safe enough. They've taken care of it. They leave it food, and it leaves us alone. The chief made contact with the god of war, and he'll send his warriors to deal with it, soon. Mother isn't happy, she says it brings bad luck to have a taniwha on the island."

"I'm sure she does," Kaimana muttered. *It's also bad luck to have a cheeky daughter who has to be put in her place with stories to scare her.*

The toddler looked startled, as if she was suddenly aware she was talking to a stranger. Kaimana watched the child leave, looking for friends or family to play with.

"Hope you enjoy the celebrations," Kaimana called after her, smiling, watching the toddler find her mother and tug on the older woman's woven dress. The girl's mother listened to her daughter say something, then raised her eyes, searching for the stranger her little girl was speaking about. Kaimana gave the woman a wave, and the mother responded in kind, a look of recognition dawning on her face as she did so.

Guess they've not completely forgotten me, yet.

Kaimana was from Pukotala, but it had been three years since she had called the island her home. She had family here, but it was the people she travelled with that she was now closest to.

She made her way out of the grove, carrying the required provisions, her bare feet taking her quickly along the sandy path. Like many Atoll villages, Pukotala was a small collection of wooden huts thatched with dried palm leaves. It was a fishing settlement, built on the edge of the tree line, to give easy access to the water these people needed for their livelihoods, and it did not take Kaimana long to reach the beach. Her troupe's twin-hulled canoe was berthed here, moored alongside a man-made pier of boulders that stretched into the blue ocean. Her new family were on the beach, already attracting attention from the villagers after just an hour of arrival, small crowds of children gathering in groups around each of the performers, straining and nudging each other to get a better view.

Kaimana smiled. *I remember the excitement when a troupe of performers arrived on the island. It's the same all over the Crescent Atoll, on each of the dozens of islands I've visited - everyone loves when we come to perform.*

The largest crowd had gathered around the dancers. Kaimana pushed her way past the onlookers to find Old Man Rawiri - the eldest member of their band by a good generation - barking orders at his girls, seemingly unhappy with a particular foot movement that one of them could not get correct. Kaimana admired the dedication from these dancers, as she always did. Not one of them reacted to Rawiri's taunts, but instead all had pleasant smiles on their faces, doing their best to please the crowds and to please their goddess. For her own part, Kaimana could not spot the mistake that continued to anger Rawiri. All three of the girls had strong Knacks for dancing - magical gifts that allowed them to excel in their art - and to Kaimana's eyes their movements were perfect.

Eloni the pipe player accompanied the performance. Again, Kaimana admired this woman's gifts, her music, but this time Kaimana's admiration came grudgingly. One of the local children crept closer to Eloni than the rest of the crowd, and Eloni shot the child a look of pure scorn, causing him to run uneasily back to his mother. Eloni was a malcontent, always unhappy, and even now Kaimana could sense the unsatisfied sneer that threatened to break out on her tattooed jaw.

What is that woman's problem with the world? The gods have decided to make her beautiful, and she's the most successful of the troupe. Why can't she accept the gifts she's been given and be happy with them? If I ever become as accomplished as Eloni - WHEN I become as accomplished, if not better - that'll be enough for me. I'll let myself be happy and not keep looking for more.

On the islands the troupe visited, Eloni would always go out of her way to catch the eye of the important men there, the chiefs and their commanders. Indeed, a few months ago Aka was worried the troupe was going to lose Eloni, that a baby was on its way and marriage offers were on the horizon. Fortunately for the performers, Eloni continued to voyage with them, although she had not been happy about leaving that island. The chief's wife, however, had been particularly pleased with Eloni's removal. Kaimana had felt justice had been done, that Eloni's plot to seduce the chief had not worked, but with a little guilt, she would also have been relieved if Eloni had not continued to travel with the troupe.

Eloni was gifted with a strong Knack for the *koauau*, the flute. Like most musicians and artists, her Knack was a subtle one. Unlike the more mundane Knacks, which were sometimes accompanied with amber sparks of magic from a user's eyes, artistic Knacks could be difficult to spot. Often it took a trained ear to hear when a musical Knack was at work, to realise that a wind instrument was being played to perfection, to spot the musician's fingers moving effortlessly between different notes. The easiest way to spot a musical Knack at work was the effect it had on a crowd, such as the small group of older girls that were currently seated around Eloni. The young women were swaying in time to Eloni's seductive tune, their heads rising and falling ever so slightly with the pitch of Eloni's notes. Kaimana raised a disapproving eyebrow to see that the women - the girls - were breathing quickly, letting themselves be caught up in the passion that Eloni channelled through her songs.

Eloni had a number of tunes - two in particular - that were well known throughout the Atoll islands. Twice in her life so far, Eloni claimed to have sparked. Her Knack, her gift for music, had flared up and she had been inspired to compose a masterpiece, a song that would endure for all time throughout the many islands of the Atoll. When a musician's Knack began to spark, there was usually some kind of inspiration behind it. Eloni claimed that each of these sparkings had happened after a particularly heated affair, and the subject matter of her songs was therefore highly passionate. Many in the troupe did not believe that Eloni had truly sparked, as it had been before she joined them, and it rarely happened with musical Knacks - she was probably the only living person on the Atoll to have made such a claim. Kaimana had spent many a time with Kiki and Travake, two of the dancers, giggling behind Eloni's back when she was telling the tale of her spark to impressionable islanders.

Nevertheless, Eloni's songs were popular, her presence was a great boon to Aka's small troupe, and Kaimana could not disagree with the woman's skill. Kaimana would happily spend hours listening to Eloni's tunes, if she could only detach the woman's art from her temperament. Now Eloni played in tandem with grumpy Rawiri who was beating on his drum to give the girls an energetic rhythm to swing their arms and hips to. Eloni caught sight of Kaimana and rolled her eyes.

Eloni was not fond of Kaimana.

At first, Kaimana had been confused when she had elicited this reaction from Eloni after joining the troupe. From what she could tell, Kaimana had done nothing that could have offended the woman. However, as Kaimana had got to know her new family, Eloni's issues became clear. When visiting a new island, Eloni was icy towards any attractive women she came across. She did not want any competition for the eyes of potential lovers. Kaimana was pleasant enough to look at, but Eloni should not have worried about her, as Kaimana was plain compared to striking Eloni and her jade facial tattoos. However, Kaimana found herself in the unenviable position of being the only woman in the troupe who could pose any kind of competition to Eloni and her appeal to men. The three dancers, Lose, Travake and Kiki, were totally dedicated to their Knacks and to Laka, their goddess. Like many dancing Knacks, this was a lifelong vocation for them, and it was general knowledge that dancing girls were not available to be brides, despite the fact that all three girls were beauties. That left only turtle-faced Poli, and poor Poli was clearly no threat to Eloni.

Kaimana also suspected Eloni did not like her because their Knacks were so similar. Kaimana had a Knack for music also, and the ocarina was her instrument of choice. It was unusual for more than one wind instrument to be present in a troupe as small as theirs, and Eloni had made this particularly clear during the fit she had thrown when Kaimana was first invited to join. Gentle Aka had simply shrugged, saying, "The girl is good. We need more good," and that was that. Worse still for Eloni, she had been asked to tutor Kaimana's raw talent, and had not taken to that task with much enthusiasm. Those sessions had been embarrassing for Kaimana to endure, because of how loudly Eloni would chastise her when she made the slightest mistake, shaming her in front of the others. Kaimana suspected Eloni saw her as an eventual replacement.

Leaving the dancing, Kaimana scanned the beach for Aka, wanting to find out about tonight's performance. The marionette team practised nearby, handsome Tokoni and turtle-faced Poli, and they were attracting a small crowd, but no Aka. Mahina, the chanting boy, sat on a large boulder at the end of the peer, looking out at the Inner Sea of the Atoll and the tall volcano that rose out of it. A few curious villagers made their way over the uneven pier to hear Mahina chant, but they soon decided to search for other entertainment after realising how melancholy a tale he was weaving. Mahina was the youngest member of the troupe, and the most recent. From the few conversations Kaimana had had with him, she had determined that Mahina's family were either all dead, or just did not want him around any longer. Mahina never smiled, and Kaimana guiltily hated spending time with him – he always lowered her spirits.

Kaimana eventually caught sight of Aka at a wrestling match over on the far end of the beach. Tonight was the harvest festival, the walk of the Long God, and today was time to celebrate. Earthen ovens were alight throughout the village, and the cooking Knacks were working hard to prepare food for the feast. The troupe had been summoned months ago to provide music and stories for the night, and to accompany the Long God on his walk to bless this year's crops. As was true of many Atoll islands at festival times, the men of Pukotala enjoyed taking time out of their busy routines to beat each other bloody to prove their superiority.

Kaimana took a brief glimpse at the scuffle that was currently taking place. Two young men, stripped down to only loincloths, were squaring off opposite each other in the middle of the circle that had been drawn out on the sand. Both were clearly strong, but Kaimana was not certain if either of them were warrior Knacks, or just fishermen or farmers whose natural strength had gotten them this far in the competition. Sunset and the beginning of the Long God's march was not that far away, so to have remained in the competition for so long was not just a sign of luck. The combatants yelled and grabbed for each other, one throwing the other down on the sand and screaming in his face, tongue protruding violently. Many in the audience gave shouts of admiration, particularly the young women. Kaimana did not join them.

Aka was not as wrapped up in the proceedings as most others appeared to be. As leader of the troupe, Kaimana knew he was expected to partake in some of the village's festivities, to show his respect to the people of the island his troupe was visiting. Kaimana also knew Aka well, and she knew his mind would not be settled until after the performance. She saw him now, eyes gazing at the wrestlers as they pummelled each other, and she could tell he was thinking about the performance. Which tunes should they play? Where should they position themselves in the parade? What could they do to ensure they are invited back next year?

He was a kind man, and although Aka was a good few years older than Kaimana, he was still considered to be very young for a leader of a performance troupe. Aka had been born into it - his parents had been in charge of the troupe before him, and when they both drowned five years ago, he had assumed leadership. The membership of the group had changed much since then - grumpy Rawiri was the only remaining member from Aka's parents' time - and Kaimana knew that the loss of the older players had been a blow to Aka. He wanted to honour his parents, and in order to do so, the troupe had to succeed, to continue to be asked to perform and to support celebrations throughout the Atoll. Playing for a small fishing village like Pukotala was not a great honour. The greatest honour for celebration of the harvest festival would be playing at the Long God's temple, but Aka's troupe could not dream of being summoned there. The group's name had diminished much since Aka's parent's days. The fame of Eloni's two tunes was the group's main draw, but there were other performers travelling the Atoll who were much better known, with larger troupes, and it was mostly these troupes who received the invites to important ceremonies. Aka would be happy to do well tonight, if the gods willed it.

For her part, Kaimana was happy with the troupe's size and success, for now. Aka did not provide fame, but he had given her a family, and for most of the others that was enough. Only Eloni would protest that she was not getting enough attention, and from time to time threatened to find another group to travel with, but so far had never followed through with her threats. Kaimana suspected none of the other troupes were interested in entertaining her affairs and her moods.

"Everything'll be fine," Kaimana assured Aka.

At the sound of her voice, Aka looked startled, but then smiled at sight of her. His eyes returned to the combat in front of him. "Doubtful. I had a wager on the red banded one. Can't see him winning now."

A cheer from the crowd showed that Aka was correct, the contestant with the green band on his arm was declared the victor.

"You've planned this well. We've been trained well. We do harvest festivals well."

Aka looked at her distractedly again. "Oh, this?" He waved his hand. "You're right, we can do this with our eyes closed. But this is the last performance before the big one, you know? That's the one that could really make a difference for us. We have to get it right tonight, to give everybody confidence for the Pig."

Kaimana should have known. Playing at the war temple in a few weeks would easily be the biggest honour Aka's troupe had been afforded since he had taken leadership. She could feel her own pulse quickening at the thought of playing in front of such a large audience, and in front of the war god himself, but then took a deep breath and closed her eyes.

Can't let myself get nervous now. No point in letting thoughts of that performance ruin the one tonight.

She looked at the troupe leader again, and found him gazing at Pukotala's mountain, his eyes on the green peak but his mind still elsewhere.

"There's a taniwha in the hills, you know," she said.

"What?" The panicked look on Aka's face was almost comical.

Kaimana smiled. "Don't worry, it's not true. Just a story a little girl told me. She said it lives in a cave up in the hills. I know those hills like the back of my hand. There were never any taniwha on the island when I lived here."

As she said this, Kaimana's eyes rose back to Pukotala's green mountain, and she pursed her lips.

It was a good story though, wasn't it? A taniwha in the hills. An uncle that never returned. A village under threat from an unseen monster.

"Doesn't it seem like a strange story for a little girl to tell?"

"Kaimana," Aka said, looking at her firmly. "Leave rumours well enough alone."

Kaimana smiled and shook her head, dismissing her leader's concerns. "There isn't a taniwha here, Aka. It was just a little girl, just a bedtime tale to keep her from misbehaving. I like the sound of it though, you know? Like, maybe there's a song in there that needs to be played?"

Aka knotted his forehead, distracted and stressed. "Do not go into those hills, Kaimana. I forbid it."

She turned to her troupe leader, shocked that he thought he had the authority to tell her what to do so sternly. His sudden air of superiority made her clench her fists in frustration.

Aka missed these signs of irritation, as he had already turned from her, walking back to the troupe canoe, shaking his head worriedly.

As Aka wandered off back to his players, Kaimana caught sight of the Long God standing on the edge of one of the village's stone piers, staring off towards the Atoll's central volcano. The god of the harvest wore a simple black cloak, a mask that Kaimana could not make out from this distance, but one that would show his flat face. He carried a tall staff decorated with crimson streamers. Kaimana shivered. It was traditional for the Long God and his brethren to visit and take part in the harvest celebrations.

This was, of course, not really the Long God. He would be at his own temple tonight, many day's journey away from Pukotala, taking part in celebrations there. It was more likely that one of the other farming gods would choose to bless a small village with their presence; possibly Kane, god of the sweet potatoes, fat Yam, or Haloa, god of the kalo root. However, none had chosen to visit Pukotala this year. Despite the fact that the gods of the Crescent Atoll often walked among their people, visiting them and blessing them with their presence, Kaimana had never seen a proper god before, at least as far as she knew.

Most of the rest of the troupe had. Just before Kaimana had joined them, Laka, goddess of performance, had chosen to accompany Aka's troupe for a few days as they travelled the Atoll. Anytime the others spoke of this humbling experience, Kaimana instantly felt like an outsider visiting a close-knit family, even after travelling with them for three years. Their time with Laka had clearly been a huge honour, and a very important part in the lives of most of the performers. Kaimana yearned to experience something similar herself. Eloni had soon realised how hearing about Laka made Kaimana feel, and she took ample opportunities to speak about the number of times she and Laka had accompanied each other on the flute as the troupe's canoe had moved between islands.

Such a happy time seemed so far away from the pressure that now weighed down on the troupe. A successful performance for Nakoa the pig god could attract the attention of other deities, could earn the troupe respect from the priests of other gods, thus securing more performances of this nature in the future.

Kaimana's eyes moved from the Long God to the huts of the fishing village, and sighed.

Well, if I'm going to do this, now would be the time.

She had another meeting she had been putting off for a while. With the knowledge they only had a few short hours before the performance, Kaimana went looking for her parents.

Kaimana's mother and father were fishing Knacks. Her mother specialised in pearl fishing, her father the net. They shared a small hut that was a short walk inland from the beach. Kaimana stopped in her tracks at the sight of her parent's home, drawing a deep breath as nostalgia rolled over her. This was where she had grown up. Part of her had been filled with joy when she had found out the troupe was finally returning to Pukotala, but she was also worried about how her parents would react upon seeing her again. They had not wanted her to leave.

Kaimana stood outside the dried grass door of the hut. "Mama? Papa?"

Movement inside betrayed the fact that at least one person was at home. The grass door parted and her mother's head emerged. "Kai?"

The older woman rushed forward and embraced Kaimana. Her mother had multiple lines of grey streaking through her hair, but other than that it was difficult for strangers to believe this woman was actually Kaimana's mother. "Preserved by the sea's salt," some would say, referring to the fact that Kaimana's mother looked a lot more youthful than she should. Despite this, Kaimana noticed a number of new lines across her mother's forehead when she held Kaimana back to study her face.

"Are you well? How are they treating you? What do you eat?" Her mother's eyes widened and she threw her head backwards. "Rua! Kai is here, Kaimana is home."

Kaimana's father emerged from the hut also, and she could not help but grin at the sight of him. He did look like a man in his forties, but had a large smile plastered over his face, as always. The jolliest fisherman in Pukotala, people often joked. Just as often they would attribute this jolliness to Rua's beautiful wife and two fine daughters.

He gathered Kaimana up in a similar hug. "My baby," he whispered.

Kaimana and her parents spent the next happy hour catching up. Her mother boiled some breadfruit and they sat on the ground outside their home, talking of distant family members, local village gossip and asking all about Kaimana's adventures with the troupe. However, as the conversation continued, the bright sheen of Kaimana's happiness upon seeing her parents started to waiver. More and more, their conversation turned away from interesting news about themselves and their friends, and turned to fishing, and their successes when fishing, and interesting facts about fishing if you happened to be remotely interested in fishing. Kaimana's attention began to drift as her mother started to talk about the pearls she had discovered in the years since Kaimana had left home.

Kaimana tried to change the conversation with a joke. "So, I was told today there is a taniwha in the village."

She was surprised to see how startled her mother and father were at the mention of the monster.

"It's real?" she said, but the looks on their faces answered her question for her.

11

"It's fine, we keep it happy," her father said. "After it ate some of our men, the chief decided to make it an offering of meat every week, so it bothers us no more."

Kaimana's eyes were large, and she felt suddenly uneasy, fighting a strong urge to look behind her, to the trees beyond her parents' home, in case something was lurking nearby.

"Are you sure? Who else has seen it?"

"Kai, don't go sticking that busy nose of yours into this, this is not for you," her mother warned.

Kaimana gave a short laugh. *Stick my busy nose in? I wish people would stop telling me not to go and see this creature. Why would anyone in their right mind want anything to do with a monster?*

"But, has anyone else actually seen the taniwha?"

Her parents looked uneasily at each other.

"Nobody alive has seen it," her father said. "The only one who returned to us after sighting the monster went back to its lair, and now he's no longer with us. They bring it meat, and when they return the following day, the meat is gone. We have a taniwha now, and we are fine."

"Perhaps it'll protect us," her mother ventured. "There are stories of lucky taniwha. You must know some."

Kaimana nodded absentmindedly, her mind busy with the notion of her familiar island suddenly harbouring a dark secret. There were tales of many different ilk of taniwha, beings made from magic by the gods or by great wizards. Some were fearsome beasts, destined to be tamed or vanquished by the warriors of the Atoll. Others were known for protecting the inhabitants of the islands. A river might have a particular taniwha attached to it, ready to defend the nearby villages from invasion by other islands, or by other monsters. Indeed, the Inner Sea inside the ring of islands created by the Atoll was known to be home to a taniwha in the shape of a white dolphin, who was said to help struggling canoes that ventured too close to the fiery goddess' volcano home. However, none of these helpful taniwha ever ate people.

The girl's story is true. Kaimana shuddered at the thought of the taniwha killing the men from the village, but at the same time there was something about the monster's closeness that intrigued her. *A taniwha lurking somewhere in the hills. What does it look like? How did it get here? So many unanswered questions.*

Kaimana realised her hands had absentmindedly made their way to the clay ocarina that hung from her belt, and her fingers were making the motions for a slow, slightly off-key tune that mirrored the dread she now felt. She shuddered.

"So... What are your plans now, darling?"

"Sorry?" Kaimana was taken aback by the question. She had been too busy contemplating the island's monster.

"Your mother and I were wondering, what are your plans after the harvest? Should we clear some room for you for a while?"

"Father..." Kaimana hesitated, picking up on the anxious looks from her parents. "We have a big performance coming up. For Nakoa. It'll be a great honour."

She trailed off. The disappointment on her parents' faces was painful. They had thought she was coming home.

"I see," her mother muttered, dejectedly. "I see."

And here it was. The same conversation they had had just before Kaimana left the first time. Her parents could just not contemplate a life outside the one they chose for themselves.

Kaimana shook her head. She could not help but feel angry with her mother and father for dismissing her calling. "What would I do if I stayed here? I have a musical Knack, I'm no fisherman. I'd be useless to you here, a burden."

"Yes, we know about the Knack," Kaimana's father said. "But you hear stories, you know. About people who develop more than one Knack. Or learn new ones. Or who think they have developed a Knack for something they really want to do, but they blind themselves to their true calling in life."

Kaimana stared at her father in open disappointment. *They know I'm no fishing Knack.*

"We'd hoped that maybe spending more time with your sister would help," her mother added.

"Yes, did you know last year she surpassed even your mother's record for pearls caught in a single season? She sparked three times last year. There are now plenty of young men eyeing her up for a future wife, when she comes of age."

Laka, preserve me. Preserve me again from pearl fishing and the eyes of young men who want to tie me down with a wedding band and children.

"Mother, father, I play the ocarina. This is me."

Her mother shifted awkwardly, and the older woman turned her eyes up to look at her husband. "Yes, dear, but..."

Kaimana's father finished the thought that both of them shared.

"But, what kind of future does this give you, playing your tunes? It's not as if you've achieved anything yet, have you? Your sister's Knack sparked three times in the last year. Three. Have you even sparked yet?"

"Sorry?" Kaimana realised her hands were trembling now, the anger and frustration she was feeling were brimming too close to the surface. She tucked her hands under her legs to get them back under control. "My Knack doesn't work like that. Musicians, artists, we don't really spark, most of us never will. Instead, we inspire other people with our songs, our stories. You know this, we spoke about it last time."

"When you left you made lots of big claims," her mother said. "Your name would be known all over the Atoll. The music you were going to make would be sung all over the islands."

Kaimana's cheeks burned at the memory of those words coming from her lips. *I had been so sure it would happen, that it'd be so easy once I was out there on the Atoll.*

"But we've heard nothing about you, and we've asked. Every musician, every traveller who visited the island. None of them had heard of you."

"Is it too soon?" her father said. "Does it take this long for your songs to make their way around the Atoll?"

"Chief Hiapo says most musicians and storytellers die as paupers." It was Kaimana's mother speaking again, but Kaimana found she could no longer look at her parents as they barraged her with questions. *It's like you've been practising this conversation, this lecture. I bet you've both been talking about this ever since you learnt the troupe was coming back.*

Her mother continued. "He said it's only after musicians are gone that their work is remembered. Is this what you want?"

Her father took her hand, but Kaimana was unable to return his gentle squeeze. "We want to hear your music. Let us hear you play, play us something you have written."

Kaimana looked at them both, with teeth clenched. *I have nothing to play for you. I'm still learning. I've had no... inspiration. Yet.* Her parents' questions forced Kaimana to admit her deepest shame. Despite her years travelling the Atoll, visiting most of the inhabited islands on the northern curve of the Atoll Ring, she had no achievements to tell them about. Certainly nothing to rival a record catch of pearls.

She stood stiffly. She loved her parents, but right now she was doing her very best to stop herself from screaming at them. "You'll hear me tonight, during the festival. I should go now. I need to prepare."

She hurried down the path back to the beach, frustrated at the lone tear that escaped her eye as she pounded the dirt with her feet, using her heavy steps as a small release for her anger.

In the three years she had been away, she had seen ten times more of the world than most born on Pukotala, but there had been very little Kaimana had felt worthy of committing to song. Life in the troupe was a life of work - practising her ocarina, helping man the canoe when at sea, chores when they were ashore. Not the stuff of legends to entertain crowds of people. Kaimana knew how to compose, and had a few casual ditties to her name, but they were born from small, unimportant moments, like a particularly brilliant shoal of fish she spotted under the troupe canoe one morning, or watching island children climb trees to steal coconuts. Certainly nothing she was willing to play for her parents as proof of her art.

But I know I have it in me to make something great once the opportunity finally comes. At that, she raised her eyes to the mountain towering above the village, squinting at the sun setting behind the tall peak. *That is, if the people around me allow me to get out there and live my life a little.*

Her nose wrinkled as she thought of Aka and her parents commanding her to stay away from the rumoured danger. Then, she lowered her gaze to her own hand, confused. She continued to clutch the ocarina at her belt, her fingers still subconsciously making the motions for the ominous, unfamiliar tune they had begun when her parents had confirmed the existence of the taniwha.

Kaimana looked back at the mountain, heart beating slightly faster, a nervous smile forming on her lips. A distant buzzing, possibly the ringing of a bell, seemed to be sounding in her head. She narrowed her eyes as she contemplated the setting sun.

A couple of hours before we start to play. If I'm quick and careful, nobody will ever know I've been gone.

Kaimana watched the sun begin to dip itself into the waters of the

Outer Sea, well beyond the limits of the Crescent Atoll. From her vantage point on the steep hillside of her island, she had a good view of much of the Atoll. The Atoll was a wide ring of small islands, a ring that would take weeks, if not months to circumnavigate. Within this ring, surrounded by deep blue waters that were good for fishing, but were dangerous for people to sail on, stood the tall volcano of Leinani, the fire goddess, the creator of the Atoll. Kaimana shuddered slightly as she gazed at the goddess, thankful for the steady stream of vapours that lazily drifted from the volcano's top. The goddess was calm today, as she had been for many years. All of the Atoll knew when Leinani was angry, as the land shook and lives were lost.

She returned her gaze to her current surroundings. Kaimana knew these hills well, from childhood explorations, and had a fair idea where the cave was that the young girl had told her about. She had never been inside this particular cave, but knew of one that sat atop a stone gully from which the stream that her family fetched their water from sprung from the earth. This was where the taniwha was supposed to now be living.

I just want a glimpse, just to see if the story is true. Maybe that'll be enough to find something to write a small song about.

As she moved further up the island's mountain, the land became tougher to move on. The greenery turned to larger rocks and boulders that Kaimana needed to use both arms to struggle over.

If I was a taniwha, this is exactly the kind of place I would hide myself in, away from those pesky villagers. I just hope he won't mind me disturbing his peace and quiet.

The cave finally came into sight. It was set about twice Kaimana's height into a small cliff. Because of the beginnings of the stream that trickled out of it, plant life loved the area despite the rocky ground, and Kaimana found herself slipping on moss and lichen as she climbed the short distance up to the cave mouth.

I must watch myself here. I'd make a lot of people most unhappy if I was to crack my skull and break my promises before the performance.

Finally, she was standing in the cave entrance. In all of her childhood explorations she had never scaled this cliff, due to the final steep climb and ancient parental warnings about leaving caves well enough alone. Most caves dotted about the island were disappointingly shallow, but this one receded into darkness, refusing to betray where it ended.

The sight of a recently chewed goat bone at the lip of the cave gave Kaimana cause to hesitate. Despite her doubts about the story, her heart began to beat faster, her fingers moving again to the clay ocarina at her waist, tapping rapidly on its empty holes.

The offering the village made to the taniwha. It might not have been a monster that ate it, probably some local predators or scavengers.

Despite these thoughts, the sight of this small object finally made Kaimana doubt what she was doing. She knew monsters were real, she knew it was perfectly possible that one had chosen to live in her former home.

What I should do right now is climb carefully down those rocks and head back to the village and warm my fingers up for the performance.

But Kaimana also knew that leaving a mystery such as this would eat away at her, causing her much unhappiness until she returned back to the island. She knew herself too well. She could not turn away, not when the secret to unlocking her first song might lie just beyond the veil of darkness.

She shuffled gingerly forward into the cave, the gurgling stream tickling her bare feet. Inside smelt damp, as one would expect with all of the water around, and she was pleased to find no hint of rotting flesh in the air that one might expect from a taniwha's feeding ground. Light faded quickly, and as Kaimana rounded a corner, she had to pause to allow her eyes time to adjust to the darkness.

Then she gave a loud gasp. There it was. The taniwha.

The monster was sleeping, its eyes were closed. It was massive. Kaimana would have to climb about three times her own height to reach the top of the creature's head. Its body receded further back into the cave, blocking any progress down the passage. Its head reminded Kaimana slightly of a dog's head, with a stout muzzle ending in a large nose. The creature's dark skin was decorated with intricate swirls, very much like the facial tattoos that many of the men and women of the Atoll chose to wear. The creature was also covered in what appeared to be random patches of green fur.

No, Kaimana realised in surprise. *Not fur. Moss.* She studied the still form of the taniwha for a few moments longer and then let out a relieved gasp. It was not breathing. It was not alive.

She stumbled forward slowly, not fully trusting her own conclusion. Gently, Kaimana reached out a hand to touch the taniwha's lower lip. It was deathly cold. Kaimana allowed herself one audible giggle of relief.

This isn't a real creature at all. I should have known by looking at the swirls on its face. They're too much like artwork to be something living. This is a statue, a sculpture. Somebody has carved this taniwha by hand.

"So, who made you then?" Kaimana asked the massive sleeping statue as she became braver, knocking on the monster's solid chin. "Wood? You're made of wood?" She studied the creature's face - it was far too large to be made out of just one tree. "I can't see the joins. Whoever made you must have been a skillful Knack indeed. Last time I checked, there were no woodcarving Knacks on Pukotala.

"What are you here for, then? A nasty surprise for anyone who comes into this cave? Some kind of guardian for the stream's beginning?"

Kaimana looked around the cave, her eyes now fully adjusted to the dull light that crept around the cave corners. The rocks here were plain and uninteresting. Kaimana had a sudden burst of sadness for this beautiful, imposing statue that had remained hidden for so long.

"I bet you're really lonely up here, aren't you?" Kaimana sat beside the solid wooden carving, running her finger through one of the creature's decorative grooves. "I'll let you into a secret - I'm lonely too. I've left my family, I couldn't bear a life of fishing. I'm a musician, you see. But my new life... I don't have many friends. Nobody close to me at all. Sometimes I think I feel like you do, trapped here in this dark, wet cave."

Kaimana let her head rest against the taniwha's mouth, sighing with a forlorn smile on her shadowed face. "Don't worry, boy. We can be friends for each other, right?"

The taniwha moved.

To her credit, Kaimana did not scream. Her first instinct was to throw herself across the cave, well away from the massive mouth she was practically lying inside, clutching the rocky wall opposite the beast with a focussed panic. She held her breath, and looked back at the monster.

Did I just imagine that? How could something like that actually be alive? It's as cold as stone.

There could be no doubt about the movements she saw next. The giant creature shook its head, dislodging some of the rocks from the cave roof above, and opened its eyes.

Kaimana took one look at the green glowing eyes, eyes that

were very clearly gazing at her, and she ran.

Heart screaming inside her chest, Kaimana stumbled in a panic back to the cave mouth, breath escaping excitedly from her lungs. No noise came from behind that might signify some kind of pursuit, but Kaimana did not let her feet stop moving. She descended the cliff face carelessly, not looking at where she put her hands and feet, too concerned she might be facing mortal danger for the first time in her young life.

Kaimana fell when she was halfway down the cliff.

She landed on her bare arms on the rocks below. Nothing important appeared to be broken, so she picked herself up and struggled over the stones and boulders, eager to get as far away from the taniwha before it pounced.

Kaimana turned and paused just before the cave mouth disappeared from view. There was no sign of the monster. She could not help the huge grin that broke across her face at that moment.

A real taniwha! And I touched it! The others will never believe this...

Kaimana's fingers beat on her ocarina in time to her running, a silent staccato accompaniment to the patter of her bare feet on rock, grass and sand. The sight of the taniwha and the stories and music that were now racing through her mind brought an excited smile to her face, but one look at Aka when she arrived back on the beach only moments from the beginning of the performance warned her to calm down. The dark scowl on his usually kind face helped to quell Kaimana's excitement, and she quickly decided that the sharing of her taniwha tale would be best left to another time.

He walked over to her, brushed her hair back, and removed his now-blood coated hand. "How did this happen? Where have you been?" His eyes narrowed as he spoke, studying her.

Kaimana was shocked to find that the side of her head was indeed bleeding. She must have opened the cut after her fall, and the excitement of her find had dulled the pain.

"Somebody clean her up," Aka barked. "This is the last thing we need just before the march."

Eloni rolled her eyes and made her way over.

The troupe leader turned back to Kaimana again, this time with pleading eyes. "Please, cause no more upsets. You know how important this is to me."

To us, Aka, Kaimana thought, but wisely remained silent.

"What in Laka's name have you done to yourself now?" Eloni muttered as she sealed Kaimana's wound together with some kind of paste. "Just remember, when the god begins to walk, follow my lead. I'm the main player tonight, you're my accompaniment."

Kaimana nodded. *You don't need to remind me. When is it any different?*

She watched the gods assemble, ready for the procession. The Long God was there, of course, the patron god of all farming on the Atoll. In accompaniment were other gods who were strongly linked to the harvest. Haumi, goddess of grain, Rongo, god of breadfruit, Yam, god of yams. Much like the Long God, none of these were the actual gods come to visit the island. Instead, they were played by locals, villagers who had earned or requested the honour of portraying the deities that lay close to their hearts. Kaimana's eyes widened as the actor portraying Yam waddled past, a young overweight child in a loin cloth and tapa mask. She grinned and uttered a silent prayer of thanks that Yam himself was not watching from somewhere.

Night fell and the torches lit across the beach. Aka brought his Knack to play, beating a large drum that he hung from his neck, accompanied by Eloni on her flute, walking beside him. The players kept to the shadows; it was the Long God and his brethren that people wanted to see and pay homage to. The Long God walked with his tall staff, streamers blowing in the cool night breeze that whisked across the sea. Behind him his family followed, silent and serene or whooping and rolling, as befit their characters. At the very rear of the procession walked Kaimana, playing her ocarina softly, a distant echo to the beat and rhythm provided by her elders. The villagers of the island lined the beach as the gods and the troupe walked past, cheering and offering thanks to the harvest and the coming season of growth. Kaimana even caught sight of her parents huddled together, smiling at their daughter's music. Her heart swelled in size at this moment.

But then the screaming began.

It was an old woman running from the village, shouting at the top of her voice. "The taniwha. The taniwha has come."

"No," was all Kaimana could utter, just at the moment her eyes fell on Aka's face. The young man looked as if his world had just been taken away from him. A feeling of dread began to bubble in Kaimana's stomach.

Kaimana ran over to the old woman, straining to hear her words above the noise of the small crowd she had already attracted.

"Saw it clear as daylight. It strutted right out of the trees, taller than my house. Raided my oven, dug it right up, gobbled up the goat I was cooking for the feast."

"What did it look like?" Kaimana shouted, hoping to call the elder's bluff. "What colour was it?"

She realised her mistake quickly after this, as the crowds parted slightly so all could catch a glimpse at the young musician.

"Grey," the old woman said. "With green hair hanging from it."

Green like moss and seaweed. My taniwha.

"Kai, your head," came a voice from beside her. It was her mother. "You have blood in your hair. Where did it come from? Kai… Kai, did you wake the taniwha?"

All took a step back from Kaimana and gasped. Kaimana felt the hairs down her back prickle as the dread in her gut spat and hissed at her. She said nothing, but had good sense to withdraw from the crowd's accusing eyes.

This can't be anything to do with me. Please, Laka, let there be a mistake, let something else have happened.

She ran to the village, desperate to find signs of the taniwha's passage, and possibly the monster itself. The old woman's earthen oven had indeed been dug up, and the huge tracks that had been left outside her hut could not have been caused by any natural beast of the islands. There was no doubt now in Kaimana's mind that the taniwha had come to the village.

Was this my fault?

Many in the village seemed to think so, judging by the angry glares that were being thrown in her direction as news of her mother's suspicions spread. The worst was when Aka returned from a brief consultation in the chief's hut. The rest of the troupe waited on the beach, huddled together, whispering. Kaimana sat outside of the group of performers. She knew too well that she would be pushing her luck otherwise.

Aka strode towards them, his face emotionless. "Pack your

21

things. We've been asked to leave."

Kaimana ground her teeth in frustration with her own curiousness. Framed by the silhouette of the fishing village torches, she caught sight of the shadows of her parents looking at her with disappointment, then turning away and walking back to their huts.

The troupe quietly made their way to their canoe and loaded their things onto it. They were very much removed from the villagers of Pukotala now, despite the fact that they were only a short walk from the closest huts. The villagers worked to repair the damage to their small community. The only job the troupe had to do now was to leave.

Kaimana was devastated. She had shamed her parents, and she had brought bad luck to the group, surely reducing their mana – their worth and power – in the eyes of the gods. As the canoe moved away from her former home, she strained for one last glimpse of her parents. They did not come to watch her leave. She clutched her clay ocarina, holding it tight as her past life disappeared into the dark. Despite her sadness, her fingers continued to move silently across her instrument, and the song that they were forming did not mirror the breaking of her heart. Instead, they reminded her of her curiosity, of her brief encounter with a world so alien to her own life. Even now, with the pain she was experiencing, her thoughts remained on the taniwha in the cave.

There are so many questions I want to know the answer to. Why is the monster there? What is going to happen to it now?

Kaimana heard a gasp from behind her, from the dancer, Kiki. Kaimana turned and the rest of the dancers saw her and stopped what they were doing, standing and staring.

"I don't believe it," Eloni said, stepping forward to get a closer look at Kaimana's face.

"What is it? What's wrong?" Kaimana said, worried now at the reactions from the troupe.

Aka came over to her, a look of wonder on his face. "You - you don't know? Kai, look at yourself."

Kaimana thrust her head over the side of the boat to look at her reflection in the waters of the Atoll. It was immediately clear that her eyes were glowing a bright amber, and at that moment Kaimana caught a glimpse of a small spark shooting from her eyes, illuminating the dark water and hull of the canoe. Her fingers continued to move on her ocarina, working their way through the motions of the song that Kaimana's mind was silently composing.

Kaimana was sparking. She was beginning to create her first masterpiece.

QUEEN ALISI
AND THE
WHALE

A tale from the Crescent Atoll

Back in the early days of the islands, one in particular was ruled by a great queen, known as Alisi. Alisi was known well throughout the land for her fairness and generosity towards her people, but the reason her name is now passed down from family to family is because of the pet taniwha she had tamed and became close friends with.

Queen Alisi's taniwha was in the shape of a great whale, but had been blessed with strong arms instead of the normal fins that whales have. These great limbs allowed Alisi's taniwha to catch many fish for her, and helped her and her people to build great palaces by the sea. Alisi would often ride atop her taniwha when she travelled from island to island, and people marvelled from miles around at the sight of this proud woman and the strong friendship she had forged with such a creature.

One of Queen Alisi's neighbours - Isileli, chief of the fat island - was very jealous of this magical creature, and he wanted it for himself. Once, after visiting Queen Alisi's island, Chief Isileli demanded that he travel home atop of the whale. He refused to get into his canoe. Queen Alisi felt uneasy at the man's demands, as he had not been the most gracious guest during his visit. However, she also knew that the rudeness of her guest did not excuse her from being a good host, and she knew she could not refuse the man's request.

"You may ride her," she instructed the chief, "but mind that you are kind to her. She shall bring you to the beach of your island, and she will shake herself to tell you it is time for you to dismount. You must do so immediately, and then she will return to me."

Chief Isileli thanked Queen Alisi for her hospitality, and wore a great grin on his face as he mounted the taniwha and set forth for home.

The taniwha took Chief Isileli straight to his island, and used her great arms to pull herself onto his beach. With half of her body still in the sea, Alisi's whale shook herself to tell Chief Isileli to dismount. Chief Isileli had enjoyed his journey on top of the whale greatly, and now that it had come to an end, he did not wish to give her up.

"Bring me further onto the beach," he urged the giant creature. "I am wearing my fine clothes and do not wish to get them wet."

Alisi's taniwha felt uneasy at this request, but did as she was instructed as her master had commanded her to look after the visiting chief. Using her great arms, she dug deep into the sand and pulled herself forward until only her great tail remained in the water. Once this far forward, she again shook herself to tell Chief Isileli to dismount.

"I wish to slide down your back, to dismount at your tail. But if I do so now, I shall find myself in the sea, and my fine clothes will be ruined. Pull yourself further ashore so I may leave you safely."

The taniwha felt more uneasy about this request and refused to do so, instead shaking herself again to let Chief Isileli know it was time for him to leave.

The greedy chief sneered and shouted to his people who were hiding in the trees beyond the beach. "Bring ropes and bind this whale. I would have her as my own."

Alisi's taniwha struggled against her attackers, but was now too far inland to move herself towards the water. She was able to use her great arms to crush many of Chief Isileli's men, but unfortunately their number was too great and soon many ropes had been thrown over her body, binding her to the earth. Alisi's taniwha struggled and rolled, and her blowhole filled with sand as the great creature panicked at her capture. The queen's whale choked on the sand and died on the beach.

Chief Isileli was most disappointed at this. He had wanted a live taniwha as a pet. However, wanting to make the best of a bad situation, he gathered his people together.

"Let us have a feast," he said to them all, "to celebrate the death of this great monster."

The chief's people dug great ovens into the beaches along his island, and inside them they roasted Queen Alisi's whale. They feasted well into the night, and danced, drank and sang, congratulating themselves on fighting such a great battle.

The next morning, the smell from Chief Isileli's ovens drifted over the seas, and Queen Alisi was awoken by the scent of whale flesh on the breeze. She instantly felt sick to her stomach, fearing the worst. She sent some spies to Chief Isileli's island, and they confirmed her fears. The chief had killed her taniwha and his people had feasted on it.

Queen Alisi's rage was furious. She gathered all the warriors she had on the island, numbering about forty, and prepared to set sail to seek revenge.

Before she did so, a group of women stepped forth. "Queen Alisi," they begged, "please do not do this. We are a peaceful people, with few warriors among us. Chief Isileli, however, has an entire army. When he sees our war canoes coming, he will summon all his men and destroy our husbands. Instead, let us, the women of the island, carry out the revenge you seek."

Many of the gathered warriors began to laugh at this suggestion, but Queen Alisi waved for silence, wishing to hear the plan.

"Chief Isileli will not expect any trouble from us," the women explained. "He will think we are merely visiting the island, to see the great warriors who worked together to kill a taniwha. This will allow us to work our magic on the army, and on the chief. When we have made them fall into a deep sleep, we can steal Chief Isileli away to be punished."

The warriors were uneasy about letting their wives travel alone to Chief Isileli's island, and they were most unhappy about letting them use their magic with other men, but the queen saw it as a good plan. She disguised herself as a washerwoman and joined the women on their canoe to Chief Isileli's island.

When they arrived on the island, the canoe of women was welcomed with open arms. Chief Isileli's armies were still celebrating their victory over the taniwha. Queen Alisi's women danced with and entertained the warriors, using their magic to make them all fall into a deep sleep.

Queen Alisi herself entertained Chief Isileli, who did not recognise her through her disguise. Her magic was strong, but her heart sank as she realised that even after entertaining him for most of the night in his private chambers, the chief's eyes remained open. Soon it would be daylight and the warriors would wake from their magical sleep. The moment for revenge had almost passed.

Then the queen's eyes narrowed. She danced closer to the chief.

She gave a smile of deep satisfaction when she realised she was not looking at the chief's open eyes, but at a pair of brightly coloured sea shells that rested upon his eyelids. The chief had noticed many of his warriors falling into a deep sleep, and had placed the shells on his eyes to fool any enemy that might be attempting something.

The queen quickly dressed and summoned the other women. They stole away in the night, bringing the sleeping chief with them.

It was a long time before the chief was released from the clutches of Queen Alisi, and by then he had been punished many times over for the death of the whale, and was a changed man for the rest of his life.

CHAPTER TWO

The troupe were not happy with Kaimana, and she could not blame them.

It had been a few days since they had left Pukotala, and the dark mood brought on by their dismissal had not gotten any better. Nobody had mentioned the incident to Kaimana since, but she could tell they all blamed her for their downfall.

There's no proof the taniwha came because of me, she thought. *It's a taniwha, by the goddess. It does what it wants. If you live close to a monster, expect to receive a visit from time to time.*

However, Kaimana also knew that even if the beast's appearance was a coincidence, no harm would have come to the troupe if she had not visited the cave in the first place.

The only thing that saved Kaimana from outright conflict with the other members of the troupe was the fact that she had begun to spark. From the corners of her eyes she could see many of them look at her with wonder, especially the younger performers. For most of them it was the first time they had seen a musician sparking. Eloni was the only other troupe member who claimed to have experienced it first-hand.

It was a curious experience for Kaimana. The glowing and sparking of her eyes had caught her by surprise at the beginning, but she got used to it quickly. What was more unsettling was what was going on inside. She could feel the spark in her head, like a treasure hidden in murky waters waiting to be discovered. It was like a living thing, happy but hungry, demanding that all of Kaimana's time was devoted to crafting a masterpiece. Every movement of her hands on her ocarina, every whistled tune she played and practised brought the song closer into focus, as if it was waiting for her to find it but she could not quite tell exactly what it should look like yet. At the moment it was ill-formed, yes, but even at this early stage, Kaimana could tell it was going to be beautiful. She had cried when she had first realised this, after the initial shock of the change inside her. A small part of Kaimana was proud that it was her name that would be attached to this song, that her name would live forevermore on the lips of the storytellers and musicians of the Atoll. However, a much stronger reason for the tears was the fact that Kaimana knew already her composition was unbearably beautiful, and she would soon be able to see it, to know it in all its intricacies, and share it with the world.

It was because of the taniwha, she had no doubt. Her encounter with the creature, that sense of discovery after the recent disappointment of being reunited with her parents. Those powerful emotions had mixed together in her mind, causing her Knack to spark. Kaimana's favourite section of the song so far, the section that she felt was most fully formed, was a high, sharp, racing series of staccato blasts on the ocarina, quickly plummeting down the musical scale. This was inspired by her flight from the monster in the cave, and she could feel her heart beating just as fast when she played this part of her song, could feel her spark burning happily whenever she played it. When Kaimana practised this section, in the corner of her eye she would spy the dancing girls pick themselves up and begin to sway rhythmically. Whether the girls were deliberately trying to encourage Kaimana, or if it was further evidence of the power of her infant masterpiece, she could not tell, but still it made her smile.

My first admirers.

Although the troupe would know the truth, Kaimana of course would not name the song after the events of her own life. People preferred stories from the past, stories of characters they already knew well. Kaimana fancied she would claim that this song told the tale of Queen Alisi meeting her taniwha for the first time - it made more sense to keep it close to the truth, just as Eloni used her own experiences to craft *The Taming of the Fire Goddess.*

Maybe I should ask everyone else what they think. They'd like that, if I let them name it.

The troupe's double-hulled canoe was large enough to carry all of the players, allowing them to live comfortably together while at sea. On the Atoll, anything man-made that could sail on the waters was called a canoe, ranging from small hollowed-out logs that a single person could paddle with an oar, to the large war canoes of Nakoa's personal fleet, each of which could house a small army. The troupe's canoe had the luxury of a great sail that carried them between islands, sparing the performers from the drudgery of rowing, except only on the calmest days. Unlike some of the larger water vessels owned by the most important island chiefs, however, there was no interior for even the troupe leader to sleep under. Because of this, each of the troupe had a certain part of the canoe that they called their own while at sea. Aka and Rawiri shared a large woven awning in the middle of the vessel which they slept under when not in charge of the voyage. Kaimana had adopted the stern, and would happily perch there, practising on her ocarina. Like all who lived on the Atoll, Kaimana and the rest of the troupe were experienced in travelling by water, and all were expected to take turns to help when at sea. However, because of her sparking Kaimana was currently excused from those duties. Having her complete her composition would be a great boon to the troupe, and so she was given as much time as possible to focus on it, for fear she might lose her spark before the song was finished.

They were travelling south now, to the pig god's temple. The Atoll was large, and it would take them a good week of travel to get there even if they did not stop, but Rawiri and his dancers in particular demanded time on solid land to practice their art. The marionettes were also difficult to handle at sea, so Tokoni and Poli were happy to stop at uninhabited islands or small fishing villages and hone their skills. Aka had also managed to get Rawiri to agree to do some fire breathing for the important performance - a feat the old man hated due to the havoc it caused in his gut for weeks afterwards. He needed to prepare special potions for the spectacle, and to pray to Laka for protection and inspiration during his performance.

As Kaimana's *kahuna*, Eloni was expected to continue to train with her, even though it had been many months since the woman had attempted to speak to Kaimana about their art. Aka appeared to be happy enough if the two sat and played close to each other, and normally that was all they did. No longer acting like teacher and pupil, they sometimes played in harmony, but more often than not, these sessions would turn into unspoken battles, each trying to rise above the other, to be the one controlling the story of the music.

When playing together the day after leaving Pukotala, Eloni took her flute from her mouth and spat over the side of the canoe.

"You're on your way out, you know," she said.

Kaimana looked at her. She wanted so desperately to say nothing in response, but knew she could not help herself. "What do you mean?"

"That stunt back at your home? Being asked to leave the harvest festival is bad for all of our mana. Aka will get rid of you before we reach the pig god's temple. Maybe feed you to the cannibals if any get too close."

Kaimana shuddered at that last threat. Eloni was harmless enough - all aboard the canoe suffered from her bitter tongue during a voyage - but the jibe about cannibals reminded Kaimana of where they were sailing. This part of the Atoll was indeed known for the tribes of flesh eaters that lived here. The pig god had chosen to build his temple in the middle of the area of the Atoll that gave him most opportunity to practice his art of war. Most Atoll islanders who ate human flesh were civilised enough to only do so to people who had angered them, but one always heard stories…

Eloni arched an eyebrow, giving a satisfied smirk that she had said enough to make Kaimana doubt herself. Eloni gathered her cloak and made her way to the canoe's bow to practice alone, and to flirt with handsome Tokoni, despite the fact he was far too young for her.

Poor Poli. Kaimana watched the marionette girl look with a pained expression as Tokoni opened himself to Eloni's flirtations, allowing the older woman to stroke his bare arms as they spoke. It was clear to Kaimana that Poli was deeply in love with Tokoni. The pair had grown up as childhood friends, and their twin Knacks performing with marionettes had come about because of the time they had spent together playing with Tokoni's uncle's old carved puppets.

31

Poli was known behind her back as the turtle-faced girl, because the flatness of her nose and the roundness of her face and body made her look not unlike a turtle. Unfortunately for poor Poli, Tokoni had grown up to be a handsome young man, and he clearly knew it. When they worked together as a team, Kaimana had never seen anyone closer than Poli and Tokoni. But when it came to socialising, Tokoni always made a beeline for the nearest attractive young woman. Poli was left looking on, ignored.

Other members of the troupe tutted or laughed about the situation, about how different their two marionette players were, and made jokes about Tokoni's roving eyes and hands. Only Kaimana, with her deep curiosity of the world around her, was aware of how truly sad Poli was with the situation.

Ignoring the demanding protests of her spark – it wanted her to continue to practice - Kaimana made her way over to Poli, looking to move the girl's mind onto something else, and also hoping to find someone to share her own worries with.

"I'm looking forward to seeing what you've prepared for Nakoa's performance," Kaimana said, startling Poli from her distracted gaze.

Poli looked at Kaimana blankly, irritated by the distraction. "You would've seen it if we'd had time to perform at Pukotala."

Kaimana was surprised. Poli had never been close to her, but the puppeteer had also never spoken to Kaimana so bluntly.

"I… yes. I'm sorry about my part in that."

Poli gave no response, just snorted and returned to the marionette strings she was repairing. Kaimana walked away, disturbed by how much animosity she had received. Clearly it was not just Eloni who held a grudge against Kaimana this time. From her position at the stern, Kaimana eyed the rest of her band. The dancers sat in a circle together, probably discussing their time with the goddess Laka and how to further devote themselves to her. Their conversations were always similarly riveting. Aka and Rawiri were manning the sail together, chatting in short sentences. Young Mahina sat close to them, watching and listening in silence. Eloni and Tokoni continued to flirt, Poli continued to watch from her position. Every so often eyes would flick in Kaimana's direction, darken slightly, and then everyone would return to normal.

The troupe had always felt like a home to Kaimana because she had finally found somewhere she could be who she really was, somewhere she did not have to be ashamed of her musical Knack. However, a close friendship was something she still lacked. The others in the troupe were too busy, too disinterested, or just too plain boring for Kaimana to fully connect with. When she had first joined with them, Kaimana thought that the distance she felt might have had something to do with Laka, because the goddess had graced everyone else with her presence. To this day Kaimana remained jealous of the divine attention that everyone else had received, and in the beginning, she had felt that missing out on this experience somehow made her less worthy than the others, that she was not as important a part of the group. As her months with the troupe grew into years, Kaimana realised that other than her love of performance, she simply did not have a lot in common with the others. Instead of seeking out a deeper connection with the rest of the troupe, Kaimana had spent more time alone, practising her music and contemplating her surroundings.

However, now these people who were family but not quite friends were angry with her. They blamed her for affecting the mana of the troupe, for affecting their luck just before the most important performance of their careers.

Two days before the expected arrival at their destination, all came to a head. Tension was running high already because of the dangers of this part of the Atoll, with the threat of cannibals lurking nearby. The troupe had been living off of salted fish for days, not daring to land at an island and light a fire to cook for fear of attracting unwanted attention. Just as their supplies had dried up, Tokoni and one of the dancers had caught a brace of yellowfin tuna and, to the relief of all, Aka agreed to land and dig a small oven. As night set in and they waited for their meal to cook, the troupe huddled around a small camp fire. Kaimana's spark buzzed in annoyance at her as she took this time away from her song. It did not seem to realise yet that Kaimana required food and sleep to continue to function properly.

Calm, calm, she urged the strange life inside her, giving a small smile at how demanding her spark seemed to be. *Let me rest, let me eat, then we can return to our masterpiece.*

The spark's buzzing reduced, but she could sense it was not happy with her.

I seem to be having that effect on everyone, recently, Kaimana thought, looking gloomily around the campfire.

33

Despite the fact that it had been almost two weeks since Pukotala, this was actually the first time all of them had been gathered together. The canoe did not count. They were so used to existing in their own small worlds on that vessel, they may as well have been miles apart, unless they actually wanted to let each other in.

"This is a fine mess, isn't it?" Eloni ventured. "We should all be excited right now. All looking forward to the big event, maybe the biggest event in our lives, coming soon. But instead here we are, ignoring each other, everyone scared to talk about the real problem."

"Enough, Eloni," Rawiri said.

Aka looked on nervously.

"Why shouldn't we talk about it?" Kiki said. "We've been run out of a village. It's a great shame to us, to the goddess. We should be talking about it."

Kaimana's face reddened, coloured by equal parts shame and anger.

"No good will come from pointing fingers," Aka said, doing his best to calm Kiki.

However, Kaimana could already see that it was far too late. Kiki's body language told Kaimana that the dancer was not happy, and most of the other young troupe members were shifting similarly. Kaimana caught Eloni grinning slyly.

She set this up. Probably been whispering in all of their ears for days.

"I only need one finger," Kiki said in response, standing up in the campfire circle and pointing accusingly at Kaimana.

Kaimana stood up in return, staring at the finger. She realised she was shaking and couldn't quite explain why. *I'm not scared of Kiki, of the others, I know they'd never hurt me. But they'd never speak to anyone else in the group like this.*

Aka shifted uncomfortably, but made no attempt to move. Travake and Poli stared at Kaimana with accusing gazes.

Well, if nobody else is going to speak for me, I'll have to do it on my own.

"I'm sorry for what happened, I really am. I don't believe that what happened was because of me. It was a taniwha - it does what it wants. If it'd been looking for me, it would've found me."

"You were told not to go," Aka said, staring at the sand that he was moving around aimlessly with his foot. "I told you not to go, and you did. If you hadn't been there, even after the taniwha attacked, we would not have been to blame. But you did not listen."

"Yes... but a taniwha! I've seen one, can you imagine how exciting that was? Did none of you wonder whether or not the story was real, what it would look like? Our life is made up of stories, and now I've seen a character from one in the flesh. Can you not understand, I had no choice?" Amber sparks flew from her eyes as she spoke.

The troupe turned inwards to their small circle, leaving Kaimana in the dark. Taking the hint, she gathered her belongings - her clay ocarina, the woven tapa cloak her mother gave her, a jade teardrop necklace that had been her grandmother's - and returned to the canoe. Her spark burned brighter, happy that Kaimana was back to working on her tune. Kaimana's mood, however, remained dark, and she made little progress on her song that night.

Moods remained dark the next day, but only towards Kaimana. The rest of the troupe joked with each other and talked with excitement about tomorrow's arrival. Most of them were not outwardly rude about her exclusion. Only Eloni and Poli kept giving Kaimana blatant looks of hate.

Kaimana remained at the stern of the boat, sometimes playing on her ocarina and working on her song, but mostly staring at the sea and the wake of the canoe. Inside, her spark was confused at Kaimana's unhappiness. She supposed it was used to inspiring joy inside the people it visited, but Kaimana could not see past how wretched she felt about the confrontation last night, and about her actions back on Pukotala.

She looked lazily at the water beneath the canoe. The islands of the Atoll all lay on a ring of rock that the goddess Leinani had cast up from the sea bed during a fit of anger in her younger days. This ring was clearly visible from the islands or from any vessels that sailed upon it. Here the waters were not very deep at all, and strong swimmers like Kaimana's mother and sister made their livings by swimming to the bottom of it, finding nature's treasures and bringing them home again. The clear water was easy to see through, and Kaimana could make out the colourful forms of different fish swimming between the rocks and coral beneath her.

Every so often larger shapes such as rays and sharks would glide by, causing the smaller fish to scatter. She had seen a few sea turtles during her years with the troupe, but these were rare sights to be treasured.

The troupe never sailed close to the deeper Inner or Outer Seas. There, the water was a much darker blue, almost black, and the bottom was endless as far as Kaimana was aware. Much larger animals lurked in those depths, and those dark waters were dangerous to travel on. The Inner Sea surrounded Leinani's volcano, giving the people of the Atoll another reason not to travel there. The Outer Sea was endless, and impossible to navigate once sight of the islands had been lost. Kaimana felt much safer here on the Atoll ring, where it was easy for her to see everything that was happening below the water's surface.

She glanced beneath the canoe, and realised the seabed was silent and still. In a place normally rife with life, this was unusual. Kaimana's eyes narrowed as she studied the waters behind the canoe. Often small fish would run when larger predators were close. It was not uncommon for smaller sharks to prowl the waters of the Atoll ring, yet the fish of the Atoll were used to these animals, and Kaimana did not expect to see them in such a panic.

Her eyes settled on a larger patch of water some distance behind the canoe. This dark pocket probably marked a gap in the Atoll ring, a pocket of the sea bed that had somehow fallen down or crumbled away, or maybe had not formed in the first place when the islands were made. These gaps - caves, really - provided underwater shelter for larger animals that lurked in the Atoll waters.

Maybe movement in that chasm startled the local wildlife. It might even have been a bigger animal crossing from the Outer to the Inner Sea, like an orca? That's pretty rare, though.

Most of the time these larger animals chose to cross the Atoll by the great trenches on the east side of the ring, where the sea god's temple had been built. His people kept a close eye on the comings and goings of larger sea animals, and tended to have a good idea of what dangers existed in the Inner Sea. However, sometimes dangerous predators chose to cross the shallower waters.

Kaimana's eyes narrowed as she stared at the hole in the floor of the Atoll ring, hoping to catch sight of something that could have cleared the sea bed so quickly.

Then the dark water moved.

Kaimana sat up straight. She had expected to see a fin, or perhaps a movement of colour in the distance that might be the tell tale sign of something large, but far away. The water moved again, and this time Kaimana was sure that the entire patch of black was moving. That dark shape was more than three times bigger than the troupe's canoe, a canoe that could be home to fifteen people at once, if required.

It could have been a shoal of fish, tightly packed together. It could have been a trick of the light, a rock on the sea bed reflecting the sun in such a way to suggest movement. But a rising panic in Kaimana's stomach told her it was something else. She could feel her spark sense that something was amiss. Its constant buzzing halted, and the silence in Kaimana's mind shocked her.

It's okay, you're all right, she soothed the spark, worrying it might choose to leave her if it became afraid.

The dark mass moved towards the boat, and the bile in Kaimana's stomach rose along with it. The shape was massive, much larger than any normal sea faring animal. Kaimana knew it was the taniwha before it opened its green glowing eyes and peered up at her from the shallow waters.

Inside, her spark grew dimmer. Kaimana could feel its fear.

"It's here!" she shouted. "The taniwha's followed us!"

What does it want? What does it want?

Rawiri swore profusely, and grabbed a worn old spear he had stowed away for fishing purposes. Kiki and Travake screamed while Eloni and Lose ran to the back of the boat with Kaimana to see the monster themselves. Everybody else, Aka included, stood rooted to the spot, eyes wide with fear.

When Eloni and Lose reached her, Kaimana took a deep breath and turned back to the taniwha underneath them.

"There's nothing here," Eloni said, her voice laced with wicked satisfaction.

Kaimana thrust her head over the edge of the canoe and searched frantically. Eloni was correct, the water was empty and the shoals of fish were beginning to return. She felt her spark burn brighter again, relieved the danger had passed. As was typical, it began to buzz for Kaimana to continue working on their song.

Eloni turned to address the canoe. "Calm down, nothing to see here. Kaimana just decided she hadn't got enough attention recently."

Kaimana's eyes locked with Aka, and his look of shock had turned to disappointment and anger. She stood with her mouth open, lost for words.

It was right there. Someone has to believe me, the monster is in the water.

Everybody else returned to their tasks, their moods slightly darker.

Kaimana looked back at the calm Atoll waters.

Where is it now? And why is it following us?

The day they were due to arrive at Nakoa's home came, and it began like any other. The dangers of their journey remained, but tension on the canoe had abated somewhat because everybody knew how close they were to protection. Kaimana also realised that everybody's negative emotions were more firmly directed at her than at any phantom cannibals that may or may not be plotting to eat them for dinner tonight.

Any free time Kaimana had, she spent practising, which pleased her spark greatly, but she always had one eye on the waters behind the canoe. The taniwha was nowhere to be seen.

Kaimana was disappointed at how quickly everybody had decided she had been lying. Old Rawiri had remained the least doubtful, and after Kaimana's alert he had spent about an hour at her side, watching the waters below. Eventually the sniggers and blatant insults from some of the younger troupe members had caused him to back away from her, but he kept his blunt spear close at all times now. From the corner of her eye she was aware of Rawiri studying her, probably trying to discern whether or not she was deliberately being false.

Kaimana felt let down by Aka in particular. She had never been close to any of them, but she had also never given them cause to suspect her as a mad woman or a liar. Out of everybody on board, Aka was the one who knew her the best.

Kaimana spent some time focussing her attention on the troupe leader, staring at him while she blew gently into her ocarina.

He is sad.

Aka was not engaging with the others, and his normally nervous banter was replaced with monosyllabic, short sentences.

Kaimana decided to face him head on. "Aka?" she ventured,

walking up to him while he was on duty at the bow.

He turned to her and narrowed his eyes. Kaimana found herself slightly shocked by such a negative reaction, but decided to continue.

"I just wanted to say how sorry I am about disobeying you back on Pukotala. I know things haven't been easy since then, and a lot of that is my fault. Just thought you should know - I really am sorry."

Aka looked away, scanning the horizon.

Probably looking for our destination, Kaimana thought.

"You never even considered listening to me, did you?" he asked, still not making eye contact.

"What?" Kaimana said, not quite realising what he was asking her.

"When I told you not to go near the taniwha cave. At any point did you actually consider following my instructions, or did you decide to disobey me as soon as I said them?"

Kaimana was flustered. *You think I was trying to hurt you, that I deliberately did the opposite of what you asked?* She had never consciously decided she was going to disobey her troupe leader, but she knew Aka would not be pleased by that answer. It suggested she had not really placed any importance on his words in the first place. In fact, that was exactly true. She had never considered his orders were an actual command that should be followed.

Do the rest of the troupe see you as some kind of chief, a master? Should I?

"I-" she began, but Kaimana never had the chance to finish that sentence.

"Canoe! Canoe sighted!" Tokoni cried, from the port side.

Aka broke away from Kaimana and rushed over to the puppeteer. Kaimana followed and stood close behind them.

"I can't see anything," Aka said, eyes searching in the direction that Tokoni was pointing.

"There. Directly between those two islands in the distance."

Kaimana spotted it before Aka did, and Tokoni was correct. There was no doubt that a canoe was there, a tiny dot on the horizon at the moment, but unmistakably a vessel of some kind.

"Keep an eye on it," was all Aka said, returning to his position at the bow.

Kaimana watched Aka leave. Although it was his job to look ahead, now his eyes - like those of every troupe member - were firmly fixed at the dot on the horizon that Tokoni had pointed at. In most waters of the Atoll ring a canoe was not an unexpected sight. However, this close to Nakoa, the threat of cannibalism put people on edge.

Then Kiki gave a scream. Rawiri moved to her and had a low conversation. The old man walked back to Aka, keeping his voice below shouting level, but Kaimana was convinced he was deliberately letting everyone else hear what he was saying.

"There's another, Aka. Two canoes out there, now."

Kaimana turned back and followed where Kiki's hand was pointed. There was another black dot, not far from the first canoe.

Again, Kaimana could feel her spark become aware of the potential for danger. Once more it grew silent, its light dimmed.

It's fine, it's probably nothing, she told it, praying to Laka that this was the truth.

The spark continued to burn low, adding to Kaimana's growing anxiety.

Throughout the rest of the day they watched the shapes, eyes dancing between the vessels, hoping their destination would soon emerge from the horizon. As time moved on it became obvious that the canoes were moving towards them, and were moving at speed.

At midday, about an hour after the first sighting, the canoes were close enough for some of the more eagle-eyed performers to make out the occupants of the boats.

"Men," Eloni said, narrowing her eyes as she scanned the canoes, which were now about the size of Kaimana's fingernails instead of the needle eye that Tokoni had seen. "All men, I think. About four in each boat. Maybe five."

Everybody was gathered in a clump in the middle by now, except for Aka who kept his gaze evenly split between the canoes and the empty horizon.

"I see them too," Poli added. "Bright colours, they're wearing bright colours. Do cannibals wear bright colours?"

"I don't think there's a dress code," Kaimana muttered, drawing a number of angry glares in her direction.

"Could be some of Nakoa's people," Rawiri suggested. "Or others coming for the celebration. Just because of the rumours doesn't mean these are people who want to eat us."

"Do you know of any islands in that direction who might be

sending warriors to Nakoa?" Eloni asked.

Rawiri remained silent.

In another hour all could make out the canoes and their occupants clearly, even old Rawiri with his tired eyes. The canoes were the size of Kaimana's thumb now, and she could see the bright garb of the men, feathers plucked from a variety of island birds.

Travake was raving at this point, bothering Rawiri with high pitched questions such as, "Do they look like cannibals?" and "Will Nakoa come and rescue us?" Poli was crying quietly under Aka's tarp tent, having decided to no longer watch them approach.

Then one of the men in the closest canoe stood up, showing a skull painted on his chest in red ochre. He held up a club with some kind of large tooth or horn fixed to the end of it, and gave out a loud, inhuman cry.

A number of the occupants of the troupe canoe instantly began to wail, including Lose and Tokoni. This seemed to please the approaching attackers greatly, and they all joined in the shouting.

Inside, Kaimana's spark grew dimmer still, and for a brief second she thought it had disappeared completely.

Don't leave me, she pleaded, and cried real tears in relief when the spark gave a small burst of light to let her know it was still there. Nevertheless, the spark was silent and cold now. It was a selfish thing, Kaimana knew. Not maliciously so, but it was selfish. It wanted to create music with Kaimana, but did not care enough for her to die with her.

The idea of losing her spark and her song terrified Kaimana more than the men in the canoes.

Aka gave up watching the horizon. He reached under his tarp, shoving past Poli who continued to cry quietly, not reacting at all to the distress of most of her friends. The troupe leader took out a simple wooden club from beneath his bedroll.

He stood beside Rawiri, who clutched his worn spear, and spoke softly to the old man. "What chance do we have, the two of us?"

Rawiri looked at the troupe leader and shook his head. "If they come at us separately? We might be able to get one or two of them before the end. If they hit us together? We'll be a joke."

Kaimana stepped forward so she was just behind them both. "I'd like to be able to defend myself," she said quietly. *If this is it, I'd rather go like one of the heroes from the stories, like Queen Alisi or Nyree of the sky fairies. Crying quietly underneath a blanket is not for me.*

Rawiri looked at Aka with a question in his eyes, and Aka nodded. The old man then fumbled in his belt and presented Kaimana with a small fishing knife. It was made from animal bone of some kind, it was small, and had not been sharpened in a long time, but it was a weapon and she was glad of it.

"This is her fault, you know," Eloni said loudly, her eyes fixed on the approaching attackers. All in the canoe turned to her. "Her. Kaimana. This is a punishment from Laka, for what Kaimana did on Pukotala."

There was hate in Eloni's eyes, and her face was pale with fear, but Kaimana was most surprised to see that Eloni believed every single word she was saying.

"Eloni, now is not the time-" Aka began.

"There isn't going to be any more time!" Eloni shouted back. "Why are you trying to protect her, now? There'll be nothing to protect in a few minutes anyway, why can't we all have our piece of her before they do? She disobeyed you, great leader, and she displeased Laka. She tainted the mana of the troupe. This is our punishment for letting her away with it."

Kaimana opened her mouth to respond, but her words stuck in her throat. *Is Eloni right? Did I do this? Laka, is this how my story ends?*

"Laka would never do this to us," Kiki said, meekly.

"Oh yes, because gods are known for their kindness and generosity." Eloni turned to look at the dancing girl, huddled with her friends. "I love Laka too, little Kiki. My time with her is my most precious memory. But I do not forget what she is. She is a god, and they can be fickle, angry and bitter just as easily as they can be generous and kind."

She turned again to look at Kaimana. "And she is angry. Angry at this disobedient girl. Angry at this girl who lies about monsters."

"It was not a lie!" Kaimana shouted, stepping forward to defend her honour while she could. "I did see it again, in the water. Why would I lie about such a thing?"

"How can we trust you?" Eloni said. "This girl who does not follow the commands of her troupe leader? What you did is taboo on so many levels. You know these things are punished by death on many islands, by the followers of other gods? Death is to be all our punishment for your mistakes."

"This isn't anything to do with me," Kaimana shouted, releasing the anger that had been building up inside. "Laka blessed me. I'm sparking right now, in the goddess' name. She blessed me. Dammit, you're supposed to be careful with me when I'm sparking. Are you trying to kill the song before it's born?" She stepped forward again, and all of the dancing girls gasped.

Too late did Kaimana realise that in her anger she held the small fishing knife out in front of her, waving it about to wave off Eloni's smirch on her honour. To everyone else it looked as if Kaimana was threatening Eloni.

"No-" was all Kaimana could manage before Tokoni slammed into her side, knocking the knife to the canoe floor and pressing Kaimana's body over the edge of the canoe.

Inside, her spark screamed.

Shouts of protest went up from Aka and Rawiri, and possibly some others, although Kaimana could not see what was happening behind her. All she was aware of was the pain from Tokoni putting pressure on her back, the squeeze of his weight and the curved rim of the canoe edge forcing all of the air out of her lungs. Her wide eyes stared at the water below, the blue and yellow fish darting about in response to the action above. The cannibal canoes were so close now that Kaimana was certain they could begin to throw spears and shoot arrows if they wished. The attackers were the ugliest things Kaimana had ever seen, smeared in red paint and bodies pierced with bones and wood.

Her air-starved mind found it funny that she found death repulsive instead of scary.

"Here," came a voice from inside the canoe. "Let me finish this. If this is the end, I need to do this before I go to the goddess."

"Eloni." This was Rawiri, and Kaimana had never heard him more serious. "Drop the knife."

The flutist had picked up Kaimana's knife, or had produced one of her own.

"This is an offering for Laka," Eloni said, her voice much closer to Kaimana now. "Perhaps she will spare us if we give her the one that has angered her."

Rawiri started to speak again, but then an argument broke out on the boat. With rising horror, Kaimana realised that Eloni was not the only one who liked the idea of sacrificing Kaimana to the goddess of performance. Raised voices turned into agitated movement, and then cries of violence. Kaimana struggled to turn to look, but Tokoni held her firm to the canoe edge. She grunted in frustration, unable to see what was happening behind her. They were coming to blows, the rest of the troupe. *Fighting - actual, real physical fighting - about whether or not to kill me.* Kaimana pushed again against Tokoni's grip, but in response he pinned her tighter to the boat, making it difficult for her to breath. She was close to passing out, her panicked thrashing slowing and becoming less forceful.

Kaimana felt long nails dig into her scalp and grab her hair, raising her head upwards and straining her neck. Kaimana could see both attacking canoes now. The men in them were laughing at the chaos the troupe was already in, and many of them were already standing in readiness to board the troupe's canoe.

"This is for Laka," came a cruel voice behind her, and Kaimana felt a cold, sharp object press against her throat. "And this is to let anyone else out there who dares try to oust me again know what they are up against."

With tears in her eyes, in what she believed to be her last gasps of life, Kaimana watched the cannibals, now within spitting distance, as they cheered Eloni on.

The sight of their laughing faces was the last thing that Kaimana saw before a giant maw opened up under the closest cannibal canoe. Kaimana's taniwha surfaced briefly, in a flash of grey and green, closed its jaws around the canoe, and then descended. In a brief second, the first canoe had vanished.

All was still. The noise of the fight behind Kaimana ceased. The remaining canoe of attackers were motionless, their bodies frozen as they tried to comprehend what had just happened to their companions.

After that second of silence and stillness, chaos broke loose. The remaining canoe of cannibals began to yell. Some gripped their weapons and looked at the dark waters beneath, readying themselves for attack. Some of their members could not get over their fear and just screamed, dropping anything they had previously held in their hands.

Eloni's grip on Kaimana loosened. Kaimana stood up and glanced behind briefly. Those who had been panicking because of the cannibal attack - the dancers, Tokoni and Poli - were now terrified by the taniwha. The others just stood and stared at the remaining canoe, unsure of how to react.

Kaimana's gaze snapped back to the cannibals as their screams heightened. Her eyes returned to them just in time to see the waters around the canoe part, and the taniwha emerged again. As its massive jaws silenced the remaining attackers, Kaimana got a good look at the beast. It had the face of a dog, mostly a grey-brown colour, dotted with moments of brilliant green from moss or seaweed. The decorative patterns that seemed to be engraved onto its wooden skin confirmed what Kaimana had expected. This was indeed the same taniwha she had encountered on Pukotala.

The monster disappeared, leaving the scene silent.

"It comes for us now," Eloni said in a detached calmness.

Nobody on board disagreed. They all stood still, awaiting the inevitable.

Seconds turned into minutes, but nothing happened.

Summing up her courage, Kaimana peered over the side of the boat to have a look at the shallow waters beneath. They remained the calm blue of the rest of the Atoll ring, the sea bed and the families of colourful reef fish clearly visible.

"It's gone," she said to everyone else, beckoning them over to the edge of the canoe. "It isn't coming for us."

One by one, the rest of the troupe gingerly peered into the waters beneath. There was no sign of the taniwha.

Kaimana smiled in relief, and collapsed to the deck of the canoe, hands finding their way to her ocarina.

We're fine, she said to her spark, *the danger has gone. We can finish our song, now.*

There was no response.

Then Kaimana began to cry, and started to make an ugly, mourning wail, drawing confused looks from her relieved companions.

Her life had been saved, but Kaimana knew that the damage had been done.

She had lost her spark.

Night fell, Nakoa's island did not arrive, but nobody was in a state to protest. The troupe had been mostly silent since the cannibal attack, allowing themselves to go through basic routines to give their brains time to contemplate what they had all experienced. Many of them continued to ignore Kaimana, but now because they were ashamed of their own actions instead of being angry with hers.

For herself, Kaimana remained at the stern of the canoe, fingers working silently at her ocarina, not daring to breathe life to the notes she was forming. She was grieving.

The spark is gone. The song is dead.

It had been the stress of the attack. Not from the cannibals, Kaimana was strong enough to cope with that. But when her family and friends had attacked her, Kaimana had felt the spark slip away, hiding from Eloni's knife. The song she had been composing hovered in her mind like a distant memory, but one she could not recall completely and one that was fading fast.

When someone is sparking, they're supposed to be treated with respect. They're supposed to be given space and time to let their creation fully form, they all knew it. Especially Eloni. People who are sparking are not supposed to have knives held to their throats. That spark was my chance, what I'd been waiting for. Finally a chance to make my name, to show that this life was the right choice.

What does it mean, now that the spark's gone? Maybe my parents were right. Maybe I'm destined to be a fisherman's wife after all.

She hung over the edge of the canoe, staring into the black waters beneath her, brooding hatefully.

Then, Kaimana spotted a familiar dark shape in the waters behind the canoe.

Her body froze.

It approached closer, and as green eyes opened to regard her from deep beneath the surface, they confirmed what she already knew.

It's back.

She knew that her first reaction should have been to shout for help, to somehow warn the others and salvage any possible chance to ward the beast off before it ate them just like it had eaten the cannibals. However, at this moment, Kaimana did not care about the possibility of death. There was only one thing on her mind. She leaned forwards, over the edge of the canoe, allowing her face to lean towards the surface of the water.

You started all of this. You gave me my spark. Are you here to help me find it again?

The taniwha crept closer, the waters beneath the canoe dimly illuminated by the unnatural green glow from its eyes.

That's it, come closer. You inspired me to song, last time. Come and give me more memories worth singing about.

"Thank you for saving us," Kaimana whispered to the shape in the waters below her. She had no doubt it was looking at her now. "I don't know what your intentions are towards us, but I still thank you for what you did earlier."

The shape below the waters continued to swim, its massive dog legs paddling lazily as it rose closer to the surface, but did not otherwise break or disturb the water. If it chose to, the taniwha could end Kaimana's life in a second, probably without making any sound to alert the others.

But you don't have to, Kaimana thought. *Monsters kill, but that doesn't mean every monster kills. We don't have to follow that path everyone expects us to. I should know, after all. I'm a fishing girl who became a pipe player.*

"I'm glad I found you," she whispered softly to the green eyes that lurked just out of her reach.

The taniwha paused for a moment, then closed its eyes and withdrew from the canoe, allowing its darkness to blend into the night surrounding the troupe.

Kaimana lay down in the bottom of the boat for a long sleep. A fierce determination was stirring in her gut.

I will see you again. And together we can reignite my spark and finish my song.

THE
LEGEND of NAKOA

A tale from the Crescent Atoll

Nakoa was *kupua*. He was born with wondrous powers. When his mother placed him in a crib and left him to prepare food, she was shocked to return and find her babe replaced by a fish, calmly swaddled in his bedclothes.

Young Nakoa delighted in playing this trick, and learnt a number of different forms to turn himself into, including the fish, the sweet potato and the pig. His parents found him difficult to control, and although they knew he would become great, as all kupua are destined to be, they began to find him wearing and an annoyance in their lives.

As Nakoa's strength grew he would test himself by climbing onto the roof of his parents' hut, thus destroying the thatching and annoying the neighbours. When he had a disagreement with the local children this would often result in broken noses and arms, which his mother was forced to mend with her healing Knack. Nakoa found himself hated by his parents, who eventually joined with the rest of the people in his village in running him off the island.

Nakoa reacted to this insult with a great rage. He roamed the Atoll seeking loneliness and solitude most of the time, but every so often he would emerge from the wilds, looking for a worthy challenge for his strength and skill in battle. All who faced him were defeated, and through these victories Nakoa grew in confidence and bloodlust. He began to favour the form of the pig, as this animal's angry temperament mirrored how he now felt about all human life. Even when taking the form of a man, Nakoa found he could no longer get rid of the pig in his blood, and contented himself with wearing the face of a pig and the body of a man. This visage, along with his growing reputation, made all who saw Nakoa fear him. He began to attract followers, who sought him out to learn the mysteries of battle.

Nakoa was not happy. He was strong, he was respected and feared. But what he lacked was love, like the love of his parents that he had squandered.

All of this ended the day he met Leinani, the fire goddess.

He happened across her by accident. Nakoa was wandering the wilderness, having managed to slip away from his followers by taking the form of a pig and running through hidden passages in the undergrowth. Leinani had taken the form of a beautiful maiden with fiery hair, and he found her cooling her feet in a forest river, steam rising from the water where her body touched it.

He hid in the bushes, unashamedly watching her undress to bathe. Nakoa had known women before, but he had never beheld one with the beauty and power of Leinani. He would not be satisfied until he knew her love, so he emerged from the bushes and changed into a man while she was bathing in the river.

Nakoa stood by the side of the river, and Leinani smiled to see him there.

"Why, hello," she greeted him.

For his part, Nakoa was impressed she was not terrified at the sight of him, for Nakoa had not yet realised he was speaking to the fire goddess.

"I am impressed by your beauty, and by your courage. You may have heard of me - I am Nakoa, the warrior. My name is known and feared across the Crescent Atoll. I would make you my wife."

The woman laughed at him, much to his surprise and annoyance. "And you, little man, may also have heard of me. I am Leinani, the fire goddess. It was I who birthed the islands of the Atoll from the sea at the request of the Earth Mother. My name is known and feared across the Atoll. I will be the wife of no man."

Nakoa stood speechless as the goddess emerged naked from the waters, dressed herself in front of him, and then disappeared into the woods.

Nakoa was thankful he had avoided the wrath of a goddess as dangerous as Leinani, but his heart continued to hurt when he thought of her. He spent weeks wandering the island in a rage, trying to get the image of Leinani and her beauty to leave his mind, but he could not.

Finally, Nakoa knew he had no choice but to approach Leinani again. This time, he brought her a gift - the head of the high priest of Tangaloa, the sea god whom Nakoa knew brought great displeasure to Leinani.

He found her again bathing in the same spot, and was pleased to see her smile when she saw him approach.

Nakoa knelt by the side of the water, and produced the head of the priest, brandishing his bloody sword as proof that he was responsible for the deed.

Nakoa bowed his head. "My lady, I bring you the gift of this infidel who dared to speak out against your beauty and your power. I am Nakoa, tamer of the Atoll and widow-maker of the wives of all men. I would make you my wife."

Leinani smiled and yet again emerged from the water. She stood beside kneeling Nakoa, his head still bowed low. Leinani picked up the dead priest's head and lightly kissed him on the lips, scorching the dead man's ruined flesh with her touch.

"I do not want a man who kneels before me. I am Leinani, scourge to my enemies and feared also by my friends. I will be the wife of no man."

She robed herself and left him again. Nakoa was beside himself with rage and despair, and spent weeks moving about the Atoll, weaving a path of vengeance through all he encountered.

Eventually, Nakoa decided he could not yet give up, that he would not leave himself unsatisfied. He sought another gift for Leinani, one with much more value. He hunted and killed the great sky dragon by climbing up to the realm of the sky fairies using only a slender spider's thread. It had been foretold that the sky dragon would eventually destroy the Atoll and all who lived on it, thus erasing Leinani's greatest work.

He found Leinani bathing again, and this time stood at the edge of the water, looking the goddess straight in the face. He held the cold heart of the monster up for Leinani to see.

"I am Nakoa," he said. "Killer of the sky dragon and greatest warrior in all of the Atoll. I would make you my wife."

Leinani smiled at him once again, but continued to wash her fiery red hair. Nakoa stood at the edge of the water impatiently, watching the steam from the river curl into the air above them. Finally, Leinani came out and stood at the bank beside Nakoa, graciously taking the sky dragon's heart from him.

"I do not want a man who waits to take what he wants. I am Leinani, lover of hundreds and mother to thousands. I will be the wife of no man."

Nakoa stared at her in equal mixes of fear and rage as she donned her clothes and left once more.

As she left he took upon himself the form of a great boar and tore through the Atoll, carving deep trenches in the ring of the Atoll that forever opened up the waters surrounding Leinani's volcano to the beasts of the Outer Sea.

Finally, Nakoa realised he agreed with the woman he loved. He had allowed his obsession with her to make him forget who he was. He was Nakoa the kupua, the warrior. He would claim what was rightfully his.

Nakoa sought out the unnamed god, the god of war. In a great combat that lasted a year and a day, they fought until Nakoa's blade found its mark and took the head of his enemy.

He found Leinani bathing once more, and threw the unnamed god's head into the waters beside her.

"I am Nakoa," he began, "the new god of war. I take what I want, and I want you."

Not waiting for Leinani to respond, he leapt into the water beside her, taking her in his arms.

Leinani gave a grin of satisfaction. "Finally my love, you are worthy of me."

They joined there in the river, and the heat of their passion caused the river to turn to steam. Water has never again run down that passage.

Nakao finally had what he wanted, to be loved by another. But this was not to last. In their throes of passion, the rage that had turned Nakoa into his beast-like form melted away, and as he was locked with his lover, Nakoa turned back into a proper man. Leinani was shocked by this transformation. She had never before encountered such passion. For the first time in her life, Leinani was afraid.

As Nakoa lay satisfied on the dried up river bed, Leinani silently gathered her clothes and ran. When Nakoa realised she had disappeared, he searched the entire island for her, but there was no sign of his love.

Eventually, Nakoa took to the Inner Sea, and made the difficult journey to Leinani's volcano home. There he was greeted not by his love, but by one of her priestesses.

"She will not see you anymore. She does not want to be your wife," said the girl who knew that the delivery of this message would be the end of her.

Nakoa was full of anger, and he slew the priestess where she stood. As he did so his pig-like features returned, and the rage fell upon him like never before.

Nakoa left the island and has not seen Leinani since. But his rage and anger are legendary, and his name is feared all over the Atoll.

✦ CHAPTER ✦
THREE

When morning came they were greeted by the sight of a tall mountainous island, much larger than the other small, uninhabited landmasses that had dotted the horizon for the last few days.

Unusually for an island on the Atoll, there was no beachside village for them to land at. Instead, there was a long stone pier, decorated with tall poles with red tapa streamers flying from them. At the end of the pier stood two warriors, their chests bare and their faces decorated with angry curved lines.

Many on the Atoll chose to mark themselves with intricate tattoos, mostly to give thanks to the gods or to highlight godly boons that had been bestowed on individuals. Eloni had chosen to have her lips and chin tattooed green to give thanks to Laka, and to show that she had been blessed with a musical Knack that came from her mouth when she played the flute. Individuals whose Knack came from working the land or sea, such as fishermen or farmers, often had their arms or hands decorated to show the strength that the gods had placed in them. Warrior Knacks, blessed by Nakoa, had their entire faces tattooed red, to show the war god's rage that each of them held within. Kaimana had often considered getting similar tattoos, possibly on her hands to highlight the delicate finger work her ocarina required, but so far had not followed through with this thought.

The troupe disembarked with little conversation. Tension still lingered from the events of the previous day. They were also anticipating the importance of this performance.

Kaimana almost understood why they had attacked her. That did not make things any easier. They had all, one by one, approached Kaimana to mumble their small apologies. All, that is, except Eloni. Kaimana caught a glimpse of the older woman's face when Poli came to speak with Kaimana, and Eloni was clearly smirking at her. Kaimana had gripped her ocarina in anger, and was worried that the strength of her rage might crack it.

Just wait, Eloni. My spark will return, and then it'll be my turn to smile again.

Nakoa's warriors barked a short welcome to Aka at the end of the pier, and then turned to lead the troupe up into the hills. Despite their muscles, the men did not offer to carry any of the heavy equipment the troupe had with them. These men had been given their strength for battle, not to haul other people's burdens around.

The walk took about half an hour, and it was steep going. Kaimana was thankful for her small ocarina, but also offered to carry some sacks for Poli and Tokoni, aware they had the largest amount of equipment. Tokoni passed some of his marionettes over to her, and she saw he was unable to look her in the eye.

When they finally arrived at the temple, Kaimana was not disappointed with the sight of it. It was easily the largest building she had ever seen, about ten times as wide as the largest hut on Pukotala, and more than three times as tall. Thin red flags flew from poles attached to the top of it, much like the streamers that had decorated the pier. As the group walked into the building, the entrance hallway led them to an open-air courtyard, the paved floor of which was busy with the war god's warriors. Kaimana was intimidated to see so many bare chested men together, especially as they were all making so much noise. Some were lifting weights, others wrestling, others fighting each other with clubs and swords. Those who were not taking part in these activities were cheering loudly.

Kaimana noticed many of the men leering at the troupe as they entered, particularly at the trio of dancing girls. The girls, humble and devoted to Laka as they were, appeared not to notice, but

Eloni certainly did. Kaimana rolled her eyes at how the older woman's hips began to sway more expressively, how her head darted around, doing her best to make eye contact with as many men as possible.

Many of the men ogled Eloni, but just as many pointed and laughed at Poli and her turtle face.

Kaimana's eyes narrowed. *I do not like them, these brave men.*

Aka, with old Rawiri as his second, was brought before a muscular man whose entire body appeared to have been tattooed in honour of his god. Nakoa himself was nowhere to be seen, and Kaimana was thankful. She had enough to deal with at the moment without seeing a god for the first time.

After a brief exchange, Aka motioned for the troupe to head back outside. They carted their belongings out of the temple and placed them at a campsite some distance away.

"We are not permitted to spend any more time than we have to inside the temple grounds," Aka explained.

"Unless any of you are willing to fight," Rawiri added, jokingly.

There were no takers, and handsome Tokoni paled noticeably at the suggestion.

It was no surprise that the troupe had been asked to leave the temple. Priests tended to hate travelling performers. Not for the frivolity and mirth that they often inspired, but because performing troupes threatened to infringe upon the services that priests served to their people. They both shared stories, the history of the islands. Most priesthoods felt that this was an honour best left in their pious hands. However, nobody ever wanted a priest to lead an important celebration, to inspire fun. On those occasions priests stepped aside and argued as little as possible about performers being called to practice their arts.

This did not mean the priests enjoyed the experience, however. This was not the first time Kaimana had experienced a cold shoulder, and she and the others prepared themselves for a night sleeping under the stars.

As they all prepared to settle down, Aka gathered the troupe together around a small campfire.

He looked at them all seriously. "About what happened yesterday," he said in measured, nervous tones. "We all made mistakes. We thought it was the end. We have to move past it." He lowered his head, as if he was struggling to decide what to say next.

Kaimana felt the eyes of the troupe on her now, their collective gaze bringing back the sting of her loss. She clutched her ocarina tightly again, wishing her anger away. Kaimana did her best to keep her eyes locked with Aka, and nodded to show she agreed with what he was saying.

That's what he needs from me now, she thought, although her heart ached at the pity that many of the troupe regarded her with. *They can't imagine how it feels, to have lost what I have lost.*

"Tomorrow is the most important day in this troupe's life, most important since Laka left us, anyway. This is it, performing for a god. We can't look back, we have to give it our all. We need a good rest." His eyes fixed with Kaimana as he said this, the seriousness of his tone making it clear that this was a command, much like the one she had ignored on Pukotala.

As night fell most chose to settle down and get to sleep. Kaimana was surprised yet pleased to see Tokoni and Poli sharing a blanket together, huddling in the warm night. She was certain there was no passion in their embrace, that they were turning to the person they trusted the most in a time of great stress.

Who knows what might blossom from that closeness.

She tried not to envy the contentedness she could see on their faces.

Eloni, however, chose not to rest. There were new men for her to attract, and as soon as curious eyes emerged from the temple, she went up to them. Kaimana knew Eloni would not settle for just anyone - she would be looking for an island chief or an underling that might be poised to soon rise to a new position. This is what she had tried on previous islands.

Kaimana watched the older woman as she flirted with three young men, all tattooed and muscular. Then, to her horror, Kaimana saw Eloni indicate in her direction. Kaimana stood open-eyed as the three men broke away from Eloni and made towards her. Eloni followed after them, displeased.

"She says you speak to a taniwha," the largest of the warriors said, upon reaching Kaimana.

Looking at them now, Kaimana realised these were not much more than boys, but boys that had probably been trained since birth to inherit the warrior's Knack. She knew herself that she was older than all three of them, and she was not long past her twentieth year.

56

"Not so much," Kaimana replied. "I've seen one. Three times now," she lied, not wanting to let anyone know about that final, intimate encounter she had had with the beast.

Another of the warriors poked at her. "You see it again, tell it Akahata is looking for it." At this, the boy turned to the other two warriors and they all gave a chuckle.

Eloni arrived, flustered and unamused. "What's going on? What are you laughing about?"

"Your friend has found me a monster to hunt," one of them said, catching the eyes of his peers as he jested. "Going to make me famous in the eyes of Nakoa."

The trio laughed together again and wandered off back to the temple, Eloni trailing at their heels.

Kaimana stood in puzzlement.

They want to meet a taniwha? Of course they would, these warriors. She knew from the stories of Nakoa and those he had inspired that warrior Knacks wanted nothing more than to prove themselves in battle, or to die trying. *What better prize could one of these younglings lie at the feet of their god than the head of a monster?*

Kaimana glanced around the clearing, an unexplainable fear settling over her. The taniwha had followed them in the water from Pukotala. Would it follow them onto Nakoa's island as well? It was impossibly large, and clearly very strong, but Kaimana doubted that even a taniwha of that size could stand up to the war god's armies.

If the taniwha follows me here, it will not live for long. There must be hundreds of young warriors like Akahata who would give their lives for the chance to win the war god's favour. Only one of them needs to succeed and the taniwha will be dead.

Is my only chance of getting my spark back in danger?

For a brief span of time, Kaimana tried to follow Aka's orders, tried to go to sleep, but she knew it was no use. Now that she was worried about the monster following her onto the island, she would find no rest until she had confirmed her fears.

Quietly, not wanting to attract the attention of the rest of the troupe, she slipped into the trees. It had seemed like a long climb up to the temple, but travelling back down the hillside unencumbered by any equipment was not a difficult journey.

A quick peek at the canoe in the water, a check of the beach for any tracks, that's all I need to calm my mind.

She hurriedly stumbled through the trees, moving between patches of moonlight to help her find her footing.

Kaimana walked onto the beach just as the taniwha was emerging from the water.

She caught her breath at the sight of the monster. This was the first time seeing it in all of its glory, not hidden in a dark cave or under the sea. The beast was three times as long as the overlarge troupe canoe, and almost three times Kaimana's height. It was dripping with water, much of it draining from the greenery that clung to the nooks and crannies on the beast's hide. The creature's eyes continued to glow green, illuminating the intricate markings that appeared to be some kind of godlike sketches all over its body. She realised now these markings extended much further than the taniwha's face.

The monster stopped as soon as it caught sight of Kaimana.

She was not as frightened as she had been at the sight of the creature on the previous night. If it was interested in eating her, it would have done before then. Instead, Kaimana's intense curiosity took over. She had so many questions to ask of this creature, so much that she wanted to find out.

But this was not the place.

"You must leave here, it's not safe," she said.

The beast cocked its head at her, questioningly.

"There are warriors here. They want to kill you."

The taniwha paused for a moment, and then made a sound that Kaimana first thought was the monster coughing. She quickly realised however, the taniwha was laughing.

Not able to help herself, she also smiled at the idea. Now that the monster was standing in front of her, the sheer size and power of the creature made the idea of the three young warriors posing a threat totally laughable.

"I know, it seems silly, I know. But there are many of them. I have heard of armies taking down a taniwha, and I don't want to see it happen to you. There is a god here also, and I think he would mean you harm as well."

The monster stopped its laugh at the mention of a god. Kaimana did not get the impression from the creature's demeanor that it was particularly concerned, but she had certainly got its attention.

"I think," Kaimana continued, motioning towards the water, "it'd probably be safer for you to return to the sea."

The taniwha took a brief glance at the ocean behind it, undulating calmly in the moonlight, but then gave a grunt and turned back to Kaimana, moving towards her, further inland.

Kaimana's brow creased and her heart began to beat faster, becoming more panicked. *Does it not understand me? How can I get something that size to do what I want?*

She ran forward to stand in front of the beast. "What do you think you're doing? There are men up there that want to kill you. Hide away, for now."

It shook its head, almost shrugging, and then continued to amble into the forest, moving in the direction of the temple and the pig god.

Stupid animal. I'm not going to lose you just after finding you, not before you inspire me again.

Kaimana had no doubt the combined forces of Nakoa's armies would be sufficient to kill the taniwha, but how could she stop the monster from moving towards them?

A sudden burst of inspiration hit her.

"Don't you want to come with me?"

The taniwha turned its head and cocked it again, looking at her curiously. She was pleased to see it was not laughing, and a surge of nervous joy swelled deep in Kaimana's heart. Since their close encounter last night, Kaimana had suspected - hoped - it was not the troupe the taniwha was following, but her.

"I was thinking of going for a walk along the beach. Maybe doing some fishing. Wouldn't you like to come?"

The taniwha continued to look at her, otherwise unmoving.

Unsure about how next to proceed, Kaimana decided to start walking away.

"It's such a lovely night," she shouted, turning her head away as she spoke, "I just wanted to see the moonlight over Leinani's island."

Kaimana walked a few more steps, heart pounding. *Is this going to work, or is the monster going to walk towards his own death?*

Her silent question was answered by a soft rumbling from behind. She gave a start, and turned to see the taniwha bounding over to her, a much more animated movement than she had expected from the large monster. She paused for a brief moment out of sheer terror. Then she remembered her intention, and continued to walk along the beach, drawing the taniwha away from the temple.

"It seems lonely, don't you think?" Kaimana indicated the distant volcano as she spoke.

Really? I've got the experience of a lifetime, the chance to speak with a real taniwha, straight from the stories, and this is what I choose to talk about?

The creature did not seem to mind. It paid little heed to the volcano, but appeared to be content to plod alongside Kaimana, taking time every now and again to sniff at pieces of driftwood.

"My name's Kaimana," she said after a while, thinking of nothing else worthy of conversation with the monster.

The taniwha turned and gave a sniff from his great nostrils, as if in acknowledgement of her name.

Kaimana smiled. "I don't suppose you can tell me your name? Probably don't even have one. Can't imagine you call yourself 'taniwha' in your own head though."

They walked silently for a while, now well away from the inhabited part of the island. "My people have different names for different types of taniwha. You seem to have been made from wood, or have wood on your skin or something."

While saying this, Kaimana made to reach out and touch the taniwha's rough hide, but thought better of it.

"Apparently some taniwha take the form of enchanted logs. Maybe that's what you are? We call them *rakau tipua*. I guess... I could call you Rakau? Until something better comes along, at least."

The taniwha stopped and gave its snorting laugh again. Then it turned its great head towards Kaimana and knocked her to the ground.

Kaimana was stunned. The blow was powerful, but Kaimana was more shocked at how unexpected the attack was. In the short space of time she had spent with the taniwha, with Rakau, she had convinced herself she was safe from it.

Clearly, I was wrong.

Kaimana groaned as she picked herself up. Rakau had moved away from her, running a few of his great strides down the beach, but was now looking at her in the same manner she had seen a cat regard a shrew before snapping its neck.

As soon as Kaimana stood up, Rakau came bounding over and

knocked her to the ground again, making her land badly on her arm, spraining her wrist. He leapt away, giving his snorting laugh once more.

He's playing with me, Kaimana thought, and then gave a groan of pain as she tried to pick herself up.

At this, Rakau stopped his laughter and crept towards Kaimana, as much as a creature his size was capable of any type of stealth. As Rakau bent his head towards Kaimana, she could swear he was frowning.

Do you look... concerned?

She took a gamble again. "You have to be careful, I'm not as tough as you."

Rakau gave a low, deep noise, a moan of sadness.

"But I'll still play, if you want," Kaimana added quickly, not wanting to lose the moment with Rakau now. She picked herself off the beach, trying not to complain about her new aches, looking around for something she and Rakau could do together.

"You like to swim, don't you?" she said, flashing Rakau a cheeky, challenging smile.

In return the taniwha growled, but Kaimana realised - or at least hoped she did - that this was his way of accepting her challenge. Without waiting for further motions from Rakau, Kaimana took off at a sprint towards the water, her feet soon dancing in the surf. She turned around to look at the taniwha and caught a glimpse of him readying to pounce, just before he leapt straight over her head, landing in the water behind her.

It was an awesome sight, this great animal, pushing itself impossibly off the ground and high into the air in an almighty bound. As it landed with a splash, Kaimana realised she was cheering.

Not thinking for a moment, not pondering the potential pitfalls of night swimming on a reef that was unfamiliar to her, let alone swimming with a man-eating monster, Kaimana dived into the waters, doing her best to follow Rakau.

Kaimana's Knack was not for fishing, and neither was it for swimming. However, she had spent a good deal of her life in the company of others who did have these gifts. Kaimana's childhood companions - she was never close enough to them to truly call them friends - had all been destined to follow in their parents' footsteps, and so they excelled underwater, even before their

Knacks had appeared. Thus, Kaimana had a lifetime's experience of doing her best to keep up with strong swimmers.

Keeping up with those children was nothing compared with trying to keep up with Rakau.

She could see well under the water. It was a clear night, the moon was full, and the crystal water of the reef was undisturbed by any nearby rivers. The moonlight painted the rocks and coral of the reef a pale blue, and this was strongly contrasted by the powerful green of Rakau's eyes, which illuminated the sea bed and even tinted the water in front of him.

Kaimana treaded water under the surface and marvelled at the taniwha. On land he had most resembled a large dog in appearance and movement, yet down here he was more like a seal, or an otter. His movements were graceful and effortless, and only needed small flicks of his legs and tail to propel him at great speed around the entire lagoon.

Kaimana found herself nervous when surfacing for air, worried that Rakau might disappear when she lost sight of him. She need not have been concerned. Soon Rakau drifted back, giving Kaimana that quizzical look he had given her earlier when he had knocked her down.

Kaimana did her best to shrug underwater, indicating her feet and legs. *I can't keep up with you with these,* she was trying to tell him.

Apparently understanding her gestures, Rakau floated closer to Kaimana, rubbing his great back up against her. She finally allowed herself to touch his hide, and was not surprised to find that it reminded her of rough tree bark.

Rakau shoved up against her again, more urgently this time. *Are you trying to tell me something?*

Another shove, and this time Rakau worked himself under Kaimana, pushing her head up to the surface. Fearful he was going to throw her out of the water, Kaimana grabbed on to Rakau's hide. She had heard of orcas who played similar games with seals that they caught, although the antics of those predators was designed to split the seals' bodies open and then feed on their innards.

Now wouldn't be a good time for Rakau to make another mistake about his own strength, Kaimana thought, gripping his body tightly and holding herself against it.

This appeared to be exactly what Rakau had wanted, for as soon as he could feel Kaimana's firm grip, he began to pick up speed in the water. Kaimana quickly realised the taniwha's intention, and allowed herself another grin.

I'm riding a taniwha. This is… I never thought… I love it!

He started out gently enough, allowing Kaimana to remain above the surface. Rakau sped around the small lagoon, bobbing Kaimana lightly up and down, just enough so that she was soaked with spray. She responded with screams of excitement, daring to stroke the back of his head to show her appreciation. Soon he began to experiment, ducking Kaimana under the water for a short space of time. On the first occasion he tried this she had not expected it, and emerged choking and coughing. Kaimana could tell by his more subdued movements that Rakau thought he had done something wrong.

"I wasn't ready. Again, again!"

She took a deep breath and they submerged. She felt the pressure of the sea water on her eyes, but Kaimana marvelled at how quickly they sped through that underwater world. Like any child of the Atoll, down here was no mystery to Kaimana, but bathed in moonlight and riding atop a taniwha it felt as though Kaimana had been transported into a dream, a world she did not quite belong in and yet relished every moment there.

She gave Rakau a brief squeeze to let him know she needed to take a breath, and he understood her straight away, rising up to the surface. Kaimana was surprised to see how far away from Nakoa's island they had come in such a short space of time. She grew even more concerned to see where Rakau was headed.

He submerged under the water again, and Kaimana's heart filled with fear. The cliff on the edge of the Atoll ring was now underneath her, and she was staring into the great gaping maw of the Inner Sea, those treacherous depths in the middle of the Atoll ring, in the centre of which Leinani's volcano belched grey smoke.

Rakau did not seem to have any worries about the change of scenery, and pushed himself forwards and down into the black depths. The pressure of the deeper water squeezed at Kaimana's head and she simultaneously screamed and let go of Rakau.

Kaimana floated in the black, shocked more by having entered the Inner Sea than by the pain in her ears. Rakau must have quickly realised something was wrong, as she felt his familiar rough body underneath, pushing her back to the surface.

Above the water, Kaimana sprawled gracelessly on the monster's back, catching her breath and nursing her head. Rakau turned his head around, trying to catch a glimpse of Kaimana. She was surprised to hear a whining from him, which she recognised as a noise of concern.

"Sorry," she said, stroking the monster's back, "We're not made to go that deep under the water. Also," and at this Kaimana looked at the darkness beneath her and shuddered, "We stay away from the Inner Sea, this deep bit."

Rakau whined again. Why?

Kaimana smiled at the question she assumed he was asking. She thought for a moment, clinging to his back. "It's dangerous, I suppose. It's forbidden? We fear Leinani, the fire goddess, and this is the doorstep to her domain. Some of our people do come here, but through work and duty, not through choice. We have many bad stories about the Inner Sea."

With that Rakau began to paddle back towards the war god's island.

Exhausted from the experience, Kaimana and Rakau plodded back onto the shore, laughing together as they did so. Rakau slumped himself onto the dry beach, as Kaimana had seen many a dog lie beside a campfire. With a grin she decided to join him, daring to rest her head close to his. She listened to his deep breathing as she lay on her back and looked at the stars.

Has anyone ever had a night like this before? Playing with a taniwha - what an experience. This is the stuff great songs are made of. I'll have to rid my face of this stupid grin before I meet with the others again.

"Please, stay here," she said eventually, deciding she should leave now before she was missed back at camp. If she was lucky, nobody would have noticed she had been gone, or perhaps they might have assumed she had embarked on some dalliance with one of Nakoa's warriors. That could certainly be the case - they did not know her well enough to assume otherwise.

"It's not safe up there. You're like a big target for them, a prize they'd love to try and take down." Kaimana rested her hand on Rakau's nose. "I couldn't bear something happening to you. Not now after we've just met."

Not when my spark is still lost.

Rakau gave a short grunt, and closed his eyes. Kaimana took this to mean that he agreed, and quietly chose to leave him, not wanting to disturb the monster as it slept. She glanced back once at the shape of Rakau resting in the moonlight. From this distance, he did indeed look like an extremely large tree trunk, or massive rock.

Hopefully none of Nakoa's men will happen by before he withdraws into the water.

She walked back along the beach, towards the pier and the hill path up to the temple. As Kaimana stepped into the woods beyond the beach, a flash of jade caught her eye. Somebody was running through the trees, back towards the temple. The jade tattoos she had seen on the woman's jaw left no doubt in Kaimana's mind about who had been spying on her.

Eloni. But how much has she seen? And what's she planning to do with what she knows?

Kaimana caught a glimpse of white as the distant figure turned to smirk, and then was gone.

The next day brought busyness and excitement. It was the day of the celebration, of a tribute to Nakoa and all he had given to the Atoll.

The Crescent Atoll was not a safe place to live. Dangers came from the sea and wind, from the animals that lived in the depths and on land. From the people themselves, sometimes, but rarely. There were a few tribes of cannibals on the Atoll, but the location of these were known well enough to be avoided. Some islands were ruled by chiefs who craved war, who would seek out neighbours to conquer and pillage. There were other oddities as well on the large ring of islands, particularly on the more remote islands of the Atoll ring. Rumours of bird worshippers who did not welcome outsiders to their ranks. Stranger tales still of men who travelled across the Outer Sea in large canoes. In particular, recent sightings of mouse men had been making their way through the villages, although Kaimana did not give these rumours much credence.

However, what was true was that her people had much to fear, whether or not the source of these fears actually existed. Nakoa's temple was a place of training for those who hinted at developing a warrior's Knack. Once trained and bled under the war god's watchful eye then these men could return to their homes to protect them, or could be bought or traded to other islands as commodities. Nakoa brought peace to the islands, or so his proponents claimed.

Kaimana had decided on the previous day that she did not like the warriors and their superior demeanour. This outlook did not much change on the day of the festival. Most were drunk by mid-morning, and had become violent or reckless. Aka's drum had been stolen, only to turn up later with the skin battered and broken, useless. He wasted much time in scavenging a replacement, and was not happy with the quality of what he had found. Most of the women in the troupe had been leered at and propositioned ten times over, except for poor Poli who had been directly laughed at. As a young man, Tokoni had gotten the worst reception of all. Warriors in training, looking to prove themselves to their peers and to the women in the troupe, would eye him up fiercely, extending their tongues in mock challenge. By midday and the time of the celebration, he was white with fear. Kaimana was worried how this would affect Tokoni today, during the performance.

Kaimana's eyes were focussed, however, on Eloni. The woman had done nothing, said nothing all morning about what she had seen last night.

What's she waiting for? Or maybe I'm wrong, and it wasn't her I saw. I was so sure it was, but there's no way Eloni would stay quiet about something that could affect my position in the troupe.

Not wanting to prompt Eloni into action, Kaimana was forced to watch the older woman, and wait.

When the time of the performance came, the troupe was led into the temple grounds. A small stage had been erected for the performers, and they all stood there, giving the marionette team time to prepare their equipment. Perched on a small stool, not requiring any preparation other than to warm up her fingers, Kaimana surveyed their audience. It was a sea of flesh and sweat, of garishly tattooed faces and a wave of testosterone that she could not abide.

I'm not going to enjoy this.

A horn sounded. To Kaimana's surprise, the ruckus from the warriors stopped at once, and as a man they stood straight and tall, turning to their left, to the entrance at the western side of the courtyard. Through this doorway came Nakoa.

Kaimana had never seen a god before, but would have realised straight away that Nakoa was one. What struck her first about his appearance was the heavy woven armour that he wore. Most of the warriors Kaimana had seen wore light clothing. Many, like the trainees she and Eloni had encountered yesterday, favoured as little clothing as possible. Nakoa was a complete contrast. His body was covered in heavy armour, woven from tight threads of what seemed to be coconut hair, studded throughout with what Kaimana assumed were various shark teeth. In his hands he clutched the largest *Kiribati* Kaimana had ever seen. This was a cutting weapon favoured by the elite of the war god's temple, a strong piece of wood whose edges are barbed with multiple rows of shark teeth filed to points. Kaimana had seen a few on her travels, but never one the size of Nakoa's.

Finally, and most shockingly, was the fact that Nakoa had indeed the face of a pig. Kaimana should have expected this, of course, from the stories. However, as she had never met a god before, she had thought the stories were an exaggeration, or perhaps that the god would have facial tattoos that reminded people of a pig. No, Nakoa had a full boar snout, complete with tusks and brown, wiry hair. This snout peeked out from the god's helmet, which appeared to be fashioned from the hardened skin of a blowfish.

Kaimana would have laughed if not for the fear that she was struck with upon seeing Nakoa. Despite his unusual features, there was no doubt from anyone in the room that this was the most dangerous creature they had ever met. Her taniwha, Rakau, was no longer top of that list. The way that Nakoa handled himself, and the way that many of his warriors shrunk back in fear at the sight of him, told Kaimana that even a great monster such as Rakau would meet his match if ever confronted by this god.

Fear took hold in Kaimana's gut. *What'll happen if Rakau is found out? Please, Laka, goddess of dance and song, keep him in the water and out of sight.*

Nakoa sat down on his throne and motioned for the performance to begin.

Despite their fear, despite how much they all felt like fish out of water, the troupe remained a collection of true Knacks, some of the most powerful performance Knacks that existed on the Atoll. They did not disappoint.

Aka had had much difficulty choosing what to perform for the war god. The most popular stories about Nakoa were those about his upbringing, particularly his early encounters with the goddess Leinani. However, these were definitely not appropriate to tell in his presence. Instead, Aka and Rawiri ended up making their own tale about Nakoa, about how he gathered together the warriors of the Atoll and fended off an invasion of taniwha from the Outer Sea. The subject of this tale made Kaimana shudder, as it was a last minute change, inspired by recent events in the troupes' lives. The last thing that Kaimana wanted was a temple full of warriors foaming at the mouth for taniwha blood, but that is what the performers were brewing.

At the front of the stage, Tokoni and Poli acted out the main thrust of the story with their puppetry. With their Knacks in full flow, eyes were drawn directly towards the wooden puppets, ignoring the darkly clad players behind who moved them. Behind this action danced Rawiri's girls, their movement becoming exciting when the story demanded it, but otherwise keeping in tune with Eloni's music and Aka's beats. The actual story itself was delivered by Mahina, his boy-like tones inspiring great devotion in all of Nakoa's followers as they heard him chant of the rise of their great leader. For her part, Kaimana was responsible for background music, filling the gaps in Eloni's song and complimenting her tune, much like the dancers complimented the puppets. She was pleased with how well things were going for the troupe, but she was all too aware of the phantom song in her mind, the one that had been taken from her, the one that she needed her spark back to finish.

I don't think I'll ever play my ocarina again without being haunted by it.

The first story finished and there was much applause. Nakoa himself did not move, but the rest of the warriors were free with their enthusiasm. Kaimana noticed that the robed members of the priesthood did not respond in the same way. Likely they were not happy with the invention of a completely new tale about their lord and master. This kind of forward thinking did not sit well with their type.

The applause continued to boom as Rawiri took to the stage to prepare his fire breathing routine. The men began to bang their feet and hands in rhythm, managing to conjure truly earth shaking vibrations when working in unison.

A wave of puzzlement rode across the gathered throng as the booming continued to get louder, much more violent a sound than was possible for the assembled warriors to make. The crowd stopped their applause, yet the earth continued to shake. Kaimana felt bile rise from her stomach.

An angry shout came from outside of the temple. This, finally, caused Nakoa himself to rise from his seat in reaction to the commotion.

It was at this point that the temple wall fell upon the war god.

No. No, please, don't let this be happening.

Kaimana stood with her mouth hanging wide open as Rakau bounded through the gap in the wall. He walked over the bodies of fallen warriors and the broken wall that covered Nakoa and roared at the gathered crowd. Several spears already stuck out of his hide. He was angry.

At this moment Kaimana noticed a glint of white to her side, and turned to see Eloni grinning at her. She did not seem at all surprised to see the taniwha here. Almost as if she expected it.

You bitch. This is your doing.

A group of men - the trio that had addressed her last night, Kaimana quickly realised - charged at Rakau with only their bare hands to protect them. The massive taniwha snapped his jaws and they were gone. A turn of his head sent half a dozen other brave, foolish young men flying across the temple courtyard, smashing their bones on the far wall.

Kaimana stood, transfixed. *Last night had been so magical, swimming together. How could a creature capable of such affection murder with so little thought?*

Rakau caught sight of Kaimana and leapt over to her. He ended his leap within reach of her and paused, looking at her quizzically.

Around her, Kaimana was aware of screaming. It was Poli, perhaps, or one or more of the dancers. She was also able to pick out Tokoni's falsetto screech. Other, more assertive shouting was also taking place behind her, although Kaimana was well aware that nobody was rushing out to rescue her from this possible danger.

Kaimana felt betrayed. By Rakau, for slaughtering so many warriors so easily, and by the goddess Laka, for allowing this to happen when Kaimana was so close to finding her spark again.

"How... how could you?" she said, tears in her eyes.

Rakau turned to deliver a fatal snap to a group of spearmen who were attacking his tail, and then looked back at Kaimana with a puzzled expression.

What have I done wrong?

"How could you kill them? Look at how many you have killed."

What Kaimana could only describe as a look of shock appeared to briefly flit over Rakau's huge features.

At this moment, an authoritative command resulted in a barrage of about a dozen spears flying through the air to embed themselves in Rakau's side. He turned to the attackers with a growl and leapt over them, raising himself up high to deliver the killing blow.

Then, at the crucial moment, he paused his front feet before they crushed the men and looked back to Kaimana, waiting.

"Run. Run from here," she whispered.

Without another thought, Rakau lowered his paws gently, missing all of the attacking soldiers. He attempted to turn around and face the gap that he had originally created, knocking down another wall with his tail as he did so.

Rakau disappeared into the forest.

The rubble that used to be the south wall moved. In an explosion of wood, the remains of the wall burst open and Nakoa stood up. His blowfish helm had been shattered, and blood now stained his woven armour, which had lost many of its teeth. However, his *Kiribati* was already in his hand, and he gave a howl of rage.

A lone warrior ran from outside of the temple.

"My lord," the man said, prostrating himself in front of the war god. "We heard rumours this taniwha was making its home on your island. We attacked it, but did not defeat it. We have failed you."

Eloni. You told them.

"Arm yourselves, my warriors!" Nakoa shouted. "Tonight we dine on taniwha!"

His men roared together. None of them, not even Nakoa, appeared to be outraged by the attack. Instead they were celebrating the hunt to come and their impending victory. Together, the largest army of the Crescent Atoll followed their god into the forest to hunt down and butcher their prey.

Kaimana hesitated for only a moment, feeling a rising desperation as her only chance to regain her spark disappeared.

They'll kill him. The taniwha will be dead, and my spark will be gone forever. That's what you wanted Eloni, isn't it?

"Kaimana? Kaimana?" It was Aka, looking at Kaimana with confusion. "Did it hurt you?"

70

Kaimana looked at her troupe leader, shook her head dumbly, and then began to run into the forest, following the path of Nakoa and his warriors.

"Kaimana, no! I forbid it!" Aka shouted, but Kaimana was already gone, disappearing into the dark trees.

THE
INNER SEA

A tale from the Crescent Atoll

There was a set of twins, a boy and a girl, and they were the strongest pearl hunting Knacks on the Atoll. At only fourteen years old, they had already proven they could out-dive men and women who had been practising their profession for decades. Both of them could swim faster than others, could dive deeper, and experienced no sickness after rising quickly to the surface. They seemed to just know where the best pearl oysters were, and often brought home handfuls of yellow and pink pearls, some the size of grapes, and never fished up ruined green pearls.

Their favourite hunting ground was the very edge of the Atoll ring, just where the seabed drops off into the Inner Sea. These grounds were seldom touched by other pearl hunters for fear of attracting the attention of the creatures that dwelt in those dark depths, and so the pearl oysters that littered the sea bed were ripe for the taking.

As their reputations grew, the twins became cockier, and started to take greater risks. Not satisfied with hunting on the edge of the Atoll ring, the twins began to dive into the Inner Sea, raiding the sheer underwater cliff face of the Atoll ring for oysters. They were rewarded for their bravery by the most plentiful harvests any pearl hunters on the Atoll had ever seen, and they beamed with pride when showing off their riches back on the islands.

Their family was impressed, but also worried. "Do not dive too deep," they warned. "Do not go too far out into the black of the Inner Sea. You do not want to be found by the things that live in the dark."

The twins just laughed.

The following day, it was the brother's turn to dive. His sister sat in their small canoe, using her knife to open up the nets of oysters her brother gathered. The brother greased himself up with fish fat to fight off the cold, and took hold of a large rock, the weight of which would drag him down to the sea bed faster than he could swim. He dived over the edge of the boat, giving his sister a casual smile as he jumped.

He never returned.

It was some time before the sister began to panic. She knew that her brother's Knack allowed him to hold his breath for a very long time, but she became uneasy when it came close to the limits of what he was capable of. Fearing for her twin's life, the sister took hold of another large rock from the canoe and dived into the dark waters.

Down and down she travelled, so far her eyes and ears became painful despite her powerful Knack helping her. Just as she was about to let go of the boulder to swim back to the surface, she saw him.

It was just a glimpse, down there in the dark distance. His eyes were closed and he was floating away from her. He was not alone. Behind her brother the girl could see a larger figure, gripping him with grey arms. This other figure was female, her face almost human, the creature's white hair floating like a cloud around her head. Where her nose should be, her face was flat, and she had two black balls for eyes. Even from this distance, the sister could see the creature's huge, pointed teeth grinning back at her. With a flick of her shark-like tail, the sea witch pulled the girl's brother down to the dark of the ocean.

The sister was forced to surface for air, and was sick over the edge of her canoe. Alone, she returned home to tell her family what had happened.

That night, after grieving with everyone else, the girl dreamt of her brother, alone in the sea witch's lair. The sister awoke to find that she was sparking - amber flames were dancing from her eyes, and she knew that her Knack was ready to help her dive further than she ever had before. The girl sealed her ears with wax, and used her grandmother's needle and thread to sew her nose shut. Then she travelled back in the canoe, in the middle of the night, to the ocean shelf marking the edge of the Inner Sea.

She dived again, her Knack flaring up like never before, the heavy boulder dragging her deeper than she had thought possible.

She dived far enough that the moonlight no longer lit the water, and only the amber from her own eyes let her see where the cliff was and the strange creatures that darted behind rock formations when she got too close.

Finally, the sister saw a cave entrance set into the side of the cliff, and she knew this was the sea witch's lair. The girl let go of her rock, and even though her lungs were now screaming for air and her head felt as if all the warriors from the village were stamping on top of it, she went inside the cave to save her brother.

He was there, kept alive by the sea witch's magic, naked and strapped to the wall of the cave with bonds made from woven kelp.

The sea witch was there also, and lunged at the sister, biting her on the arm with her sharp teeth. The girl was ready for this, and already had her grandmother's needle and thread in hand. Quickly, she sewed shut the witch's gills, and for good measure stabbed both of the creature's black eyes once with the needle, leaving it embedded in the left one. As the witch writhed about, dying, the girl untied her brother.

Unfortunately, the lack of air, the pressure of the sea and the loss of blood was too much for the sister. As she untied her brother's wrist, her spark faded and she passed out.

However, the brother had been watching his sister's bravery and was inspired by her. As the light of her spark went out, the light of his Knack was ignited. With his sister slung over his shoulder, the boy retrieved his grandmother's needle and paddled hard in the direction he thought was the way to the surface.

Their grieving parents woke in the morning to the sight of the twins pulling their canoe up onto the village's beach. Both were weary, and both had learnt their lesson. The waters of the Inner Sea are not meant for mortals.

⫸ CHAPTER ⫷
FOUR

In the darkness, Kaimana ran through the forest, eyes wide, darting to any imagined movement in front of her. The wake of Nakoa's army was easy to follow, as the tree branches and grass were trampled. It seemed as though a giant boulder had rolled through, crushing everything flat.

She knew she would be devastated if she lost Rakau now. Yesterday evening, swimming with her taniwha, Kaimana had been happy. If she was honest with herself, she could not remember the last time that she had been so relaxed, when she had last had so much simple fun.

In those few hours I experienced things that no human ever has before. I'm bound to spark again if I can just spend more time with him.

Kaimana slowed herself down when she heard voices close by. She crept forward on all fours, convinced she was close to some of the warriors now.

"It's down there by the water," a man in the darkness barked, doing his best to both whisper and ensure that his words reached the ears of those close to him. "Nakoa wants us to surround the monster. On his cry we strike as one and bring the taniwha down."

Kaimana's heart fluttered in panic. Keeping her distance from where she thought the voices were, she crawled further forward on her belly. The forest floor and branches opened up in front of her. She was at the top of a cliff, overlooking the lagoon that she and Rakau had bonded in only yesterday, Kaimana was dismayed to see Rakau down there in full view on the beach, using his brown-grey tongue to tend to his wounded side.

Kaimana glanced to her right, where the warriors' voices had come from. Sure enough, a short distance away she sighted the glint of spears hiding among the bushes. Kaimana cast her eyes along the cliff line and noted many similar glints, or rustling of foliage which suggested that dozens of bodies were hiding, readying to strike. Here, exposed on the beach, against all these men and a vicious war god, Rakau had no chance.

Kaimana had only one option to save the creature. She screamed.

Immediately the taniwha raised his head, searching for Kaimana.

Many of the warriors reacted by rushing out of the bushes, some towards Kaimana, some tumbling down the scree towards Rakau. A demon-spawned bellowing told Kaimana that Nakoa was displeased, and she felt bile rise in her throat at the thought of angering him.

However, her ruse had worked. Upon sighting the warriors pouring from the undergrowth, Rakau turned tail and dived into the water. Kaimana breathed a sigh of relief. After seeing Rakau swimming last night, she knew he could more than handle himself if any dared to follow him in the water.

At that moment, as Rakau disappeared beneath the waves, the closest group of warriors came upon Kaimana and grabbed her. She did her best to struggle, but they quickly overpowered her, pulling a bag over her head and binding her wrists and ankles. Kaimana felt instantly claustrophobic, breathing rapidly, struggling in vain against the many unkind hands that now carried her. In the distance, the war god's demonic cries rang out in the forest. She could tell by the increasing volume of these cries that she was being brought closer to him.

I didn't want Rakau to be caught, but I'm not ready to die for him either.

Eventually the bag was pulled off her head, exposing her eyes to piercing daylight. There, in front of Kaimana, in all of his glory stood Nakoa the war god.

His heavy breathing suggested either great exertion or rising fury. If the stories were true, the latter was more likely. He gripped Kaimana by the hair and pulled her roughly to her feet.

"What does this beast mean to you?" he growled. The pig's breath was foul and turned Kaimana's stomach.

She found herself unable to answer, silenced by the pain of being held up by only her hair, and by the knowledge that she was currently the sole focus of a god's rage.

Nakoa shook her. "Why did you warn it we were there?"

Laka, protect me, protect your foolish servant. I can't tell him the truth. Will he know if I'm lying? My own father knows when I lie to him, surely a war god is not easier to fool than a mortal.

"I... I did not warn it, Great Nakoa. I was afraid of it. My cries were cries of fear, not of warning." Kaimana did not fake the tears that ran down her face.

At that moment her eyes met with those of the pig god. They were nothing like the eyes of a human. These were soulless, full of anger, and Kaimana did not believe they would ever be capable of showing any kind of compassion or mercy.

Nakoa furrowed his eyebrows.

He knows. Laka, preserve me. He knows I'm lying.

"My men tell me the taniwha has been sighted before, by the performers. You are one of them?"

Kaimana nodded her head, gritting her teeth against the pain, tears running freely down her face.

"Why has it followed you here?"

Her eyes snapped open. "Me? You think it followed me?"

The pig god rolled his eyes and shook her again. "Stupid bitch. All of you, the performers. Why has it followed you all to my home?"

Kaimana's eyes rolled as she threatened to pass out from the pain, and from relief that Nakoa did not think her important enough for a taniwha to focus its attention on.

The god dropped her, and she crumpled in a heap, cowering at Nakoa's feet. Again, this was not an act.

"She knows nothing," he said to the nearby men. "Take her back to her people and confine them to the temple until I say otherwise. I want them where I can see them."

Nakoa grunted, and Kaimana heard him turn away from her. "Set traps," he barked to his warriors. "Sharpen your blades. We must be ready if it returns."

As some warriors hauled Kaimana to her feet, she took one last look at the war god as he made his way away from her, *Kiribati* held ready, flanked by a group of muscular men carrying similar weapons. He was the god of war, and she had angered him.

In the stories, when a mortal wrongs a god, things never end well for them.

Kaimana shook her arms, indicating to the warriors that carried her that she was capable of moving without their help. They let go, but continued to push her back to the temple.

Laka, allow me to live long enough to find my song and play it for all to hear.

The return to the temple was not a comfortable one for Kaimana. She had been forgotten by the war god, but his warriors remained suspicious of her. The men were not kind as they marched her back, shoving when she slowed her pace.

What was worse, however, was the look on Aka's face when she was finally returned to the troupe. The performers had been removed from the temple again, and they huddled together back at their makeshift camp. Kaimana was relieved to see them there, all uninjured, but the betrayal on Aka's face told Kaimana that her time with these people was nearly over.

Eloni spat in Kaimana's direction, then turned her back on the ocarina player.

Aka stood in front of Kaimana, his face openly questioning her. Kaimana looked at him, gutted at how hurt and angry he was because of her, considering what exactly she could say to explain her actions.

"We are ruined," Aka said, eventually. "This performance today, and with you again having fingers pointed at you… We are ruined."

In a rush of inspiration, Kaimana took the hands of her troupe leader. In his shock, he did not fight her. Kaimana stood on her tiptoes and whispered in Aka's ear.

"Aka, we have a taniwha now. He will bring my song back to me. I know things seem bad, but trust me - we will go down in legend as the performers with the blessing of a taniwha."

She withdrew from Aka to judge his reaction. His mouth hung open, staring at the young ocarina player, shocked.

"Everyone," Kaimana said, addressing the troupe in a louder

voice, "everyone, I have something to say."

The other performers were already watching Kaimana, waiting to see how Aka would react to her. None of them, not even Old Rawiri, did anything to hide the anger on their faces now.

The toughest audience I've ever had. Laka, give me the strength to let them understand the opportunity we now have.

"Everyone, I know things seem bad. And I know a lot of this looks like it's my fault. Yes, I did meet the taniwha on Pukotala, and yes, it does look as if it's following me. That's why I couldn't let Nakoa get him last night - the taniwha is here for me. He's the one who inspired my Knack to spark, and he'll do it again, I know it. The experiences I've had with him already... the songs I could already play, even without my Knack sparking. I couldn't let those warriors kill him, I couldn't turn my back on this gift from Laka.

"He could be a gift for you too, if you let him. What makes us spark? Inspiration. Huge, life changing events that give us insights into the workings of the world. Eloni, even you'll admit I'm right. That's what happened to you, and it can happen to all of us. The monster is still out there, my taniwha. Can you imagine what life will be like, living on the waves with a monster swimming beneath us? He can inspire us all, if you let him.

"Things look bad now, but can't you see we are on the verge of something nobody else has ever had? He's a gift, and he can be a gift for us all."

She had no more to say. Kaimana looked at the faces before her, and one by one they turned to Aka, waiting to see what he would do.

Aka was crying silently, twin tears running down his cheeks. He took two steps forward and slapped Kaimana's face, knocking her to the ground.

She cried out at the attack, more through the shock of gentle Aka's actions than the pain of the blow. She turned to look at the troupe leader, and her heart was deflated by the reactions of the rest of the performers. Eloni was grinning wickedly, of course, but many of the others were smiling too. Even Old Rawiri was nodding, grim-faced but nodding, showing he agreed with Aka's actions.

Aka looked at her sternly. There was sadness in his eyes, but determination as well. "I cast you out. Leave our troupe. You've already done enough to destroy my parent's memory. I will not let you poison our mana further with your madness."

Kaimana opened her mouth to speak, but then looked at the others again. Except for grinning Eloni, there was no malice in their eyes for Kaimana. Instead they were focussed on Aka, chests full of pride for their *kahuna*.

They want me gone. All of them. They think he's doing the right thing, and they respect him for it.

Kaimana looked at Aka again, and she could see the young man bracing in anticipation of her attack. She could see he was scared, and ashamed.

I'm leaving anyway, and my actions have already taken so much away from him. Kaimana raised her hand to her cheek, still stinging from the slap. *I could break him now, if I want. Aka's too gentle a soul. It would be all too easy to crush him with guilt at hitting me.*

Instead, Kaimana lifted herself up, keeping her head lowered, as if ashamed. Without looking at any of their faces, she gathered her small bundle of belongings and slipped away into the jungle surrounding the temple, aware of the eyes of every troupe member as she moved.

After entering the jungle, Kaimana did not disappear straight away. Instead, she stood behind the jungle leaves, observing the people who until recently had been her friends. Poli and Tokoni hugged each other, and smiled. The trio of dancers walked off together, holding hands, with a skip in their step as they did so. The troupe was relieved that Kaimana was gone.

Unable to control the trembling in her lip, Kaimana watched Aka speak for a short while to Rawiri and Eloni, and when the conversation was done he wandered off into the trees. Kaimana saw the troupe leader check to see that none of the others were watching him, then he allowed himself to collapse on the ground, his head in his hands, and sob.

She rubbed her face again, the sting now almost gone. Kaimana turned and walked deeper into the jungle, looking for a spot of her own to cry in private.

It was more difficult moving unobserved now. The entire island was swarming with Nakoa's men. From what Kaimana had overheard during her short capture, it seemed as though the majority of the warriors were resting from today's hunt, preparing to renew things again tomorrow. However, this did not mean all of them were inactive. Many still roamed the paths and the wilderness of the island in groups, either as deployed scouts or as ambitious men hoping to earn the favour of their god.

Despite the additional numbers, Kaimana did not find it too difficult to outmanoeuvre them. The majority of their Knacks lay in actual combat, not the disciplines of scouting that were so often important for hunting a beast. Also, they were looking for a prize considerably larger than a small island girl.

As Kaimana made her way down from the temple, her mind was buzzing.

What now, for me? I've lost the people I was closest to in the world. Even travelling together along the Atoll was not safe. Now I have to get back home on my own.

An image of her mother and father flitted through her head, the look of disappointment they had both given her at the end of the harvest festival. They had left without saying goodbye. It stung to think of that moment again.

They'll take me back, I know it. They love me. The big question is, do I want to return to Pukotala? I'll always have a home there, but that home will require husbanding and fishing.

Deep inside, she could feel the infant song that had been ruined, abandoned before its completion, its beautiful tune dampened and twisted by the fogs that it hid behind.

I know you're there, waiting for me. But I can't find you, not on my own. I don't think I ever will, now. Without my troupe to travel with, without their canoe and without them to protect me, I can't seek the taniwha again.

At this moment Kaimana reached the beach that ringed Nakoa's island. There in front of her, beached just where the jungle greenery turned to sand, was a small canoe.

Most living on the Atoll had access to these boats, and it was not unusual to come across half a dozen abandoned vessels when walking around any of the inhabited Atoll islands, but the sight of this canoe at this moment in her life caused Kaimana to drop to her knees in shock.

"Laka," she whispered. For a brief moment, Kaimana fancied that she felt her song stir, urging her to complete it. *This is for me, I know it. Laka, you're trying to tell me to do this alone. I should take this canoe, find Rakau and reignite my spark.*

81

Kaimana's eyes raised to find the looming volcano in the distance, and she shuddered.

It's not safe, out there. There are cannibals, gods and, yes, taniwha. And more. All of which will not let a young woman travel safely alone.

She thought again of her family, of the life that waited for her back on Pukotala.

There's no choice here. She looked once more at Leinani's volcano, shuddered, and then pushed the canoe into the water.

Kaimana had made her way down to the south side of the island, knowing that the stone pier and the beach she had shared with Rakau the previous night would still be swarming with warrior Knacks. Because of this, she was able to paddle her small canoe away from Nakoa's island without facing resistance. All the while as she paddled she looked into the salty blue beneath her, desperately seeking a hint of green that might suggest that Rakau was close.

It was not a green glow that told Kaimana the taniwha had returned. Instead, she felt the canoe rise out of the water, and she had to catch her breath to stop herself from shouting at the disturbance. When Rakau finally did open his eyes, illuminating Kaimana in green, she found herself and her canoe beached on the great beast's stomach. Rakau had risen beneath her, floating on his back, and was now regarding her with what she interpreted to be some sort of smug grin.

Kaimana got out of her canoe, walked over to his large face, and hit him.

The taniwha's expression turned from smugness to shock, but thankfully not anger.

She hit him again.

He pawed at her with one of his great limbs, pushing her down roughly, but not using any real force. This movement was accompanied by a whining querying.

Why?

"You killed them," she hissed. "All of those people, now dead."

Rakau grumbled again, and indicated with the light of his eyes to deep marks on his belly and arms. The point of a warrior's spear still stuck out of his right paw.

Kaimana waved her head. "I know they were attacking you. I know you were defending yourself. But so many? Did you even try to save their lives?"

82

The taniwha was frozen in confusion now. Obviously, this line of questioning was totally alien to him.

"Promise me," Kaimana pleaded. "Promise you will never kill again."

Again, no reaction from the great monster.

A tear threatened to slip from Kaimana's eye. She took Rakau's lack of response to mean he would not make the promise. Sadly, she moved to push her canoe off of his belly, back into the ocean.

"I cannot travel with you," she said. "I cannot pretend to be happy with you taking lives."

She turned from the monster and began the long paddle back to Nakoa's island. Her journey was interrupted by a gentle nudging of the canoe's stern. Looking down into the water she saw one of the taniwha's green eyes staring up from below. Rakau rose again, once more lifting the canoe out of the water.

He whined at her.

"I want to travel with you," she explained. "I want to leave this island, leave behind the people I came here with. But you must promise me - no more killing."

Silence again from the beast, but Kaimana saw something different in its eyes. Affirmation. Rakau was agreeing with her.

Kaimana sat silently in the canoe as the taniwha paddled slowly through the waters. *What do we do now?* And then, oddly, she felt a pang of guilt about the promise she had just forced Rakau to make.

He's a monster. Monsters kill. That's their nature. What I've asked him to do is like someone asking me to stop playing my music, or to laugh or play when others do so. What have I done, asking him to stop being what he is?

She lowered her hand from the canoe and stroked the taniwha's belly as these thoughts busied through her mind, trying to recapture some of the friendship she had felt with him during that night on the beach.

"We have to leave here," she said, eventually.

Rakau raised what passed for an eyebrow at her, questioningly.

"You cannot stay here," she said. "The war god is after you, now. You will be hunted and killed."

Rakau snorted at this, but Kaimana clicked her tongue to chide him.

"Yes, I know you're strong, but they are many, and they have a god at their side. You would fall. But I don't know where you'll be safe. There're no villages on the Atoll that I know of that would accept you. You'll be hunted everywhere you go."

Kaimana fancied that the green of Rakau's eyes dimmed slightly as she said this, and with surprise she felt a sudden pang of empathy for this great creature.

You're used to that, aren't you? Being hunted. Bet you've been hunted for most of your life, if you've spent most of your time on the Atoll, close to people. I wouldn't be surprised if I'm the first person who has attempted even a basic conversation with you.

The monster lowered himself back into the water, allowing Kaimana's canoe to float again on the waves. The taniwha surfaced some distance ahead of Kaimana, and motioned with his head.

He wants me to follow him.

Kaimana picked up her small paddle and started to push forward, not knowing where she was going and trusting this large beast with her life. Oddly, she had complete faith that the creature would not lead her into harm.

In the distance, from the far end of the war god's island, a hunting horn sounded. Nakoa and his armies would not be far behind them.

THE BIRDMEN
OF THE
BROKEN ISLAND

A tale from the Crescent Atoll

This is the story of how the Birdmen came to the Broken Island.

The island had been at war with itself for two generations. Two peoples had lived on the land, but the names of these tribes are now forgotten. An ancient slight had made these people develop a great hatred for each other. Some said that the argument had to do with land. Others that it was over a beautiful woman.

No matter why the feud began, what is important was that it was bloody and brutal. People were butchered on sight. Entire villages were put to the torch. Captives were taken from each side, and instead of being ransomed off or used as slaves, they were burned alive, allowing the screams of the dying to fuel hate in the hearts of the enemy.

Slowly but surely, the people of the Broken Island killed each other. When the last spear was thrown, they cut down more trees to make new weapons. When the last tree was cut down, they mined great rocks from the earth and threw them at each other, scattering the rich brown soil of the island into the sea in their quest to harm each other.

Finally, the remaining people of the Broken Island could no longer fight. They lay on the ground, looking at each other with contempt, but were too fatigued or hungry to lift even a finger to harm each other anymore.

Only then did they see what they had wrought upon themselves.

There was no greenery left on the island. All of the trees had been cut down for spears, or burned when the villages and villagers burned. All of the good roots and fruit from the earth had been destroyed, thrown away when the soil had been tossed into the water. No earth remained on the island to grow anything on, and no seeds remained to grow food from. The animals had all fled or had been killed, caught up in the chaos that had possessed these people.

From this madness, the hero Rongo appeared. He was the son of one of the warring chiefs. As Rongo lay beside his dying father and wife, he finally saw the mistake they had made.

"People of the Broken Island," he shouted to the remaining men and women, "Listen to me. Stop this madness. We shall all be lost. Let us live together as one people, and let us thrive once more."

Weary of the conflict, all who remained agreed with Rongo. There were only enough survivors to create one village, and life in that village was difficult. There were no trees left to make huts out of, so Rongo's people were forced to dig their homes out of the rock. There was no dirt to grow things in, and no seeds left to plant, so Rongo's people were forced to rely on the sea for their food. However, without wood for boats or plants to make spears or nets, catching fish was hard, and most of what they fed on were limpets, mussels or seaweed. The passing birds were the only source of life that visited the island, yet because the Broken Island had nothing of worth left on it, the birds never stayed.

Rongo felt the pain of his people, and within him guilt welled up.

One morning, the day after his youngest son had passed away due to starvation, Rongo fell on his knees at the sight of a great albatross that glided near the island but chose not to visit it.

"Great Albatross," Rongo pleaded, "Help my people. Give us food, give us protection, and we shall always be yours."

It was the wild plea of a desperate man. But the albatross answered.

For you see, this was not a normal albatross that hovered near the Broken Island. This was the Albatross Spirit, one of the many great bird spirits of our world. It heard Rongo's cries and said to him, "We will help you, my people and I. Return to this cliff when the moon is new again, and you will see what we have for you."

Excited, Rongo returned to his people to tell them the news. However, none believed him, all thinking that the talking albatross was a sign of growing madness.

Nevertheless, when the moon disappeared from the sky all of

the Broken Island journeyed with their chief to that cliff, and they were amazed at what they saw.

The albatross was waiting, but it was not alone. Other birds of the Atoll were there too. The common gull, the great moa, the wise owl and more. Each of these birds spoke to the people of the island.

"We have left a gift for you," they said. "One of our eggs. We have hidden them on your island, or in the seas surrounding it. These are no normal eggs, as we are no normal birds. The man or woman who finds these treasures shall be imbued with our powers for the course of exactly one year. You may use these powers to protect your people, and to provide for them.

"After a year, the man who has the power of the egg will die, and return to us. Then another egg shall be secreted away, for the next Birdman to find.

"The eggs are waiting to be found by the greatest warriors. Go now, and make us proud."

With that proclamation, the bird spirits vanished.

There was much commotion among Rongo's people. All wanted the power to provide for their families, yet few among them were willing to pay the price that was being asked.

Finally, a small number set out to search the island and claim the eggs. Some climbed the steep cliffs on the north of the Broken Island, searching for hidden eggs in the recesses where small gulls used to stop on their winter journeys. Others ventured up the barren hills and mountains that decorated the centre of the island.

Rongo watched his people working, and his heart was proud. Rongo's eyes, however, were drawn south, away from the Broken Island. There, just within sight of his home, were small sharp rocks that stuck up from the Atoll bed. He remembered visiting them once, when his father still had his canoe. The bird spirits had mentioned that the eggs might be hidden close to the island, and Rongo fancied that these rocks might hide their treasure.

Trusting to fate, Rongo dived into the sea. To most people of the Atoll this would be an achievable swim, but you must remember that Rongo and his people had suffered much, and without proper food even the climb to meet with the bird spirits had exhausted them all. Nevertheless, Rongo swam until his heart almost burst, using all of his energy to reach those distant rocks.

Luckily, or perhaps due to some unseen hand, none of the

predators of the Atoll seas were interested in Rongo that day. As the sun began to set, Rongo reached the rocks. Pulling himself up onto the tallest one, he spotted a lone albatross egg, sitting in an empty nest. Rongo cracked the egg open and consumed it, gaining the power of the Albatross Spirit.

He returned to the island and used his new power to provide for his people. When the Broken Island was discovered by invaders, Rongo used his new magics to fend off the attackers. To his frustration he found that his powers would not help new food to grow on the Broken Island - the land had been too thoroughly destroyed for that - but now Rongo was able to claim food from the sea to give to his people. Others emerged from their hunt for the eggs with new powers - one had claimed the power of the Moa Spirit, another that of the Owl, and more followed in time. Together, this grim group of magicians spent the final year of their lives doing what they could for the people of the Broken Island.

After that year those who had claimed the power of the bird spirits fell dead, and there was much mourning. However, true to their word the spirits hid new eggs that in time were found by new people, and the Broken Island continued to thrive.

To this day, the Birdmen of the Broken Island survive. On the first new moon of the new year the young, proud warriors of the tribe roam the islands and the rocks beyond the shore in search of magic that will make them lords for a year, and will protect their people for the rest of their existence.

CHAPTER FIVE

Kaimana paddled alongside Rakau in her small canoe. She had enjoyed being carried on the taniwha's back that night in the lagoon, but would not risk travelling the Atoll that way. The images of him consuming the cannibals and breaking the bones of Nakoa's warriors still weighed on her mind, and Kaimana found she could not bring herself to fully trust this beast, despite how friendly he often acted towards her. She looked at the dark waters beneath her canoe. The area around her vessel was pitch black, and rippled under the surface. If she panned her eyes a short way away, the normal aqua blue of the Atoll floor shone through. However, beneath her swam a giant taniwha. Reactions built from a lifetime of stories caused a shudder to run up Kaimana's spine. Not for the first time on this journey, she panicked, gripped the oar tight and looked around for the safest place she could paddle to if the monster below her decided to strike.

Kaimana, what are you doing? You have no clue where you're headed or what to do next.

She had felt like this once before, years ago, when Aka's troupe had first arrived on her island. It had been not too long after Kaimana's Knack had made itself known, and the decision to leave home had not been an easy one, despite the excitement that had come with it. For most of her life, she had expected, and had been expected, to live and die on that small island. When Kaimana had chosen to leave with the troupe, who had only berthed at Pukotala for two days, she had been putting her life into the hands of a group of unknown people.

At least they had been people.

This time, Kaimana was relying on a murdering beast. She looked down again at Rakau swimming under her canoe, his shallowly submerged bulk dwarfing her by at least ten times. She had seen him devour boats larger than this small canoe in one bite. She did not have enough fingers or toes to count the lives she had already seen him responsible for taking, but for some reason Kaimana realised she was a lot more content at travelling with this taniwha than she had been when first starting out with the travelling troupe. This thought scared her.

What scared Kaimana more, however, was what to do next. Part of her had expected her spark to return as soon as she had decided to travel with Rakau, but in the days that they had spent travelling together, there was still no sign of it.

It's the stress, Kaimana thought. *Everyone knows the worst thing for sparking Knacks is stress, even the more mundane Knacks that spark more often. I'm all alone out here, I've nobody to speak to, and I know somewhere out there the war god is hunting us down. There's no chance the sparking will start again while things are like this. I don't even know where we're going to. I'm just trusting Rakau does, and that he's bringing me somewhere safe.*

Rakau did not seem to breathe, or if he did need to, he held his breath for hours at a time. After leaving Nakoa's island, Kaimana paddled straight south for at least a day. She was unsure whether or not great alarm would be raised by her disappearance, but she was certain that Nakoa and his warriors would by now be hunting Rakau. Hopefully they did not know which direction the two of them had travelled in, but going by the efficient reputation of how those warriors operated it would only be a short amount of time before their trail was found. The Crescent Atoll was large, but not large enough for a giant monster and a young woman travelling by herself to go unnoticed.

Only once on that first day did Kaimana spot any sign of life. On the horizon, two black dots signified two canoes. Upon spotting them, Kaimana became aware of the fact that the black shadow was no longer underneath her canoe. As soon as she realised Rakau was gone she stood up and yelled for him.

"Rakau, come back. Come back here, now. You promised me no more killing."

After a short while, the black shadow returned. Mournful green eyes looked at her from below, but she could not tell if he was upset she had stopped him from taking any more interest in the distant canoes, or whether he was upset she did not trust him.

The canoes appeared to follow them for a bit, probably curious themselves about Kaimana's small boat travelling all alone. However, before evening came, they disappeared, telling Kaimana that the canoe owners had better things to do.

That night they found an uninhabited island to sleep on. Kaimana lit a small fire and cooked some mahi-mahi that Rakau caught for them both. She curled up under his belly and fell into a deep sleep, more comfortable and content than she had been for a very long time.

"We can't just keep running," Kaimana told Rakau in the morning, as she dug up the roots she had left to roast under the campfire during the night. Her arms ached mightily from the rowing of the previous day. "They'll find us unless we get somewhere safe. Are we just running away from them, or do you know where we're going?"

Kaimana glanced at the monster for some kind of interaction, but he showed no response, other than his constant eye contact telling her he was still listening.

"Where are you leading me?"

Rakau immediately rose and shook his head. Kaimana stared as he made his way into the water and submerged. Realising this was her companion's way of telling her that breakfast was over, Kaimana finished gathering her food from the makeshift oven and paddled out to her canoe.

The taniwha was already moving, but Kaimana stopped paddling immediately when she realised where he was headed.

"No," she said.

The black shadow continued to move, closer to the Inner Sea, and to the dark volcano that it held at its centre. However, when Rakau noticed he was no longer being followed, he turned back.

His head peeked out from below the surface, raising above the water to give Kaimana an inquisitive look.

Kaimana shook her head again. "No, not her." Kaimana

shuddered, daring to contemplate presenting herself before the goddess Leinani. "She doesn't care for mortals and our concerns. I wouldn't survive the trip to see her, let alone actually finding her."

Rakau's face gave the impression that he did not agree, but instead of debating, he sniffed at the air. Kaimana watched intently as he circled the canoe, sniffing the sea breeze.

Eventually, the taniwha gave a growl and dived back underwater. Travelling again, Kaimana was thankful to find he was now heading south, along the Atoll ring and no closer to the Inner Sea. She picked up her paddle and followed.

After a few hours of travel, and the passing of a number of islands that did not seem of particular interest, Kaimana realised that Rakau was headed directly for a small island that had appeared on the horizon.

From a distance, the landmass did not appear to be noteworthy, not being particularly hilly or mountainous. In fact, it was raised just high enough out of the water for the sandy beaches to turn green and brown with plant life and soil, but otherwise there were no features that Kaimana could spot on it, except for a dense coconut grove close to the western shore.

Two things that Kaimana saw made her heart beat faster. First, a hut was on the northern side of the island, the side that she and Rakau were now closest to. It was a small building, but a thin plume of smoke coming from it told Kaimana it was occupied. The second thing that caused her heart to quicken was the sight of Rakau pulling himself up onto the beach beside the hut. He had swam ahead of her without her noticing.

Kaimana panicked. She did not know why the taniwha had led them here, but she knew she could not risk him making contact with any more islanders. The best result would be that the islanders would run and hide, and then later inform Nakoa's warriors when they inevitably came across this island on their taniwha hunt. However, Kaimana's greater fear was that the islanders might do something stupid like attack Rakau, causing him to forget his promise.

She paddled with all of her might, pitching forward in the canoe when it ran aground on the beach close to the hut. By this time, Rakau could no longer be seen. Kaimana knew she still had time to catch him because of the lack of screams, so she jumped out of the boat, not taking the time to pull it out of the tide, and ran.

"Rakau! Come back!" She knew shouting would attract the attention of anyone else close by, but she would rather they focussed on her than on the monstrous moving log that was about to invade their home.

Kaimana rounded the hut and stopped in her tracks at the sight before her.

Rakau was there, sniffing the air inquisitively. Right in front of Rakau's nose was a small man.

The man was not particularly unusual looking. He was smaller than average, although compensated for this by the roundness of his belly. He wore a simple *piupiu,* a grass kilt, but nothing else, allowing the perfect sphere of his gut to hang over his waistband. He was bald and was carrying some kind of digging tool. What was most unusual about him was the complete absence of fear on his face at the sight of Rakau. In fact, the main emotion that Kaimana got from this little man's body language was that of annoyance.

"Now, I've told your kind before, you're not welcome here. So stop sniffing me and scram."

Yes, definitely annoyance.

The man sighted Kaimana and gave a deep sigh. "Oh great, now you've done it." He stepped over to Kaimana, rolling his eyes, raising his hands high. "Okay, girl. Let's ignore the fact that you're trespassing for a moment. What I want you to do is to pay no attention to the terrifying monster standing right here, back away slowly, and please don't scream. I've got a splitting headache from last night and really am not in the mood for loud noises."

Kaimana's forehead creased. *Why isn't he scared of Rakau?*

The man rolled his eyes again and took another step towards Kaimana. This time he spoke very slowly, clearly thinking that Kaimana was an idiot. "I am going to be fine. This monster is not going to hurt me. Run away and get out of my face."

Kaimana's confusion turned to annoyance. "Rakau," she said.

The taniwha looked over to her immediately. Kaimana smiled at the power she felt with that small movement. She was in control.

"Why've you brought me to see this rude little man?" she asked.

Rakau gave what Kaimana could have sworn was a chuckle and padded over to her. The taniwha stood just behind Kaimana, and she lifted a hand to lay it on the monster's muzzle.

"Now," she addressed the little man, satisfied to see him looking at her in shock. "Tell me again to get out of your face."

The man looked at them both with his mouth wide open, then threw his hands into the air. "All right, I give up. Come inside, I'll sort out lunch, and you can explain this bloody situation to me."

He walked up the steps to his hut and then turned round and shouted, "No!" He indicated towards Rakau with a finger. "The last time I had a taniwha in here, I had to rebuild my hut from the ground up on the opposite side of my island. New plan. You two wait here, I'll bring food out."

Kaimana laughed as the small man spun on his heels and disappeared into his hut.

Rakau sat down on the earth, and Kaimana joined him.

"You know this man?" Kaimana questioned.

Rakau just grunted in response.

The small man brought back some plates with simple fare on them. Roasted yams, with some tuna to accompany. These were just for Kaimana and himself. For Rakau he had brought a sizable reef shark, uncooked, and Kaimana had the good sense to not ask where it had come from.

The little man fretted and groaned as he moved his belongings, but eventually settled down to eat in front of Kaimana.

"Now," he grunted, with a mouthful of yam, "since you've already upset my day, do you mind telling me why you don't have the good sense to be running a mile from that thing?"

Kaimana hesitated. Given that they were being pursued, she knew secrecy was important, but she could not help but feel her host would know straight away if she was lying. Also, he appeared to be able to tolerate monsters more than most, so perhaps he could be trusted…

Kaimana took a good amount of time explaining her entire tale, including her current quest - to find somewhere safe to hide from Nakoa.

At the end of the account, the little man turned his gaze towards Rakau. He spat the remainder of his food out, showing the taniwha he was unimpressed. "So she wants to be safe. And you took her to see me. Shouldn't your kind know better than that?" He picked up another yam from his plate and bit into it. The look on his face suggested the root had gone bad, but Kaimana suspected it was more due to his dislike of the current situation.

"Why would Rakau take me to you?" she asked.

The little man stood up and took a bow in front of her. "Guess

I have to introduce myself, then. My name is Yam. The god of yams."

Kaimana was still for a moment. *A god. This ugly man?* Like many on the Atoll, Kaimana expected to be overcome with awe upon meeting a god for the first time. There was very little to inspire awe about the man in front of her.

"Really?" That was all she could manage.

Deflated, rolling his eyes yet again, Yam sat down to the earth with a thump. "Yeah, I didn't see that reaction coming. I've never been treated like that before," he said, sarcastically. "You know, you'd think that just once you mortals would be impressed with the fact that you in are presence of a god. The fact that I'm the god of yams shouldn't be influencing your mood here. Hello? God, right in front of you, serving your dinner. You're welcome, by the way."

Realising her reaction might be taken as an insult, Kaimana did her best to backtrack. "No, I mean, yes, it's very impressive. Well done."

Yam looked at her, unimpressed. "Well done at being a god? Or for the dinner?"

"Both?" Kaimana suggested, realising that neither was going to be a good answer. "I'm sorry, I'm really bad at this." She sat down and put her head in her hands, but could not help the grin that wanted to spread over her face.

"And now I'm funny. Fantastic. Excuse me while I take another drink." And with that Yam took a swig from the earthen jug he had with him.

Probably some kind of fermented yam beer, Kaimana reasoned.

"No, you're not funny," she said. "Not at all. I'm not laughing at you, I'm... But, a god? A real, actual god?"

Yam raised his bottle to her. "Sorry to be such a disappointment," and took another swig.

Kaimana shook her head. "No, don't you see? This is amazing! A few weeks ago I thought I knew where my life was heading - a future filled with travelling and performances. But now, I've made friends with a taniwha, and now I'm eating with a god? Amazing!" She was genuine in her excitement.

This appeared to puzzle Yam. He glanced at Rakau. "Is she for real?"

The taniwha grunted one of his chuckles in reply.

"You think you're friends with a taniwha?" Yam said, moving

his bottle between Kaimana and Rakau. "Girl, he doesn't even know what that word means, 'friend'."

Kaimana forgot her excitement for a moment and rushed to defend the taniwha. "Of course he does. Well, I mean, I think so. We've only started travelling together, and we've not called it that before…"

Kaimana felt a soft push from behind her, and turned to look into Rakau's eyes.

Of course we are, they seemed to say.

She smiled back and laid her hand on his nose, softly.

Yam let out a breath of air as he took all of this in. "Touching. You're making me emotional," he said, his face indicating otherwise.

Kaimana pursed her lips. God or no, he was starting to get on her nerves.

"Well, it's been a while since I've been able to say this, but that is new to me. Human girl and taniwha, best friends on the run. Exciting stuff." He took another drink. "So, dare I ask: why d'you need a god?"

Kaimana picked up her plate. "Rakau is being hunted by the war god, Nakoa. I guess he thought you might be able to help."

Yam nodded as she explained, continuing to eat and drink. He watched her expectantly after the short explanation, until he realised she was now finished. His mouth dropped open, and his face turned red. "Wait, what? Lady, I've got bad news for you. You've found *a* god, but not the god you're looking for. Want to improve your harvest or find the best place to try out some new crops? I'm your guy. Anything other than that? Someone else's problem. Sorry."

Kaimana was instantly deflated. "Oh. Well, can you make any suggestions, then? You're all related, right? The gods? Can you think of any brothers or sisters who would know the answer to our problem? Where can Rakau go to be safe?"

"Well, that's easy. Stop messing around with the small fry and head straight for the big players." Yam indicated to the west with his bottle. Kaimana followed his hand, but the gnawing doubt in her stomach told him exactly who he was talking about. "Leinani there knows everything about every island on the Atoll. She made them, after all. If she's still doing her job properly, she'll know where you can hide from our brother."

Kaimana was despondent. *Why does everyone keep pushing me where I don't want to go? Don't they understand that people don't sail on the Inner Sea?* "Leinani? But, I was hoping for... Isn't there anyone else a bit less dangerous?"

"Less dangerous? Like me, you mean?" Yam's eyebrows furrowed in anger. "So, instead of some dangerous fire and brimstone goddess, you'd rather have a safe and cuddly god of yams? Maybe you could try the god of potatoes next. Or maybe the god of snails. Heck, I don't even know if there is a god of snails, but they exist so there's probably someone out there somewhere taking responsibility for them."

Rakau chuckled behind her, but Kaimana was starting to lose her patience with this small god with a chip on his shoulder.

Yam continued, either unaware or uncaring of his guest's rising emotions. "No girl, you aren't after a useless little god like me. A question like yours, a quest like yours, it's a big one. Don't you realise this is a real story you're caught up in? I thought that would've been clear to someone in your line of work. A girl and a taniwha travelling the Atoll together - this isn't something that's going to go away, this is not something people are going to forget about and dust under the rug at the end of the day. You can't just chat to a little farming god and sort the whole problem out quietly. You need one of the big guys, and you need them quick. Because the other side already has their players, and you're badly outnumbered, even with that taniwha.

"Go and see my sister. She'll sort you out."

Kaimana looked at the volcano again, darkness clouding her mind. "It's safe?"

Yam laughed. "No, of course not. Have you ever heard a good story that's safe? What'd be the point?"

Her gaze steeled. "Come with us, then. Introduce me to your sister, tell her not to hurt me."

Yam looked around himself wildly, expecting somebody else to jump out on him. After a second, he looked back at Kaimana and barked a laugh. "Me? Help you meet my sister?" Yam stood up and walked over to Kaimana and Rakau. "No," he said, and his cold face told her he meant it. Then the god of yams turned and walked away. "Night's coming. You can both sleep out here, but I want you gone in the morning."

Kaimana pursed her lips in anger. This was her first ever meeting with a god, not counting being threatened by Nakoa, and it had neither gone well nor lived up to any of her expectations. The rest of the troupe had spoken of their time with Laka with such reverence. Kaimana could not see how Yam could ever inspire those emotions.

She turned her head to Leinani's volcano in the distance. "Looks like we have no choice," she whispered to Rakau.

He gave a small whine in response.

Kaimana curled up beside Rakau's belly, running her hand over his hide as she sat there, smiling at the low contented rumble her friend made in response.

My friend. I must be crazy, thinking of this taniwha as a friend. Still, when I said it to Yam, it felt right.

She looked over to the taniwha who was now dozing contentedly.

I do feel safe with him, even after all the bad things I've seen him do. And now he'll have to keep me safe if we are going to visit Leinani's volcano.

Kaimana knew she should be terrified at the thought of heading to the volcano, but instead she felt an odd sense of excitement brewing inside her.

Soon I'm going to visit the most important god on the Atoll, with my friend the monster. Who else gets to live a life like this?

Her smile grew wider, and for a second, Kaimana fancied that her surroundings were reflecting an orange glow, as if some small spark of light had briefly illuminated them.

She sat upright, keeping deathly still.

There it was again - another amber light, light from her own eyes. The light was quickly followed by a familiar buzzing inside Kaimana's head, cautious and questioning.

Her spark had returned.

Hello! Come back, things are better now, welcome back, welcome home. Kaimana was freely crying, silent tears streaming down her face, curling around the painfully wide smile she now wore.

Inside, her spark was searching, getting louder. It seemed to be particularly interested and concerned about the large taniwha Kaimana was resting against.

This is Rakau, my friend, our friend. He brought you back to me. He's going to be in our song, going to help us finish it.

As soon as Kaimana thought the word 'song', the spark's attention fixed on it, and began to buzz greedily for Kaimana to pick up her ocarina.

She laughed. *Yes. I'm tired, but for a short while, yes. I've been through so much since you left - we've got a much bigger story to tell now, and it isn't finished yet.*

Shuffling a distance away from Rakau, Kaimana brought her ocarina to her lips, softly playing the tune that she had forgotten when the spark had left. Tired, her grin was now causing her cheeks to ache.

I knew leaving the troupe was a good idea.

That night, Yam got drunk. He did not leave his hut again, but a large amount of banging and the sounds of items tumbling and breaking suggested he was busy at something. When darkness fell, his singing began. Kaimana - her spark content to allow her rest after an hour of composing - looked at Rakau and laughed at the suddenness of it, but she could not help feel a small amount of concern as well. What was a god capable of whenever he got drunk?

The songs were rude and ribald, the sorts of songs Kaimana was used to hearing islander men singing when they were in their cups. However, as the night continued, Kaimana became more concerned about her host than anyone else. The singing became more angry and forceful, and was accompanied by the sound of wood and pottery breaking. Finally, when Yam was clearly sobbing through his lyrics, Kaimana built up the courage to walk up to his door.

"Yam? Great Yam? Can I be of any help?" Kaimana was unsure of how exactly she should address a drunken god, especially one who had begun things so informally with her.

Her enquiries were met by something smashing on the inside of the hut, not far from where Kaimana's head would be if the wall had not been in the way.

"Not here right now, go away. Come back later." The slurred shout was followed by huge sobs of grief.

Kaimana turned to look at Rakau. He was lying where he had sat for dinner, clearly unconcerned by the events. She looked at her friend with a question in her eyes.

What do I do?

All Rakau seemed to do was shrug in response. It appeared that the damaged emotions of a harvest god were beyond the concern of a taniwha.

Kaimana turned back to the hut and tried again. "Yam, I'd like to come in, please. I don't think you're being honest with me."

Silence from inside, followed by a few more sobs. Ignoring her spark, dimming anxiously, Kaimana took a deep breath and entered.

Other than the destruction that had been caused over the past few hours - many broken clay bottles and plates, some ruined furniture - there was nothing unusual about the inside of Yam's hut. In fact, it reminded Kaimana of her own family home back on Pukotala, complete with fire for cooking and a lone bed for sleeping in. The various implements that lay around the room suggested Yam's godhood did not keep him from living a fairly regular existence. There were tools for farming the fields, for washing and cooking. There were even a few empty coconuts he had probably collected from the grove on the other end of the island, although most of these were now smashed.

Yam himself was sitting on the sole remaining chair. He sat slumped on the seat, an unbroken and filled mug in his hand, resting on his belly. His face was red with tears, but she could tell straight away he was angry with her.

"Is - is anything wrong?" she ventured.

"Wrong? Why would anything be wrong?" he barked, indicating at nothing in particular with his mug, but swishing it wildly above his head, sending much of its contents flying over him. "I mean, I find this little island, make my home here so I can't be found, and then what happens? People can't help but come and find me, can they? And aren't they all so happy when they do that..." His mouth soured and he drained the rest of his beer.

Kaimana stepped forward, beginning to feel sorry for the little man, despite his anger and rudeness. "I - I am truly sorry if I said something to offend you, great Yam. I just, I don't meet a lot of gods. I don't know how I should react." She paused and thought. "Should - should I be kneeling now?" Realising that this very well might be the right thing to do, Kaimana began to get down on her knees in front of the god.

"Don't you dare!" he barked, forcing her to stand up again. "Not for me, don't dare do that. Get up, get up, we're all nobodies here." He forced himself out of his chair and walked towards a barrel he kept beside his bed. Yam dipped his mug into it, pulling it out filled with beer.

"Nobodies? I'm not a nobody," Kaimana said, irritated by the suggestion. "I have a Knack for music. I play the ocarina. I have a friend who happens to be a taniwha."

Yam mimed clapping slowly for her achievements, clearly unimpressed.

"You aren't a nobody, either. You're a god."

Yam laughed, now struggling to look straight at her properly. "Oh yes, what a god I am. The god of Yams. The god of jokes, more like it."

"How can you say that? You give us one of the most important foods we eat on the Atoll. You're praised every year for your bounty."

"Oh yes? You're a performer, I bet you've been to many a harvest festival. Tell me, little mouse, how do they celebrate the great Yam, god of yams? Do they dress up their most handsome warriors, put me at the front of the parade and sing my praises and lavish beautiful women on me?"

Kaimana stood silently, allowing her mind to wander back to the memory of the overweight child on Pukotala who had dressed as Yam, gaining a few chuckles from some of the onlookers, but otherwise being mostly forgotten.

Yam looked at her for a moment, then gave a large belch. "Don't answer that question. I know the answer, I've been there."

"You've been to Pukotala?"

"What? No, nowhere in particular. They're all the same though, the islands. Wanting to focus on the big ones, the Long Gods and the volcano gods. Rest of us are just a joke to them." Yam sat down on the ground this time, resting his back on his beer barrel, and continued to drink.

Kaimana knelt down beside him, considered taking his hand, but then thought better of it. "It doesn't have to be that way, though. The people of the islands don't know you. We have no stories of you, not really. All we know is what you give us. If you walked the islands, like so many others of your kind do, that would let people get to know you better."

Yam eyed her. "You think I haven't done that? Think I haven't visited humans before? That's what brought me here in the first place," and he indicated the hut they were both sitting in.

"What happened?"

"It was a harvest festival. No others of my kind were there. We can sense each other, you know. It'd been a while since I'd been out and about, so I thought it was about time to soak up some praise and thanksgiving.

"The villagers though, they didn't know me. Thought I was just some nobody coming to mulch their food off of them. Were pretty rude to me, to be honest.

"That wasn't the worst bit, no sir. That came when the harvest parade began. The Long God took his walk, and the rest of us were following behind. Not actually me, of course, but the fat joker who played me." The god fell silent at this, lost in his own memories.

"What happened?" Kaimana asked quietly, now too curious for her own good.

"He was a joke," Yam explained. "The fool was so drunk, he needed two children with him to help him stand up." With that, Yam raised his mug to her and took another swig before continuing. "They threw things at him, laughed at him. Not exactly giving thanks for this year's bounty, was it?"

Kaimana felt deeply sorry for this broken creature in front of her, and she allowed him time for silence and to finish his drink.

Then a thought occurred to her. "Where are all the people now?"

Yam looked at her, his lip curling. "I'm a god, little girl. What do gods do to those that cross them?"

Kaimana answered quietly, "They punish them." Inside, she felt her spark fade towards nothingness again. It sensed danger and was preparing to flee.

"We punish them," he nodded gravely. Then, his serious face just briefly threatened to turn into one of grief, but he quickly masked this change by raising his empty mug to his mouth again.

"We'll be away from here early in the morning," Kaimana told the drunk, angry god, and backed away slowly from him, leaving his hut.

Kaimana did not sleep for the rest of that night, but instead lay curled under the heat of her taniwha, thinking about the drunken god that slept close by, agonising over his actions long ago.

There was no trace of any other life on the island.

In the morning, as Kaimana started to pack up her belongings, Yam came out of his hut and stood there, watching her get ready. As she was about to turn and leave, a thought entered Kaimana's mind, one that she had been nursing for much of the night.

She ignored the warning buzz from her spark, urging her to steer clear of danger, and Kaimana ran up to the god of yams and gave him a kiss on the cheek. Looking at the shock on his face, Kaimana spoke to him. "We don't remember Leinani for her volcanoes, you know. Although she does use them to remind us of her, those aren't the stories we tell of her. We talk about her romance with Nakoa, of her encounters with islanders that dare to cross her. When we talk about the Long God, we don't speak of farms and produce. We talk about his quest into the Sky Kingdom and his affairs with the Sky Fairies. When it comes to the god of the seas, we are more interested in his war with his brother than what he provides in the water.

"You're the god of yams, and we should worship you for this, better than we do. But if that really means something to you, and if you want the islanders to know you, you need to leave this island. There are no stories in farming yams and coconuts for the rest of your existence. Get out there, on the Atoll, and live some stories for us to tell about you."

She hugged Yam once more and then left for the beach without giving him a chance to respond.

Rakau slipped into the water first, and then turned and looked at Kaimana inquisitively.

She stole a glance at the dark volcano again. "I guess we don't have a choice," she said. "Time to visit Leinani and find a home for you."

And finish the story that I am putting to song. Her spark jingled merrily at the thought.

Luckily, her canoe had remained on the beach last night. Kaimana pushed it further into the water and climbed aboard.

As she took one last look at the island before paddling off, she was surprised to see Yam running towards them. The god's belly was dancing as he jogged, and his face was red after just a small distance of travelling.

He was shouting at them. "Wait for me! Wait!"

Smiling, Kaimana stopped paddling. She watched the god trip into the surf, and then he fell face first into the water, weighted down by the large pack he had on his back.

Kaimana jumped out of the canoe and ran to pick him up.

"I can do it myself, I'm fine," he barked, as he grabbed the side of the canoe and tried ineffectually to pull himself over the edge. "I've been walking on beaches since before your great-grandparent's ancestors were born."

Rolling her eyes, Kaimana gave him a little push and then jumped in after him.

She picked up the oar again and looked at her new passenger.

"What?" Yam questioned her, angrily, still huffing and puffing.

"What changed your mind?"

Yam nodded his head, eyes lowered. Then he gave Kaimana a look of grudging respect. "I guess - I guess I've got some stories out there to make." He broke her eye contact and turned red in the face, flustered. "Don't make a big deal about it, okay? I've been planning something like this for a while, got nothin' to do with you. Just needed a canoe because I'm a terrible traveller, and I fancy watching you two make a complete mess of things in front of my sister. Always nice to know there's someone out there who's got it worse than me."

Kaimana pursed her lips in annoyance at the stubborn god, used the paddle to turn her canoe towards the volcano, and started to push towards Leinani's home.

THE
LAVA RACER

A tale from the Crescent Atoll

Fainga was the chief of an Atoll island. He was well loved by his people and he tended to his island and lands well. Because of this, his farms were fertile and provided well for his people.

Fainga's island was a large volcano. This volcano was nothing compared to Leinani's home, but it was still an impressive sight, and provided Fainga's people with the rich soils that allowed them to thrive.

The chief's favourite sport was lava running, and he would challenge all on the island to this activity whenever their volcano was active. He had his wood smiths carve him a thin sledge that was capable of making the sharp turns needed to manoeuvre down flows of molten rock, and he thrilled at showing off for his people. Fainga's lava racing was well known throughout the Atoll, and people travelled for days to watch him compete if they heard that the volcano was flowing.

One summer's day, Fainga was challenged by his rival, Ekewaka. Theirs was a friendly rivalry, but one that had lasted for many years. One year, Fainga would get to the bottom of a lava flow first, and on the next Ekewaka would be the victor.

On the eve of this competition the two relaxed together in Fainga's hut, joking about tomorrow's challenge. It was at this time that Ekewaka was visited by a strange woman with fiery red hair.

"Give me your sledge," the woman demanded of Ekewaka. "Give me your sledge and tomorrow I will best the chief of this island upon the fiery slopes."

Ekewaka laughed at the stranger, but Fainga looked thoughtful. The red haired woman repeated again, "Give me your sledge."

Ekewaka turned to Fainga and grinned, "What do you say,

friend? Instead of a true competition, would you rather humiliate this woman who has too high an opinion of herself?"

Fainga stroked his beard and spoke. "What will be our bargain? What do you want of me if you win?"

Without hesitation the woman said, "That you promise to never again race the volcano. That you shall leave well enough alone that which should not be tamed."

Fainga raised his eyebrow. "And if I win?"

"You will not win," she replied.

"So, I can name my prize then?"

The fiery woman nodded.

"I claim you. I shall own you for one week and a day, and will parade you around my island in victory, bound to the sledge that I shall best you upon."

The woman grinned and nodded, then left with Ekewaka's sledge.

The next morning, both competitors met at the foot of the volcano. They nodded at each other and climbed the mountain together, silently.

The local priest waited for them at the top. There he gave the signal to go, and both took off at high speed.

Fainga had to admit that the woman was fast, much faster than he had anticipated. She appeared to know exactly which patches of the molten rock would carry her at speed, and she had an uncanny ability to avoid the slower moving, cooler patches of lava.

However, Fainga was faster. He had lived all of his life racing on the mountain, and he also knew that his reputation would never recover if he allowed this upstart stranger to best him. So, through desperate action and skill, Fainga reached the bottom first, claiming victory.

The woman was furious at her loss.

"Again," she said, simply. "We must race again. I raise the bet."

Fainga shrugged. "I have already beaten you. Why would I want to race now?"

"Name your prize," the woman said.

"You," Fainga replied. "I claim you, for a year and a day. You shall belong to me, body and soul, and shall do whatever I bid of you until your term is finished."

The woman nodded. "If I win," she said, "you will never race on the mountainside again. You will leave this island in disgrace."

They shook on the new terms, and then climbed the mountain once more.

At the top, before they began their race, the woman looked at her own sledge in dissatisfaction.

"We must exchange sledges," she demanded. "I see now that yours is better than mine. The last race was unfair. We must exchange sledges before we begin."

Fainga laughed and shook his head. He knew the woman's words were correct - his sledge was indeed better, as it had been carved for him by the finest woodworking Knacks on the Atoll. He was not willing to give it up.

"We can continue this debate after you belong to me," he barked at her before setting off on his descent, before she was ready.

Smoke began to flare from the woman's hair. Fire danced in her eyes. Because, unknown to Fainga, he had been challenged by Leinani, the fire goddess, and now she was angry with him.

"I shall show you how to ride the fire," she said, and stamped her foot. The volcano above her erupted, and a fast moving wave of molten stone belched forth from the mountain top. With her bare feet, Leinani mounted this wave and rode it down the mountain, gaining on Fainga, spouting violent threats from her mouth as she came closer and closer to him.

Fainga looked around and panicked. He focussed on his sledge like never before. He took risks and shortcuts that he had never dared to use in the past, doing all he could to save his life from the raging goddess. He used the soles of his feet to push himself onward, burning them to the bone as he did so.

So it was that Fainga, chief of the island of Raiatea, won his lava race against the volcano goddess.

He waited for her, on the beach at the bottom of the mountain. He lay in the surf, panting, exhausted, a nervous grin on his face. No others dared come near them, fearing Leinani's wrath.

She came to him on a slow-moving flow of fire. The air around her hummed in anger.

Fainga bowed before her, his smile growing larger. "My lady," he said, "I appear to have bested you. This means, I believe, you are mine for the next year. And one day." He looked at the goddess hopefully, as if sharing a joke with her.

In response, Leinani reached into the fire at her feet, and pulled up a writhing flame, which she cracked like a whip. The flame lashed out at Fainga's face, burning an ugly line down its right side, sealing his eye shut.

He cried out in pain, falling to his knees and splashing salt water into the wound.

"I mean no disrespect! You are right, of course, it would not be fit for a man to claim ownership of a god. It is enough for me to know I have beaten you. Let us be done at that."

The whip cracked again, carving another wound on Fainga's face, and taking his other eye.

He screamed again, pleading with the goddess. "You are right, of course you are right. It must have been a draw, I could not have beaten you. Let us forget the whole thing happened. It was a foolish notion."

Blinded now, Fainga could no longer see Leinani, but could still feel the heat of her presence. More than that, he could also feel the rumbling of the earth beneath his feet, and knew then that the goddess was feeding the island's volcano with her rage. It would not be long until it erupted violently.

"Do not punish my people for my crimes," he whispered. The rumbling continued, and Fainga knew Leinani stood before him, watching impassionately.

He sighed, all pride leaving his body with that breath. Quietly, he spoke again. "You won. I was wrong now, I see. A mortal could never beat a goddess, I was wrong. You won our race, and I will leave my island now as punishment."

He could not see the goddess' reaction, but the trembling of the earth subsided, and the cooling of the air around him told Fainga that Leinani was gone.

In the distance, he could hear the shouts of his people, moving closer now that the goddess had departed.

He did not, however, wait for them to arrive. He did not want to further risk the goddess' anger and what it might mean for the survival of his people. Blind and broken, using his sledge as a raft, Fainga, chief of Raiatea, turned from his island and disappeared into the sea.

His story reminds us all that mortals cannot hope to best the gods, not when they are the ones who make the rules.

CHAPTER SIX

To Kaimana's annoyance, Yam did not take turns to row. She had been unsure whether or not to offer him the chance to do so, and he certainly did not volunteer. In fact, the god of yams did not appear to travel well, and spent his first day in the small canoe looking decidedly green.

"I don't think that's a great idea," Kaimana said when she realised that the liquid Yam was drinking was more of the beer he had got drunk with during the previous night. "Drinking when travelling disagrees with most, especially those who've spent most of their time on land."

"Oh, really?" he replied, face dark, voice loud. "That goes for gods too, does it? Have you asked many gods about their experiences with beer on the ocean waves? Or, perhaps, just perhaps, you've assumed that because I've chosen to take this form, I suffer from the same weaknesses as your inferior bodies? Girl, I am a god, and we do not get sea sick."

Kaimana wisely did not smirk when, less than an hour later, Yam was emptying his contents over the side of the canoe.

"I know what you're thinking, little mouse" he shouted between retches, "but this has nothing to do with the beer." After another bout of dry heaving, he continued. "We gods are sensitive to sources of magic, to things that are wrong on the islands. Must be that insufferable bond between you and the beast that's upsetting my gut."

What irritated Kaimana more, however, were the strange looks that Yam shot her whenever she was talking to her spark. Now that it was back, her spark's hunger for Kaimana's attention was insufferable, and it did not understand why she could not devote all her time to it. Most of her day was spent rowing, now, and after a session of intense buzzing Kaimana felt she had eventually convinced the spark that she had no choice. However, after this argument Kaimana caught Yam glancing at her with a raised eyebrow and knowing smile, which caused her to blush furiously. She was used to having the spark to herself, and was sure that Yam and his godly powers were encroaching on these moments, yet he said nothing about it.

Kaimana had a much more difficult time convincing her spark that Rakau was still important to them. All it wanted was for her to abandon the monster, find a small island with food and solitude, and finish their song.

But, can't you see, she thought, addressing the spark, *the song is all about Rakau, now. It started in his cave, the chase, and it has grown so much since I've been spending time with him. We can't finish the song until we finish his story, and to do that we have to get him to safety.*

The spark again relented, but Kaimana felt it continued to regard the taniwha with jealousy and suspicion, especially when Kaimana spent free time with Rakau instead of composing. Kaimana argued that this was helping her to understand the monster, so they could better portray him in their music.

This was not the truth. Although Kaimana's heart had broken at the loss of her spark, and she was overjoyed when it had returned, and remained excited at the thought of the song they were weaving together, what became a joy for Kaimana over these few days of travel was her time with Rakau. They travelled for long stretches, making for the edge of the Atoll ring that opened onto the Inner Sea. They were lucky enough to find small islands to stop at in the evenings, and it was at these times that Rakau and Kaimana played.

Kaimana's favourite activity was a re-enactment of their first swim together, allowing the taniwha to take her under the shallow Atoll waters and explore the reef at speeds she had never experienced before. Rakau himself seemed to prefer time on land, and took much joy in doing his best to hide from Kaimana on the beaches, rocks and forests of the islands they stopped on. Despite his size, Rakau had a gift for the game, using his dark hide as camouflage, and Kaimana would often struggle to find him. What tended to give Rakau away were deep coughing chuckles, after which he would emerge from the undergrowth or swamps he had dived into.

"Not natural," Yam would protest at these times when the playful pair left him lying on his back on the beach, doing what he could to settle his stomach. "Girl and a monster shouldn't be getting on like this. It'll lead to bad things, you'll see."

Kaimana smiled at the god's grumpy demeanour, but a twist in her own gut warned her of her own similar fears. Rarely in the stories did mortals fare well when concerning themselves too deeply with the affairs of gods and monsters.

On what was to be the final night before setting sail on the Inner Sea, they could not find a suitable island to berth at. The one they had been making towards as the sun set turned out to be inhabited by a few small families, their handful of huts a future village in the making.

Yam stared at the small settlement from the distance, his eyes wistful.

Kaimana put her hand on the god's shoulder. "You could go to them, you know," she said. "I can't take Rakau, of course, but we'd wait for you here. I'm sure these people would praise and remember a visit from you for the rest of their days."

The sweat on the god's forehead glistened in the setting sun, and Kaimana could read the temptation in Yam's eyes. However, the god grunted and waved his hand, dismissing the notion.

"I'm here to find my story, not grow more roots," he said. "And for the record, gods do not appreciate it when mortals tell them what to do. Best get that into your head now, before you meet my sister."

On the following morning, Kaimana woke and saw that Yam was already up. He was standing in the canoe, facing the rising sun.

Kaimana sat up straighter when she realised that Rakau's head was above the water, and that he too was staring in the same direction as Yam.

"What is it?" she asked.

Yam shook his head. "Not sure. Something though, something with power. Looks like we can both sense it," he said, indicating the taniwha.

Kaimana wrapped her cloak around her to ward off the morning coolness. "Power? A god, you think? Is it Nakoa?"

Yam let out a deep breath. "Don't think so, no. I've met him once, after he did away with my brother. Wasn't a fan of him, and he didn't take much notice of me, but I'd recognise him again if he was close. No, this is something else. Maybe someone else."

"Another god then?"

Yam turned to look at Kaimana, his face grumpy and confused. "Could be, mouse."

Kaimana felt her spark sing in excitement, and she stole another glance at the dark volcano that had haunted her skyline for the past few days. If they had found another god, perhaps this one would be able to help them against Nakoa. Kaimana might be spared the dangerous journey across the deep after all.

"We'd better go then," she said loudly, making sure Rakau could hear her. "We don't want whoever it is to disappear before we get to them."

Rakau turned around in the water and looked at her, whining. He was not happy about something.

"What is it?" Kaimana asked.

Yam answered for him. "It's strange, this feeling. Not bad, just... different. Not felt something quite like this before. Bit like you two, being so close - maybe this power shouldn't be here."

Kaimana stopped rowing, her own emotions now mirroring Rakau's uncertainty. "Do you think we shouldn't go? It's too dangerous?"

Yam shrugged. "Like I said, it just feels different. If you want dangerous, you know where to go," and he looked at Leinani's distant volcano. "That way?" and he motioned east again, where he and Rakau had sensed something. "Could be danger. Could be something else."

Kaimana looked at the volcano one more time. Inside, her spark shrank away, fearful of the stories of Leinani's anger. Kaimana caught her breath at this movement, for a moment thinking her spark was going to disappear again.

"It's worth it, then. Let's have a look, and we know the volcano is there if things don't work out."

They travelled for half a day until the source of their unease peeked over the horizon. It was, of course, an island. This one was different to most on the Atoll because of how tall it was. Most Atoll islands had started life as large rock formations that peeked just above the sea waters, remaining above the surface long enough to collect sand for beaches, attract vegetation and then animal life. The islands came into being over years of the ideal conditions attracting life. This new island jutted out of the sea like an arrow from a wound, thrusting high into the sky. The sides of the island, as far as Kaimana could see, consisted of mostly cliff. Looking up at the rock face from the sea, the island appeared to be barren and devoid of life. It was, however, large. There was plenty of room on it for living things to hide, which gave curious Kaimana all the excuse she needed to get out and explore.

As the canoe drifted closer to the massive rock, Yam became restless, shuffling about on his seat and looking around in paranoia.

"You know," he said, "I'm beginning to think this is a bad idea. Something feels wrong. I think you'll be better off with my sister."

Kaimana studied the island, eyes narrowing. "What's wrong now?" she asked. She did not fancy the idea of facing the volcano god, not now that the option of something else was so close. She could see no problem with the rock ahead of them.

Yam shook his head. "Not sure. It just feels wrong."

Kaimana bit her lip. Her mind returned to the stories, when mortals chose to ignore godly advice. Again, these situations never turned out well. However, most of the gods in those stories held a bit more renown. What could the god of yams really know about danger? Also, Kaimana was conscious of her spark, and how it quivered when she thought about approaching any closer to the volcano.

"We'll be careful," she said, finally. "Let's take a peek, but if anything strange happens, we can head for Leinani.

"After all," and with this she smiled at Yam, "I'm travelling with a god and a monster. What could go wrong?"

They eventually found a sparse beach on which to land. The rocks upwards formed a sort of natural staircase, one that even Rakau was able to mount.

"We're not the only ones here," Yam noted. "Doesn't that thought just fill you with excitement?"

Kaimana ignored the god's sarcasm as she had spotted the signs also. The rocks they climbed were worn smooth, probably by generations of feet plodding up and down them. The plant life had been cleared from the natural stairway. This suggested that the regular movement of bodies up and down this stretch of cliff kept the plants at bay.

Upon rising up the cliff, the rest of the island appeared very strange to Kaimana. It was mostly flat, but almost entirely devoid of life. Some dead trees dotted the landscape, and many large boulders, but there was little else to tell of. Even the few wisps of grass that grew on the ground were straw-like and yellow.

Kaimana looked at Yam, whilst resting her hand on Rakau's side. "What is this place?"

Yam shook his head and Rakau just grunted, turned his head to the mountains in the middle of the island and walked towards them. The rock field in front of them was strewn with large boulders, which Rakau walked around or nudged out of the way with his large bulk as they moved past.

"We're being watched," Yam muttered, continuing to look in the direction they were travelling.

"Where?" Kaimana said, darting her head all over the place, desperate to see what he was talking about.

"I keep seeing them behind the rocks. Look closely, there are people here."

Kaimana eventually saw them, noticing small movements out of the corner of her eye. From what she could tell, the scampering figures were human, but they wore strange garb, mostly covered in feathers.

"Hello?" she shouted, but gained no response as the people darted out of sight.

"Don't seem to be interested in speaking with us," Yam grumbled, "but they also don't seem to be completely terrified by the sight of your friend. Unless they're gods - which they aren't, by the way - then I gotta ask why they don't seem to mind having a monster strolling through their lovely field of rocks."

This did strike Kaimana as odd. Any villages she had had much experience with would have started screaming and making a lot of noise at the sight of a taniwha on their island.

"Do you think they've seen a taniwha before?"

Yam shrugged. "Maybe." He turned to look at Kaimana, grimly. "How about this thought: maybe there's something else in their lives that already terrifies them, scares them enough that the sight of our friend doesn't unnerve them. There is no power in these people, anyway. What we're sensing lives up there." Yam indicated with his head to the top of the central mountains, and Rakau grunted in agreement. "But I'm going to tell you again, we shouldn't be here. Best get back to the canoe while we can, and head on to my sister. At least we know what's lying in wait for us that way."

A big part of Kaimana agreed with the god, and she thought again about the fire goddess. As the image of a flame-haired woman formed in Kaimana's mind, she felt her spark shy away again, growing dimmer as it had just before it had left her the first time.

I won't take you there, she promised the spark, and in response it pulsed brighter again, happy. *We'll find something to help Rakau here, and then we can finish our song.*

Not responding to Yam, and trying to ignore his stare as she spoke to her spark, Kaimana kept walking. After a moment, Yam threw up his arms in disgust and followed her.

"Foolish mortals," he grumbled, "let's see what kind of mess you get us into now."

As they continued to climb, they spotted more of the natives. Kaimana could not tell whether they had darker skin than most islanders, or if it was just because they were covered in mud. The natives did not stick around long enough for Kaimana to get a good look at them, although they did eventually become braver, and approached the visitors in larger groups. Still, every time Kaimana turned her head to get a better look, they darted behind nearby rock formations.

As the trio climbed higher, they came across the homes of the natives. Whereas most islanders on the Atoll created huts for themselves out of the island vegetation, these people lived in the caves of the hills and mountains. A winding, well-used path snaked up the mountain and Kaimana, Rakau and Yam followed it. Lining this path were a large number of natural caves, which contained small fires and bright, wide eyes watching the strangers walk past. Nobody responded to Kaimana when she tried to address them, and she thought it best not to linger. Neither did anyone seem interested in doing her harm, although she thought this was mostly due to the large monster that was her walking companion. Best not to let him get too far ahead.

When they finally reached the top of the mountain they found the largest collection of trees they had seen since getting out of their canoe. The mountain top was flat, and contained a circle of six dead trees, hanging from which were numerous rags and other flying things - faded tapa ribbons and dried seaweed - creating the impression of leaves where there were none.

Yam and Rakau walked as if in a trance, wandering into the centre of the circle of trees. Kaimana heard a low rumbling coming from nearby, and quickly realised it was Rakau. She put her hand on the beast's side.

"What is it? Everything okay?"

"It is not," Yam replied. "Look."

Kaimana followed Yam's gaze. He was looking into the branches of the trees that surrounded them. There, camouflaged by the rags of branches, Kaimana saw the source of the power that her companions had sensed.

Each of the trees had a person skulking inside of its branches, camouflaged by the rags and dead things that hung from each lifeless limb. Each of these individuals was dressed in a different way, but some similarities were shared by all. Most of their clothing consisted of feathers. They also all wore masks, each painted or shaped in such a way to suggest some kind of bird.

A large figure dropped from the tree closest to Yam. The man's chest was uncovered, showing taunt, stringy muscles. His kilt was decorated with large white feathers, and his flat driftwood mask was coated in chalk, with a yellow beak painted around the hole for his mouth. The man also carried a tall, thin spear.

"We sensed you coming. We have waited for someone of power for a long time."

"We're only having a look, we thought there might be a god

here," Kaimana responded, backing away slowly from the newcomer. She was relieved that this uncanny figure was choosing to speak with them, but at the same time was uneasy in the knowledge that they were surrounded, as the creaking branches in the trees reminded her.

The man's mask darted to Kaimana for the first time. One of the figures in the trees above barked a laugh.

The man on the ground then turned to look at Yam. "It is you I speak to, god of the Atoll. We have waited for you for some time. We are the Birdmen of the Broken Island."

Two more figures dropped from the trees. One was a female, her breasts bare, sporting similar white attire to the first, although grey feathers also flecked her costume. The other was a man, much larger than the first, with a round belly and fat legs. Both of these also brandished weapons, the woman a thin, jagged stone dagger, the man a large club. They too wore masks, but unlike the original speaker their masks were not flat, and neither were they painted. Instead they had been worked into the shape of long bird beaks.

The original speaker continued. "We speak on behalf of the totems that have gifted us their strength. I am the Albatross Lord, the first of our kind. These are Gull Knave and Moa Chief. There are others, above you."

A hissing overhead made Kaimana turn her head upwards. In the tree closest to her she managed to catch a glimpse of a black and white shape moving amongst the rags.

"I think it was a mistake to come here," she said, both to Yam and Rakau, but also attempting to address the original speaker. "We mean you no harm, and shall leave your land at once."

The Birdmen did not appear to be unnerved by the sight of Rakau. Instead, Gull Knave and Moa Chief began to circle the taniwha, their weapons ready. It was Rakau who looked unsure, moving his eyes between the two Birdmen. Yam was not looking much better, his face having become pale and dotted with sweat.

"We do not address the child," came a female voice hiding in a tree on the opposite side of the circle from Kaimana. Kaimana could make out the speaker moving around inside the tree, again covered in white feathers. It was the eyes on the flat mask of this person that really unnerved Kaimana, however - they were the wide, predatory eyes of an owl.

"We do not address her, we speak to the god."

"Owl Queen is correct," the figure who had identified himself as Albatross Lord said. "We do not concern ourselves with invading mortals. She will be dealt with in time. It is you we wish to speak to," he said, indicating the quivering god with his weapon.

"She speaks for me!" Yam blurted out, visibly shaking now. He turned to Kaimana and hissed, "You brought us here. Get us out, now."

At the god's words, Kaimana felt her stomach clench. Inside, her spark began to dim again, shivering.

Another low growl came from above, where the black and white feathers shuffled about.

Kaimana slid closer to Rakau. There was a rumble coming from the taniwha's throat.

"What do you want from us?" she asked.

Albatross Lord cocked his head. "From you? Nothing, besides another breeder. Our people will be pleased with you. It is the god we require, he is our main prize. We have been gifted power, from our totems, but one such as he could change the lives of our people."

Kaimana shook her head to dismiss the fear of a possible future of being a 'breeder'. "What about Rakau? The taniwha? Do you not fear him?"

The growling figure in the tree barked a hoarse laugh, and Kaimana was unnerved to see all of the visible Birdmen smile as well.

"He will be fine sport," came a gravelly voice from the tree above, "but he cannot stand against us. He is made of wood, is he not? His carcass will provide for our people."

On saying this, the figure dropped from the tree to the ground, with the female dressed as an owl doing the same some distance behind him. Now, Kaimana got a clear look at the final Birdman. His cloak was mostly black feathers, speckled with dots of white throughout. Like the Gull Knave and Moa Chief, this man also had a carved wooden mask, but this one was painted or charred black, creating a hideous visage to look at. This man's weapon was an overlarge, black sickle.

"Magpie King, Owl Queen," the Albatross Lord addressed the new arrivals, "What shall we do with this, the first god that has entered our island?"

Yam turned to face the Magpie King now, the god's entire body vibrating.

"What is your realm?" the Magpie King barked at Yam. "What is your power?"

"Yam," the god stuttered. "I-I am god of yams. Yams."

The Magpie King and Moa Chief spat.

"Yams? A farmer? What kind of power is this? Useless to us."

As the Birdmen spoke, Kaimana's eyes darted around the dead copse of trees. Beyond the dead trees were numerous large rocks, and the path back down the mountain. If they could somehow get past the Birdmen, getting back to the path and the canoe would be their only chance. Kaimana realised she was panicking, taking shallow, quick breaths. Her spark had almost disappeared again, terrified of the threat of these newcomers.

"Useless?" the Albatross Lord rebuked. "It is not the stuff of legends, but to us his could be the greatest gift. We who are no longer able to grow on our land, we may finally be able to do so again."

Yam finally found the courage to speak. "You wish to c-call upon my powers? I might grant them to you, although you clearly do not worship me. Grant me and my companions safe passage from your shores, pray to me and you may find your prayers will be answered."

The oversized Moa Chief responded to this suggestion by jumping forward and knocking Yam onto his belly.

"Foolish god," the Owl Queen sneered, walking up behind the Magpie King and resting an arm on his shoulder. "We will take what we need from you. We do not pray. We know not the meaning of safe passage."

In her growing terror, what Kaimana was most aware of now was Rakau, his muscles tensed to pounce. The Birdmen appeared to be mostly focussing on Yam, aware that despite the god's diminutive appearance, he was probably the greatest threat to them. Rakau in turn had his gaze mostly focussed on the black robe of the Magpie King, and the large spear of Moa Chief.

Gull Knave stepped forward. "I will take the girl to the village. The chief has given my totem much honour this season, and I will give her to him as a reward." She pointed her knife at Kaimana. "Move now, girl, before I mark you with my blade."

Kaimana stood where she was, and shook her head frantically, both outraged and fearful of the woman's suggestion. She could not find the power to speak.

"Very well then," Gull Knave said and took a step towards Kaimana.

Rakau's rumble became a roar. All of the Birdmen turned to the taniwha, waiting to see what he would do next.

After a tense pause, the Magpie King snarled. "He knows he cannot beat us. This is why he does not attack."

"No," Kaimana said, finally finding her voice. She also found a smile to wear on her face, because she knew what was coming. "He is not attacking you because he made me a promise."

"Rakau, I release you from your promise."

What happened next was a blur for Kaimana. The massive taniwha leapt at Gull Knave, snapping his colossal jaws down on the woman. Or, he would have if she had still been there. At the same instant that Rakau had pounced, each of the Birdmen leapt back into their trees. Kaimana had to blink again to figure out what had just happened, as the speed of the movement was so quick it appeared that the Birdmen had just vanished.

They're fast. Unnaturally fast. Rakau, we have to run. You can't win this fight.

In another breath, the Birdmen descended again upon the taniwha, striking at once with all of their weapons. Kaimana felt her heart break as Rakau screamed in pain, and a luminous green liquid spurted through the air.

Kaimana did the only thing she was able to do in the face of such a clash. She ran.

She was not ashamed at her choice. Kaimana was a mortal woman, not long from being a girl, and she was in the company of monsters and gods and they were at war. There was no chance of survival if she stayed to watch.

The cacophony behind her was accompanied by the cracking of rocks and trees, and the path that she ran down was peppered with debris. A small stone hit Kaimana on the back of the arm and remained embedded there, the shock of the impact sending her tumbling to the ground. She took a deep breath and began to run again, speeding down the stony path.

None of the natives were in view, now. *Wonder how many times they've seen this happen before?*

She slipped and tumbled down the mountain, and when she

felt she could run no more Kaimana found one of the mountain-side caves and slunk into it. This particular opening was not that deep, and thankfully was uninhabited. A pile of still-warm ashes told Kaimana it had recently been occupied, but they appeared to have decided to move elsewhere at the sound of the battle up above.

Just need to get my breath back and I'll do the same. Another run like that should get me to the canoe. If it's still there. Just a few more minutes...

Inside, her spark struggled, but she held on tight to it. Despite the pain in her arm, and despite the fear of being found by one of the Birdmen, one thought chiefly occupied Kaimana's mind.

This is my fault. If I'd listened to them both, Yam and Rakau, we wouldn't have come here. They'd still be with me. But I wanted to protect my spark.

The infant song called for her attention, wanting her mind to focus on it instead of the guilt that was rising inside her. For the first time since Kaimana had begun to spark again, she ignored it.

She listened to the conflict high above. The sounds were not as constant as before, but every so often, a loud crash, thud or roar would let her know that events were still ongoing. She tried not to think of the wounds that were being inflicted upon Rakau.

He's my friend. A monster, yes, but a friend. He attacked them to protect me. I don't want him to be hurt.

When she thought of Yam, she was only frustrated.

He's a god. I know he looks after yams, but surely any god should be able to best those five Birdmen. They have powers, yes, but the way they were talking, it sounded as if they were given to them. Surely whatever Yam holds within his being is greater than that?

After catching her breath, she got up and moved towards the cave opening. The crashes above continued, but Kaimana knew it was time to move. If Rakau and Yam survived, they would be able to find her again. They knew where she was going next. If they did not survive... well, Kaimana was certain they would not want her to sacrifice herself for nothing. Her arm ached where the stone had forced its way under her skin, and she pulled it out, accompanied by a spurt of red. She was proud that she did not cry out in pain, and tore a little of tapa cloth from her dress to bind the wound with.

As she was finishing with the knot, she heard a loud thump outside.

"I can smell you, you know. Can hear your heart beat."

Kaimana could hear it too, thudding in her ears at the sound of the gravelly tones of the Magpie King.

She looked frantically out of the cave entrance. She could see nothing, but was certain he was close by. Would she be able to run fast enough to get away from him before he found exactly where she was?

"We have your friends. The god came willingly enough, and my companions are taming the beast. He shall be lumber for us soon enough." Her face sagged at the thought of Rakau dying because of her choices.

"Come quietly now, and you will be harmed as little as possible."

Not the most tempting of offers.

Nodding her head in affirmation, Kaimana took a deep breath and sprinted, pointing herself in the direction she believed the canoe to be in.

She was only seconds out of the cave entrance before something landed on her back, sending her sprawling to the ground. She hit her face on the hard rock underneath. Inside, her spark began to scream.

"There you are," the Magpie King rasped.

Kaimana rolled over onto her back to look at the dark figure standing above her. The man's bird mask covered his entire face except for his eyes, in which she could see cruel mirth at the position he had her in. His sickle was attached to his belt now. He did not need his weapon to catch this particular prey.

Something inside Kaimana snapped. This man thought she was weak and defenceless, easy prey for someone of his abilities. The rage that began to build inside her at this thought startled her spark, causing it to pause and watch what was happening in morbid fascination.

Kaimana spat at the Magpie King's face. "I'll never give in to you. You may as well kill me, if you think I'll come with you willingly."

The Magpie King nodded, and as he spoke she could hear the smile in his voice. "My queen told me you looked like an obstinate one. I shall enjoy beating it out of you."

Her spark screamed again, and threatened to run.

Do not! The spark halted, as if in shock at the command in

Kaimana's voice. *You do not get to run from me again.*

The Birdman kicked Kaimana in the side of her gut, sending her sailing through the air, over one of the boulders that decorated the Broken Island. Kaimana landed on her side with a snap, and she knew straight away that something inside - hopefully just a rib - was broken.

She had never known pain like this before in her life. She knew she should be terrified. However, Kaimana also knew that if she gave in to her fear now then all was lost.

She scrambled around on the ground for some dirt to throw into her attacker's eyes, but there was none to be found on this barren island. Instead, her hand found a small stone, just large enough to fit into the palm of her hand.

Kaimana closed her eyes and whispered a prayer. "Laka, goddess of music, my patron, hear my prayer. Give me the strength to live past this day, give me the strength to craft you a tale these islands have never seen before."

At that moment, the Magpie King leapt over the boulder to land beside Kaimana's prone body. She heard his smile again as he spoke. "Now let us end this, little girl."

Kaimana threw the rock at the Magpie King. The Birdman laughed at her act, as well he should have. A small rock against this force of nature was a pitiful weapon. Kaimana's aim was true, and the rock flew straight at the Magpie King's exposed eye, but was a simple enough task for the man to turn his head and the stone bounced ineffectually off of his helm.

This turn of the head was all the time Kaimana needed. In the second that the Magpie King's attention was diverted, Kaimana sat up, grabbed the King's sickle from his belt and did what she could to plunge the blade into the man's stomach.

This resulted in a yowl of pain from the Magpie King, but Kaimana did not wait around to savour her victory - she used this opening to turn and flee again. She could not help the smile of success that played across her face, even though she knew this desperate act would do little to help her. The blade had not bitten deep, and in seconds he would be on her once again, this time angry and bleeding.

But I stood my ground as heroes in stories are supposed to do.

Behind her, the scream of pain turned to anger and Kaimana realised her assailant had leapt high into the air. She jumped to the side, narrowly missing being crushed by the Magpie King's landing. However, her jump caused her to sacrifice her footing, and she tripped and fell to the ground again.

Knowing there would be no chance to throw another rock, no other chance to steal his weapon, Kaimana turned around to look at her attacker. One of the Magpie King's hands was clutching his belly, which wept red.

"I will kill you for that," he whispered.

Kaimana nodded. "I expected nothing less. But I've marked you for life, now. You'll always remember me."

Her spark tugged away from her again, struggling for survival, and she relaxed her grip on it, allowing it to escape. Kaimana closed her eyes and waited for the end.

Instead she was greeted by what felt like an explosion. Kaimana opened her eyes, just in time to see the Magpie King's legs protruding from Rakau's mouth, broken at impossible angles. Another crunch from the taniwha and the Birdman disappeared.

Rakau was covered in deep cuts and wounds, each of which oozed green blood, luminous like his eyes. One large spear remained stuck deep into his side, and Kaimana recognised it as Moa Chief's weapon.

It was Rakau's eyes that most worried Kaimana, however. They were filled with a rage that shocked her. Since travelling with Rakau, she had begun to think of him as a companion, like a trusted pet almost. She had allowed his tenderness around her to let her forget that there was a reason these monsters had a reputation for being bloodthirsty and vicious. He was hurt, his blood was up, and that meant he was unpredictable.

Kaimana should have been just as wary of Rakau as she was of the Magpie King. Instead, she ran forward and threw her arms around the taniwha's neck. "You came for me," she whispered in his ear. "You didn't leave me."

As she embraced the monster, she was surprised to feel a familiar buzzing inside of her. It was her spark, still with her, appreciating the reunion with the taniwha. Kaimana smiled. *Thank you for staying,* she told it. *This, these dangers, what a song they'll make.* She could feel the spark jingle in cautious agreement.

Rakau shook his head and the anger in his eyes dissipated. He exhaled deeply, and to Kaimana's surprise, he collapsed into the dirt.

"You're hurt," she said. "Stay still."

The taniwha did not argue, so Kaimana moved backwards to inspect his wounds, keeping her hand always in contact with his rough skin so he knew where she was, that he was not alone.

Most of the cuts aren't deep, and if he heals anything like a human, they shouldn't be a problem. One or two of the larger cuts are going to need dressed, and they'll definitely scar. That spear will be tough to deal with.

Rakau's once-patterned skin was now irreparably broken.

The worst wound, as Kaimana had predicted, was the one in which Moa Chief's spear remained lodged. The weapon was so deeply buried, she could not see the tip of it, and the blood that oozed from this cut was much darker than the rest.

Kaimana walked back to Rakau. "I have to remove it," she told him. "I think it'll hurt, but afterwards it can heal."

For the first time, Kaimana saw fear in the taniwha's eyes, and she did something that surprised even herself. She ran forward to give the taniwha a hug, and kissed him on his cheek.

"I'll be as gentle as I can," she promised.

Rakau gave her a weak smile.

She moved back to the spear and took a grip of its shaft. Rakau gave a loud roar at the touch and shook himself, throwing Kaimana to the ground, pain blossoming from her own injuries with the impact.

She dusted herself off. "Please don't do that. It'll never get better if I don't."

She took a hold of the spear and pulled on it again. Rakau roared once more, and this time the spear shaft broke. The taniwha turned his body away from her, raising the wound high into the air where she could not reach it. Even from this distance, Kaimana could see the remains of the spear still lodged under the taniwha's skin. Rakau shook his head.

Kaimana looked at him in disappointment, but also with worry. Without the long shaft to pull on, she knew she would not be able to work the weapon free without time or help.

"We need Yam," she said, eventually. "Do you know where he is?"

Rakau grunted, indicating the top of the mountain, where the encounter had begun.

"Is he all right?"

Rakau gave another grunt, this one non-committal.

Kaimana turned to look again at the top of the island. "We have to go back to get him."

The two wounded companions made their way stealthily back up the mountain path, finally coming upon a ridge that allowed them to look unobserved onto the ring of trees. There they saw the answers to their questions. The four remaining Birdmen were together, and by their movements they were very agitated. The one that called himself Albatross Lord was particularly angry, shouting and beckoning towards the others. The Owl Queen had her mask off, and seemed to be wavering between crying and uncontrollable rage. It appeared they already knew of the fate of the Magpie King.

Yam was there also, in a heap in the middle of where the ragged trees had previously been. The trees themselves were no longer standing, destroyed in the battle between Birdmen and taniwha. Yam was still, and Kaimana could not tell whether he was alive or dead.

She turned to Rakau, who was breathing heavily beside her. The taniwha was badly wounded, and the spear in his side needed attention, fast. There was no chance of Rakau taking on the Birdmen by himself.

Kaimana looked back at the prone god on the ground.

We're going to have to leave him. Maybe this will turn out to be the story he was looking for, the tale of the Birdmen of the Broken Island. He'll be the god they captured, a small side note in a larger story, much like the previous god of war that's often mentioned when talking about Nakoa's rise to power.

At this moment, Yam turned over on the ground. His movement was ignored by all of the Birdmen, still arguing amongst themselves. Kaimana's eyes widened. Yam was completely unrestrained. He must have offered no resistance to his attackers. They seemed to believe he was fine to be left there cowering before them as they dealt with other matters.

Let that be their last mistake.

Kaimana turned to Rakau. "I'm going to do something that'll look pretty stupid, but I want you to stay hidden for as long as possible, all right?"

Rakau, exhausted after the climb, raised what passed for his eyebrows in a question.

Kaimana smiled wearily at him. "Just trust me."

Then Kaimana stood up, now in plain view of all on the mountaintop.

"Yam, god of yams. Do not lie there in the dirt in front of these warriors. That is what a farmer would do, a coward. You are not a farmer, nor a coward. You are a god. Show them the truth of that."

At once, the Birdmen realised where the noise was coming from. Owl Queen was the first to react, crossing the space between the ragged trees and Kaimana's hiding place in a heartbeat. Her thin dagger was drawn, and would have impacted with Kaimana's neck if the musician had not rolled out of the way, and if the Owl Queen had not been intercepted by Rakau's teeth.

The taniwha was not able to deal with this combatant as quickly as he had the Magpie King. Rakau did not have the element of surprise this time, and he was tired. Hopefully exhaustion was his only issue - he had lost so much of his green blood by now, Kaimana feared there might be worse in store for him. Nevertheless, the Owl Queen jumped away with one less arm, which now dangled uselessly from one of Rakau's eye teeth. This grave wound, however, did not stop the woman from continuing to attack. She realised this was the creature that was responsible for the death of her mate, and wanted revenge. Her face contorted more with rage than with pain, she lunged again at Rakau, drawing another blade with her remaining hand. Kaimana knew that Rakau might not survive this attack, especially when the other Birdmen joined in.

Where are they?

Kaimana turned back to the others - the Albatross, Gull and Moa. She could not see them, only the green trees and Yam remained on the mountaintop.

She had to double-take before she realised what she was looking at.

Yam was no longer lying in the dirt. He was standing in a crouch, with his fingers buried into cracks in the mountain rock. He was moving his fingers softly, much in the same way as Kaimana had seen her mother kneed her father's back after a rough day on the sea. Yam's eyes were closed and he was muttering, a soothing smile playing across his face.

Kaimana realised the green trees that she was looking at were completely new. She was also quick to realise that there were three of them - one for each of the remaining Birdmen. She squinted and ran closer to Yam to get a better look at what was going on. The greenery was not trees at all, but a mass of what appeared to be long shoots or vines growing from the ground. At that moment, the hand of the Albatross Lord burst from one of these clusters of vines, brandishing his weapon blindly. Some of the new shoots broke free of the main column, grabbed his hand by the wrist and yanked it back under the green.

She realised then that these were the leaves of the yam root. This was Yam's power at work.

With a laugh of surprise and triumph, Kaimana ran over to the god. He opened his eyes and looked at her, smiling through his exhaustion.

"Look at what these stupid people did to their island," he said. "Stopped growing things on it, ruined it through fire and war. But, they didn't get everything. Some roots remained, deep under the stone, waiting to be found."

His smile left his face and he looked at her seriously now. "I would never have had the strength to do this without you, mouse."

She smiled back. "Yes, you would. Do you think those roots were there by accident? This is your story, god of yams. This is how we will remember you."

He nodded, both excitement and exhaustion playing across his face.

A series of loud thuds behind them drew Kaimana's attention back to Rakau's conflict with the Owl Queen. With the shock of her companions being dispatched so quickly, Rakau appeared to have gained the upper hand. The woman's legs were in his mouth, and he was thumping her viciously and repeatedly to the ground, a series of wet cracks marking the end of the Owl Queen's reign.

Exhausted, Rakau dropped the body of his foe and turned to plod slowly towards Kaimana and Yam, each step pained.

The harvest god stood up and greeted the taniwha. "Look at you, a proper monster. And me, a proper god. Together, we could see off armies."

In response Rakau collapsed into the dirt. A trail of dark green was trailing behind the taniwha, leading back up to the broken body of his enemy. Rakau lay still, lifeless.

THE
FIRST CANOES

A tale from the Crescent Atoll

We do not know where the canoes came from. We know they belonged to a people not unlike us, living on islands far across the Outer Sea. They travelled across the waters in canoes the size of whales, bringing entire families with them.

We do not know why they came. Perhaps they had been cast out from their homeland, exiled and in need of somewhere to start anew. It may be that they were lost, cast adrift by an unexpected storm, far from familiar shores. Or it is just possible that they had been inspired to explore, leaving the safety of their own islands to find a part of the world they could call their own.

What we do know is when they first arrived here, to where we now live, there were no islands for them to make homes on.

There was only Leinani.

It must have been an intimidating sight for those weary travellers, a colossal red headed woman standing naked in the sea before them, towering up to the clouds. Or perhaps she had taken the form of a volcano, giving them a tempting possibility of dry land - we are no longer sure exactly what they saw. What we do know is that Leinani was there, and she was not happy at the presence of these animal-worshipping intruders.

To rid herself of these people, Leinani called up fire from the depths below, igniting the wooden canoes and consuming the generations of travellers that briefly gazed upon her magnificence.

Unknown to Leinani, or perhaps by her own divine decree, one woman survived. Blinded and scarred by the goddess' flames, this lone swimmer somehow found her way back to her people. It was from this woman that humans began to learn of the danger that awaited them across the waters, but also about the divine majesty of the goddess that walked the waves.

It took generations for them to return. Perhaps it took this long for them to work up the courage to approach the goddess again. It may be that this time had to pass before the winds and ocean currents were aligned to bring people back to these waters. It has also been said that a few hundred years is all it takes for people to forget the horror of countless deaths, instead only recalling the majesty of the living goddess.

This time a score of vessels survived the journey to Leinani. Once again they found her emerging from the waves, steam rising from where her bare waist parted the sea.

Once again she looked upon the visitors with scorn.

She called her then-lover, Tangaloa, god of the sea, to deal with this irritation. Tangaloa withdrew his waters from the canoes, lowering the canoes to the sea bed. Then he allowed the waters to return, splintering wood and filling lungs.

Pleased with her lover's work, Leinani regarded one of the human women as she struggled beneath the waves, the light in her eyes growing dimmer.

It was then that Leinani noticed something that caught her interest. When the previous group of outsiders had come, they had brought with them tokens of their animal gods - mouse feet, bird feathers, snake fangs. This dying woman had a wolf's tongue in a small bottle hung around her neck. However, beside this bottle hung a carven image of a woman on fire.

Leinani smiled when she realised that somewhere over the seas, her story was spreading. She strained her ears, and far in the distance, the faint murmurings of worship in her name floated across the waves.

Intrigued by the notion that these small humans were glorifying her, the goddess raised the drowning woman to the surface, again allowing a single survivor to return back to her people, to further add to Leinani's legend.

Centuries passed by, and a final fleet of canoes made their way to Leinani's waters. The journey had been a dangerous one, as Leinani had asked her siblings to test these humans, buffeting them with wind, water and beasts. Only seven canoes remained.

These humans each wore the symbols of Leinani, or had her marks tattooed on their bodies. They had long forgotten the worship of animal spirits, instead dedicating themselves to the stories of the fiery goddess.

They did not find what they were expecting. Much like the other fleets who had braved this journey, the occupants of these canoes were expecting to see their goddess in the flesh, gazing upon her majesty for mere moments before she punished them. Instead, where they expected to find a goddess they found a ring of islands, summoned by Leinani from the sea bed. There, in the centre of the ring, Leinani awaited them.

"You have done what I thought was impossible," Leinani said to the supplicating outsiders. "You have impressed me. In return I give you this gift, these islands, so you may never lose sight of me."

And so the Crescent Atoll was created, made for our people to settle near our goddess, so we may worship her for the remainder of our bloodlines.

CHAPTER SEVEN

While Rakau was unconscious, Kaimana took it upon herself to clean his wounds.

"Would you give me a hand with this?" she asked Yam as she stepped around the taniwha to where the Moa Chief's spear had pierced Rakau's hide.

Yam, still heady with his victory, spluttered at the suggestion. "What do you think I am, mouse? I saved us all from our attackers. I am Yam, the warrior, feared by all on this island, not a bedside nurse for beasts. Sorting this out is hardly the task one asks of a god." Nevertheless, he moved beside Kaimana to observe the wound, worry lines creasing on his forehead.

Kaimana used one of the Owl Queen's thin knives to cut into the spear wound and was eventually able to reach in and pull forth the remains of the weapon. Rakau lost a lot more blood during this operation, and Kaimana continued to fret about how much blood a taniwha could afford to lose.

Yam, his confidence now bolstered in a way that Kaimana had never seen before, assured her that Rakau would be fine. "Calm down, mouse. He isn't like you, that creature. Not even like me. It'll take much more than a few pokes and scratches to end his story."

Still, as they slept through the night on the mountaintop, Kaimana worried. Her spark remained, even after the traumatic events of the day, and in the silence it called to her, hungrily, urging her to forget everything else and to concentrate on it. However, Kaimana pushed it to the side, focussing her attention on her fallen friend.

"I want to go swimming with you again," she whispered in Rakau's ear. He had not opened his eyes since collapsing at the end of the fight with the Birdmen. "I want to travel under the sea with you and see the Atoll by moonlight."

Her fingers found her way to her ocarina. She felt a pang of guilt when she realised she had never once offered to play it for Rakau since they had started travelling together.

Softly, not wanting to wake Yam or to disturb any of the island's other inhabitants, Kaimana brought the clay instrument to her lips and played a low, haunting tune, based on a lullaby her mother had sang to her and her sister when loud storms had raged across the Atoll at the sea god's request. For the first time since falling unconscious, Rakau stirred a little, and Kaimana fancied she saw him smile.

Amber sparks jumped from her eyes, and her infant song mewled at her petulantly, urging Kaimana to forget this child's tune and to work on it instead.

Kaimana ignored her spark, and played for Rakau until morning.

As dawn broke, Rakau finally awoke, his green eyes opening to greet Kaimana, brightening her morning in a way the sun could not.

She gave a cry of thanks to Laka, and embraced the taniwha, sobbing through her smile of relief. He remained lying on the ground, exhausted, but rubbed his head into the hug, returning the comfort that Kaimana gave him.

"What in the mother's name is that racket?" Yam asked, having been awoken by Kaimana's shout.

"He's awake, he's fine," Kaimana said.

The god looked at Kaimana, eyebrow raised. "Didn't I tell you? They are tough, the taniwha. They have to be. They attract trouble like flies to shit. Just look at what we've been through already."

"No," Kaimana shook her head. "This wasn't Rakau's fault, it was mine. I should've listened to you, to both of you. We shouldn't

133

have come here. Only your sister can hide us from Nakoa."

Yam looked out from the mountaintop, across the empty waters of the Atoll, and his face darkened. "I don't want to interrupt this tender moment," he said, rolling his eyes, "but we've got problems. He is close, Nakoa. I can sense him now, not far from us. I reckon a day's journey, at the most. He must have found your trail. Well done on hiding it so well."

Kaimana's heart sank. She had known this would happen, but the timing was terrible. Rakau had still a long way to go until he recovered from yesterday's battle.

She stroked the monster's side, speaking to him softly. "We have to leave now, or he'll catch us."

Rakau opened a heavy eye to look at his friend. The taniwha sighed deeply.

"Not far to go. Look how close the volcano is. We'll be there before evening, I bet, if we start now."

Inside, Kaimana's spark gave a yelp of fear at the thought of Leinani's volcano, but Kaimana shushed it into submission.

Taking another deep breath, Rakau pushed himself onto his feet, and began to plod slowly back down the path to the canoe.

"I hope you're feeling up to some exercise," Kaimana said to Yam, her hand remaining on Rakau's side as her friend struggled down the steep slope. "You're rowing yourself this time." She grinned at the indignant shock on the god's face. "I'm travelling by taniwha."

Yam remained in the canoe, and Kaimana rode on Rakau's back. She argued this was so she could keep an eye on him as he recovered from his wounds. Although many of the cuts had now closed, and although it appeared that taniwha recovered considerably faster than most other creatures, Rakau was still noticeably weaker in his movements. Kaimana told Yam she was going to ride on Rakau's back to keep an eye on him, but she also realised she felt safer close to him.

A deep dread welled up in Kaimana's stomach as they approached the dark blue drop into the Inner Sea, and she reached her hand to her belt, this time to touch one of the Owl Queen's daggers that she had secured beside her ocarina, in case of danger.

Much like the last time, Rakau took her over the edge of the drop, and all of Kaimana's knowledge of this part of the world was screaming at her to turn back, to jump off of the taniwha and swim to the nearest land she could find. Kaimana tightened her grip on Rakau and tried to fight off the sense of vertigo that she suffered from no longer being able to see the sea bed.

They travelled for hours on the dark waves. Before them always loomed the volcano that was Leinani's home. The stories Kaimana knew about the goddess had Leinani taking many different forms. Sometimes she was a woman with red hair, in others she appeared as a person made of molten rock. Sometimes she was the volcano itself. Kaimana did not know what to expect when they saw her. She did know, however, some of the rules that were to be obeyed when mortals approached Leinani. One had to bring a gift. One also had to be certain to not eat anything on the journey to the goddess' volcano, particularly the red berries that grew on her land. She told Yam and Rakau as much as they travelled across the water, doing her best to take her mind off of the dark below.

Yam sniffed at this information. "Most of us, the gods, can change shapes, as we wish to. It may not surprise you to know that I can turn myself into a yam at a moment's notice."

"Would that not have been a fantastic way to escape the Birdmen when their backs were turned?" Kaimana asked.

Yam was silent for a moment. "This is why we never spend too much time with mortals," he grumbled eventually, then went back to paddling the canoe.

Rakau turned to Kaimana and gave her a quick grin. It made her heart soar to see the taniwha happy and healthier again, but she still hoped they would not encounter anything troublesome on this leg of the journey. If they were attacked by the creatures of the Inner Sea, Kaimana and Yam would have to rely solely on Rakau to protect them, and Kaimana could not predict what those dangers could be, or what condition Rakau was actually in when it came to being ready to fight.

Luckily, they arrived on the volcano without any encounters. At this point, the sky had grown dark. Kaimana was surprised to see so much greenery at the foot of the volcano. Looking at this place from a distance for the entirety of her life, Kaimana had assumed the island was just the volcano, and had expected to see black rock sprouting up out of the ocean. However, there appeared to be a wide circumference of forest between the beach and the mountain, and they would have to travel through it before beginning their ascent.

"Maybe she isn't here," Kaimana said upon disembarking, knowing that the gods of the Atoll often travelled.

"Oh, she's here," Yam said, without looking back. "I've felt her presence my entire life, and would have told you on the day we first met if she was not at home. Her power and energy shouts to me wherever I am on the Atoll. You can feel her too, I wager," he said to Rakau.

The taniwha nodded solemnly.

Kaimana took a deep breath, and was about to declare that they begin to climb when she stopped, her sentence frozen in her throat.

Somebody was watching them.

Just beyond the tree line, Kaimana made out a shot of fiery red. A figure stepped forward from the trees. It was a young woman, probably about Kaimana's age. Her hair was indeed a deep red, and she was dressed in an unusually long tapa dress, flowing all the way down to her ankles.

Kaimana's first thought was that this was Leinani herself, but she quickly realised this was not the case. The girl's hair was not naturally red - perhaps some dye made up from ochre paste - and she didn't have the presence that Kaimana had come to expect from a god.

"My lady Leinani bids you all welcome," the girl said to them, smiling softly.

A priestess, then. Kaimana had not known that any people lived on this island, although it did make sense that Leinani would call mortals into her service, like most other gods on the Atoll.

"Especially to her dear brother," the priestess continued, indicating Yam.

"Don't remember her showing any particular fondness to me," Yam grumbled, not at all trying to keep the words under his breath. "You know, we only met once, at the very beginning. She didn't really favour me in any particular way."

"She told me you would be wanting to proceed straight to her," the priestess continued, "although of course my order wants to make our services and luxuries available to you before you begin your climb."

Kaimana was tempted. It had been a long time since she had enjoyed the pleasures of a warm bath, and her belly was indeed rumbling at the thought of food. However, despite the priestess' pleasantries, the idea of being on Leinani's island unnerved Kaimana, and she wanted to be done with this place as soon as possible.

"We would like to proceed, if that's all the same with you," she told the priestess. "That is, if you think the goddess would not mind us going before her in our present state?"

It was at this moment Kaimana realised how bedraggled the three of them must look. Yam and Kaimana were still covered in dirt and blood - both on their faces and clothes - from their escapade on the Broken Island. Rakau himself was worse, his decorative patterns now a patchwork of cuts and welts.

The priestess smiled. "It will make no difference to her. Indeed, she told me she was looking forward to your meeting."

This sentence both piqued Kaimana's curiosity and made her stomach knot in anxiety.

"I believe you will be able to find the way yourself," the priestess said, indicating a small but well-trodden path that left the beach into the jungle.

Kaimana thanked the girl and motioned to Rakau to follow her, which he did stiffly, his wounds seeming to be more difficult to bear on land. Yam followed both, looking up at the high mountain with a fair amount of trepidation.

The jungle quickly began to rise, turning into a mountain path soon enough. Kaimana was pleased to see the red berries of legend appear not long after the climb took them above the tree line, and she took satisfaction in reminding the others again not to eat them.

"Or apparently the goddess will bring down a storm upon us, and we shall be lost forever," she said, repeating the tale once again.

"Bring down a storm," Yam grumbled. "That isn't even her area of responsibility. And how's a storm going to get us lost up here anyway? There's only one path - just keep heading up and we'll be fine."

Despite the yam god's words, he left the berries untouched.

About two thirds of the way up the mountain, the path ended at the opening of a large cave. It was just wide enough for Rakau to fit through, and no more. Wordlessly, the three of them stood there, catching their breath after the steep climb, but also contemplating what might lie inside. Kaimana put her hand on Rakau's side, both to steady her wounded friend and to calm her own nerves. She turned to Yam and was surprised to see that the god had turned white and was shaking. She smiled, and without speaking offered him her other hand.

Yam looked at it in surprise, and took a deep breath as if to speak, face turning red in anger at the suggestion that he would take comfort from a mortal. However, after a moment's pause, he exhaled and took hold of her hand, grasping tightly. One by one, hands firmly joined, the three of them entered Leinani's lair.

Inside, Kaimana found it difficult to breathe. The massive cavern hidden under the mountain was lit by molten rock, the goddess' fire. The lava flowed in a river, in a crescent arch cutting the companions off from the furthest wall. There, hanging from the rocks of the mountain, ten times the height of even Rakau, was the fire goddess.

Leinani was asleep, or so it seemed. She had taken the form of a giant stone woman, looking almost like a colossal, sleeping statue. The goddess was bald, and completely naked. Her still form was embedded into the wall of the volcano, with her waist disappearing into the stone surface.

Kaimana hesitated, and Yam laid his hand on her shoulder. "You're up, mouse. I'll speak to my sister for you," he whispered to her, "but this is not my tale any more. You're going to have to greet her first."

Kaimana knew this was true. She gulped, beckoned to Rakau, and stepped forward.

When she had learnt that Yam was a god, her reaction had been to laugh. For so long she had wondered what it would be like to meet a god - most people of the Atoll do so at some point in their lives - and the mundanity of the encounter with Yam had shocked her. This time, however, the experience meeting this deity was exactly what Kaimana had feared. This beautiful, powerful being sleeping in front of her was terrifying. Kaimana had no doubt that she was an insect compared to Leinani, and the thought of being treated and dealt with as such, terrified her.

But this is the only way I can think of helping Rakau. Nakoa is almost upon us, and until Rakau has a chance to heal I can't let him near the war god. Leinani is our last hope.

Kaimana moved forward to a small altar that had been erected in the cave, beside the lava flow. Somebody - Kaimana assumed the priestesses - had left some flowers here, and they had been burnt into black husks by the heat of the cavern. Kaimana sat on the warm altar, took out her ocarina, and gave Leinani her gift.

She had known for a while now what she would give Leinani. Perhaps this had been why the infant song inside her had been so afraid of approaching the volcano, because it knew where it was destined to be first played. Since beginning to spark again on Yam's island, Kaimana had had little time to practice, especially since Rakau had been wounded. But in the back of her mind, throughout all of her trials, Kaimana's Knack had been hard at work completing her masterpiece.

Except it was no longer hers. The story had been originally inspired by Kaimana's adventure with Rakau, their first meeting and subsequent adventures. Yes, Kaimana was going to dress it up as Queen Alisi's story, or perhaps one of the other heroes of the Atoll, but she knew it would always be hers, and those close to her would be able to draw links between the movements in the tune and Kaimana's own experiences. Yet now, as she played her song for an audience for the first time, the memories in the tune changed. Where Kaimana had once pictured herself creeping towards Rakau's cave, heart beating wildly at the thought of what might lay inside, she was no longer there. Instead, eyes closed, Knack taking over her actions as the song breathed through her ocarina, Kaimana pictured a young god, fire in her hair, as she walked softly through the forest towards the man who would become a god himself so that he may love her. The fast paced sequence that had once been Rakau chasing Kaimana out of the cave now became a man chasing a woman, the goddess finally willingly submitting to this creature who had raised himself up to be worthy of her. And the final, piteous close that would have been Kaimana nursing Rakau's wounds on the Broken Island was now the volcano goddess, watching her lover from afar, heart breaking with sadness at what his rage had made him become.

Kaimana was crying openly as the final note from the song left her lips, as she felt her spark leave her, its job complete. All memories of the former tune - of the tune about her meeting and becoming friends with Rakau - were now gone. Only Leinani's tale remained.

Kaimana opened her eyes to see the fire goddess looking back at her. At some point during the song Leinani had awoken, and had pulled herself away from her stone bed. The goddess was still colossal, she was still embedded in stone, but she was no longer asleep. Where she had once been cold and grey, she was now alive and on fire. Her skin was the rocks of the mountain, but beneath the rocky disguise, through the cracks and faults that formed as the goddess moved, Kaimana could see red molten rock flowing beneath the surface, the true heart of her body. Leinani was no longer bald - now a full head of flame had ignited.

The goddess was smiling at Kaimana. In her hands she held an amber light, which Kaimana vaguely recognised as the song she had just given birth to, the spark that had just left her. Leinani was playing with the light, allowing it to run along her fingers. The goddess was staring at the amber spark in wonder.

Kaimana's heart was straining, and she involuntarily threw herself to the ground, lowering her eyes. The goddess was the most beautiful creature she had ever seen.

"That was... it has been some time since a mortal has given me a gift such as that," Leinani said. Kaimana had expected the goddess' voice to be hoarse and rocky. Instead it flowed like warm honey, soothing Kaimana's ears.

Kaimana bowed, blushing. "Thank you, my lady. I have been working on it for some time, for you."

"Not always for me, I think," the goddess replied, "but it fits me well." Leinani lowered herself from the wall of the chamber, bringing her glorious, terrible face down to the level of Kaimana and Rakau.

Kaimana took another look at the goddess and found herself bewitched by the bright flames of Leinani's eyes. Kaimana had never imagined that such beauty could exist in the world. She reached out with one hand as if to touch Leinani's face, but then withdrew it, both because she could feel the deadly heat radiating from the goddess, but also because she was certain she would not be permitted to do so.

Leinani smiled throughout all of this. The goddess looked over Kaimana's shoulder. "Ah, my brother. Well met."

Yam stepped forward sheepishly. "Uh, hello there, sister. It's been a few ages since we set eyes upon each other."

Leinani nodded, smiling, but Kaimana could tell her attention was already wavering. "Yes. You have been up to some mischief recently, have you not? I shall have to tell Mother, she will be most interested."

"She speaks of me?" Yam asked, shock in his voice now. The small god disguised as a man looked so out of place in the same room as this massive being.

"You? No. But she expresses an interest in all of her offspring. She will listen when I tell her of your recent story."

"I have a story already?"

"Not quite yet, not in the way that you wish. But the seeds have been sown. I daresay it shall not be too long until your name means more to the people of the Atoll than a fat child to laugh at."

Yam blushed, Kaimana assumed through anger, but he wisely chose not to respond.

The goddess' attention returned to Kaimana. "So, little one," she said, soothingly. "I assume there is a very good reason you have convinced my brother to lead you and this beast to disturb me?"

Kaimana swayed, somewhat hypnotised by the goddess' words and movement. "Yes, my lady. I mean, this is no beast, my lady. This is Rakau, a taniwha. My friend."

Leinani's swaying motion ceased. The indifference on her face disappeared, and she lowered herself to look at the pair. Kaimana now stood side by side with the massive taniwha, her hand on his jaw, the only part of his face that she could reach without standing on something.

"You have made friends with this monster?"

Kaimana was a bit surprised at how Leinani spoke of Rakau, and also a bit annoyed. "My lady, I do not feel it is fair to call him that. A monster. That's the same phrase I would use to describe one of my kind who had committed horrible crimes. But Rakau is kind, gentle. He has protected and saved my life - and the life of your brother - many times in the short space of time I have known him for."

Leinani looked thoughtfully at the taniwha. "You would use the word monster to describe a human that kills his own kind. Does this taniwha not kill, then?"

Kaimana shifted uneasily. "Well... he has, my lady-"

"Then I use the phrase correctly, child. Do not seek to reprimand me again."

"I would never dare to, my lady. And I see your point. Still, there is no malice in how Rakau kills, has killed. He does it to protect himself, or for food."

"You have no issues with your taniwha killing humans. For food?"

Kaimana shifted uneasily again. "I... I do not like it. He had agreed to stop for me. For my companionship."

"But he has killed, and recently."

"Yes. I freed him from his promise."

Leinani nodded, raising her body again, a look of satisfaction on her face. "Then you have realised - realised it is in his nature to kill. Make no mistake, my child - this is a monster beside you, this is a monster you have foolishly allowed yourself to care for so deeply. It is in his nature to kill. You know this, and so you have allowed him to do so again."

Kaimana winced. She felt Rakau shift beside her, and she knew she should continue to defend him. However, she did not want to further annoy the goddess, and she also found it difficult to disagree with what Leinani was saying.

"Just as it is in my nature, my child," the goddess continued. "And my brother's nature, and the rest of our brethren. We shape the world, and in return we demand worship, fealty and respect. Do I not speak the truth, my brother?"

"You do, sister," Yam replied. Kaimana could not help but notice the angry glare on Yam's face directed at Leinani.

Please don't do anything stupid, Kaimana begged silently. *Let us mortals get out of here before the gods begin to argue.*

"My lady," Kaimana said, turning to Leinani once more. "Whether or not I can ever be truly friends with Rakau, I have realised there is no place for him in the human world. He is being hunted by... by hunters. Something of his size cannot be hidden for long." Kaimana had almost mentioned Nakoa by name. In Leinani's presence, mentioning her former lover could have been a fatal mistake.

Thankfully, Leinani raised a fiery eyebrow, inviting Kaimana to continue.

"We are looking for a safe haven for Rakau, a home for a taniwha. I sought out your brother, and he directed me to you."

"My brother?"

Yam nodded. "I know not of such a place, sister, where this

142

taniwha could remain hidden and happy. But you, having created the Atoll from the Earth Mother, you would know if such a place exists."

Leinani nodded again. "It does."

Kaimana's heart leapt. *Rakau will be safe.* "Please, my lady, tell me where. Where shall we head?"

The goddess narrowed her eyes and outstretched one arm, with a finger pointing east. "That way," she told them.

Kaimana thought of all of the maps of the Atoll she had ever been allowed to see, and grew puzzled.

"The sea god's temple? That is all that I know of that lies in the east, just north of… of the more violent peoples. Is there something hidden near there I do not know of?"

Leinani shook her head. "No. For this task, you must widen your eyes, expand your gaze. Travel to my brother the sea king's home, yes, but travel further still than that. Finally, then you will reach the island of the taniwha."

Kaimana's eyes widened. "But… you're talking about the Outer Sea. Sailing on the Outer Sea? There's nothing out there." Even as Kaimana said this, she knew it was not true. Stories told that her people came to the Atoll from somewhere else, although details of this location are sparse.

Leinani looked at Kaimana, not responding to her outburst, waiting.

Eventually Kaimana bowed to the goddess and said, "Thank you, my lady. This is the information we were looking for."

The goddess smiled and pulled herself back up to her rocky wall. "I wish you well, taniwha girl. And, little Kaimana?"

Kaimana looked at Leinani in surprise, shocked that the goddess had used her name. "Yes, my lady?"

"Your gift to me, it is not finished yet." Leinani played with the amber spark that was Kaimana's song, still dancing on her fingertips, but then blew it and watched it float across the chamber, back to Kaimana. "It is mine now, but it is forged from you as well. It will not be complete until your story is too. Take it back and finish it for me."

The light melted into Kaimana's chest, and she felt a glow of happiness as her spark returned. It was forever changed, but was still with her.

"If you should survive this trip, I will take it as a great kindness if you return to me in the future. I would dearly love to hear my gift again." The goddess smiled a beautiful smile of dancing fire, breaking Kaimana's heart with it.

"Yes, my lady," Kaimana answered, bowed to the goddess, and then left, followed by Rakau and Yam.

"Well," Yam said, once outside, "she wasn't everything you'd built her up to be, was she, mouse?"

Irritated, and aware that Yam himself was still pale after the encounter with his sister, Kaimana glared at him as much as she dared, and then began the long walk down the volcano path.

They headed east on the Inner Sea, Rakau pulling Yam's canoe with a rope in his teeth. The yam god's journey was done, now. His sister had as much confirmed that the seeds of his story had been sown, and it would soon be time for him to leave.

"We would take you back home," Kaimana said to Yam, "but Nakoa lies that way."

Yam looked out over the Inner Sea, to the south and his small island.

"Yes," he said eventually. "He's a persistent bugger, that one. By my judgement, he has found my home, and possibly even that mess we left on the Broken Island." His eyes narrowed, as if trying to pick out something that had just breached the horizon. "I'm sure it wouldn't take him long to make his way out here in those war canoes of his. Not sure if he'd risk coming close to my sister, however."

Kaimana nodded. "You'll notice, though, that staying here was not one of the options given to us. Either Leinani thinks it would not put him off forever, or she just doesn't want us here. Either way, it'd be foolish for us to stay any longer. But, as I said, we cannot bring you home."

Yam shook his head. "Not a problem. Didn't want to go back anyway." He stretched, took out his flask and made to drink from it. Then, with a puzzled look on his face, he held the liquid in front of him, allowing some to dribble onto the sand. He put the stopper back onto the bottle, turned to Kaimana and smiled. It was an unusual sight on the grumpy god's face, and Kaimana felt it improved him markedly.

"I think it's about time I walked the Atoll for a while," he said. "You know, get my name out there, meet my people."

Kaimana gave a little grin. "You know your story won't have grown just yet, right? I have to tell it to a few people first."

Yam nodded in agreement, but looked around slyly as he did so. "True. Maybe you'll be beaten to it, though. After all, I can't imagine Nakoa is travelling by himself, is he? What kind of story are those warriors going to get once they find and interrogate the natives of the Broken Island, I wonder? What will be left once they find those yam trees - the only bloody yam *trees* on the whole Atoll, mind - and the bodies held within? You might be beaten to the telling of your story, little mouse."

He grinned. "Either which way, I've spent enough time with my farm and my coconuts. That's no way to live a life, especially one that lasts as long as mine. No, I'll do this, visit my people, story or no. I'll teach those damned islanders I'm not a god to be laughed at."

Kaimana raised an eyebrow, looking concerned.

Yam let out a barking laugh. "Don't you worry, mouse, they'll get fair warning. I'll give them a generation or two of gentle chiding before the real punishments begin."

Kaimana rode on Rakau's back as they travelled east, and Yam left them at the first inhabited island they found. Kaimana needed the canoe, to row herself back from wherever she found for Rakau, but Yam did not seem that worried.

"Oh, I'm certain my people will gift me with something or other, once I decide to move on," he muttered as he gave his goodbyes to the girl and the monster.

Despite his constant pessimism, Kaimana had grown fond of the god, but she could tell he was raring to leave them now, his head continuing to twitch towards the thatched huts that lay on the other end of the beach.

"Until we meet again, my lord," Kaimana said to him, giving him an awkward bow.

Yam smiled at this, and then grew more serious. "Little mouse, my sister is one of the most important creatures on the Atoll. That doesn't mean, however, she is always right. She told you a human can't be friends with a taniwha. I used to think that too. But the two of you, I've watched you together. Kaimana, you are happiest with him, and he with you. Sickeningly so. In all my years, I've rarely seen a bond like this, and certainly never between a taniwha and… well, between a taniwha and anything. Don't trust every word my sister gave you." He prodded one of his stubby fingers at Kaimana's chest. "Trust this, instead."

Then Yam turned without saying goodbye, and jogged off to the village, to hear them exalt his name.

LAKA'S DANCING BOY

A tale from the Crescent Atoll

Eneti was a carpenter's son. He was young, but already he was being trained in the ways of his father. Young Eneti, little more than four years old, would watch his father in his workshop, shaping canoes from whole tree trunks, or carving fine figures for the chief's daughters. Eneti's father had a Knack for woodwork, and he used his magic to find the shape that would best suit the wood that was brought to him. Eneti was destined to inherit his father's Knack.

All of this changed on the day Eneti first met the goddess Laka.

Little Eneti was walking along the shore close to his village. It was not unusual for the children of the village to wander the beach by themselves. They had all learnt to swim before they could walk, and no taniwha or enemy islanders had been sighted on these shores for generations. Indeed, Eneti would not be harmed on this day, but he would forever be changed.

Laka had taken the form of a young girl, clothed in a black dress that wrapped itself tight around her from her neck down to her ankles. Only her hands, feet and face were visible, and Eneti could see straight away that her skin was the purest white.

She was dancing.

He sat and watched her for hours. Eneti did not hide from the goddess. He sat in plain view, close enough to see every footstep and delicate play of her fingers, but she did not react to him. The goddess must have known, however, the effect this performance would have on such a young mind. Eneti was entranced by the goddess, entranced by her perfect flowing motions. From that moment, he was doomed to fall in love, with both Laka and with her dance.

The goddess looked at him only once, at the end of her dance, and she stared at him briefly with her black eyes. Then she was gone, and so too was Eneti's freedom.

It would be many years before Eneti met Laka again. As he grew, he became obsessed with dancing, and with any spare time he had he would run back down to the beach, back to where Laka had bewitched him, and would attempt to copy the memory of her movements. Even when he dutifully watched, and later helped, his father at the carpenter's workbench, Eneti's mind continued to wander back to Laka on the sand.

It surprised nobody when Eneti developed a Knack for dancing, but disappointed all in his family except for the boy himself. Despite his clear gift, Eneti's father and mother continued to pressure him to follow in his father's footsteps, to become a carpenter to support his family, and his future.

It was during the time that Eneti was mulling over these pressures, when he was twelve years of age, that Laka visited him again, this time taking the form of a giant, white-faced spider nestled in the tree he had sat under to contemplate his future.

"Why are you worried, little Eneti?"

Eneti recognised the goddess straight away, and prostrated himself before her, daring not to look at her face.

Laka tutted. "You do not have to be so formal with me. You, who have given me so much already, and who will give me more in the future."

"But," Eneti said, daring to look upwards again, "I do not know what my future holds. My father wants me to become a carpenter like him, and I think I have no option but to do as he says."

The sky seemed to darken, and Laka's eight legs lowered her fat body out of the tree, bending down towards Eneti. "I have given you a gift, young Eneti, and it is not wise to refuse a gift from the gods." There was a pause, and Eneti realised he was holding his breath. Then, the goddess continued. "There is a troupe of dancers berthed at the village on the western end of this island. If you travel through the night, you should reach them before they leave. Tell them I sent you. Honour me with your dance."

Eneti nodded, and began to run, half-terrified of Laka's threats, half-thankful she had once again robbed him of choice.

Eneti found the dancing troupe and was adopted by them. He quickly made a name for himself as a strong dancing Knack, despite having no formal tutelage. Eneti learnt from his teachers quickly, and soon surpassed all other dancers in the troupe. Indeed, the troupe found themselves requested to perform at many different islands, all requests specifying that they bring the dancing boy that people on the Atoll had heard so much about.

The women of the Atoll loved Eneti, and it was not long before Eneti learnt to love them back. He fell in love with one of his fellow dancers, and asked her to become his bride.

It was on the eve of their wedding that Laka visited Eneti again.

He was lying on his back, unable to sleep because of his anticipation of tomorrow's events. Then he became aware he was not alone in his bed. Lying beside him was Laka, taking human form again, this time of a young woman. Under the covers, she was completely naked, and as she brushed up against him, Eneti was surprised to find how cold and hard her skin felt, like touching a smoothly polished clay ornament. Despite this coldness, and despite the unusual features of her face, which appeared to be painted on with black ink, Eneti's body betrayed the fact that he wanted her.

Laka did not need to tell Eneti what she wanted. She did not need to tell Eneti she wanted him to leave his bride and to focus on his dancing, on his art. Eneti knew all of this as soon as he saw her there.

That night Eneti and Laka became lovers. He stole away from his troupe before sunrise, leaving a note of farewell to the woman who had hoped to be his wife, dedicating himself instead to honouring his goddess.

After this, Eneti travelled the Atoll, both to escape the shame of jilting his love, but also to find inspiration. He was a skilled dancer, but now sought a story worthy of being captured in his movements.

Eneti was in his thirties before he began to spark, and it was during his first ever performance of the dance born from this spark that Laka visited him for the final time, watching from the shadows as Eneti unveiled his masterpiece.

Eneti's dance was perfect. The small crowd that had gathered to witness him smiled as he moved daintily about the stage to show the rains falling, and gasped when he began to leap and fall, catching himself almost impossibly when it looked as if he would hit the floor, bounding again to signify the blows that fell in a great battle.

Laka, for her part, was entranced. The story that Eneti told through his dance was one of love and loss, and Laka was surprised to find a single tear rolling from her painted eye as the dance finished.

The goddess was the first to begin the applause.

Eneti smiled, and bowed graciously to the audience. "Thank you, thank you. But please, I cannot take all the credit, as the tale that I tell is one of great importance to all of us on the Atoll, and it is dedicated to a god that we all must remain thankful to in our daily lives. I dedicate this dance to the Long God, for continuing to give us food from the earth, and for helping us find plenty on our small island homes."

On hearing these words, Laka's mood darkened. From the shadows she was hiding in, black ribbons began to unfurl, whipping at those close to her, forcing a path to open between the goddess and the man who had forgotten her.

When Eneti saw Laka's white face glaring at him from the shadows, he collapsed to his knees.

"You dedicate your dance to the Long God?" she spat, bitterly.

Eneti could only shake his head at her. "I-I met him. I spent some time with him. He inspired me."

Laka's black ribbons grabbed at Eneti's wrists and ankles, and drew him to her.

"He inspired you?" she whispered. "You were mine, young Eneti. I made you. And I can unmake you."

Laka's ribbons tightened, and Eneti's legs and arms shattered.

The goddess faded from the shadows, and left a broken man in the dirt.

Eneti never danced again, and nobody has since dared to recreate his dance celebrating the Long God's harvest.

CHAPTER EIGHT

Kaimana and Rakau enjoyed their final days on the Atoll. They were all too aware of how close Nakoa must be by now, but still they gave themselves time to spend in each other's company. Kaimana played tunes for Rakau as he paddled onward. He pulled the canoe in his mouth, but she still chose to ride on his back, to retain the closeness they would lose soon when he found his home. At night, Rakau dove under the water and brought back mouthfuls of fish, and they would cook them on a beach and curl up together, gazing at the stars.

Finally, however, the deep dark of the Outer Sea appeared. To Kaimana's own surprise, she realised that a part of her was excited by the idea of venturing into the unknown. This excitement was tempered by how unsure Rakau seemed of those waters.

"Have you ever been out there before?" she asked him.

Rakau seemed to be unsure of the answer and did not respond. There was so much that Kaimana did not know about her friend, or of taniwha in general. How old is Rakau? Where was he born? Were taniwha even born, or were they made? Do they have parents?

She stroked the monster's rough hide as he paddled forward, the cool blue of the Atoll floor giving way to deep black as the ocean shelf dropped under them. Here she was, once again, putting her faith in this beast who she hardly knew. A beast that Leinani had warned her not to trust. And now she was returning him to his home, just before another god hunted him down and butchered him.

Kaimana had almost forgotten that this was not the reason she had begun to travel with Rakau, that the whole point had been to light her spark again and find her song. To create a masterpiece, to give Kaimana the respect she would need to join another, more popular and respected travelling troupe, or perhaps even Laka's own priesthood. Then her parents would have been able to see that it had been the right choice, to follow her Knack and her heart, that Kaimana had been able to make something of her life by devoting herself to her music. However, despite the spark that continued to sing inside Kaimana's head, alien but still hers, Kaimana's thoughts drifted elsewhere.

What mattered now was Rakau, and his safety.

Kaimana turned around to take a look at the Atoll behind them, and was shocked to see how small it looked. Rakau swam forward with strong purpose, eyes intent. She sensed an urgency in his movements that had not been there before, but whether this was because he was remembering something about this part of the world, or if he was just as scared as she was, Kaimana could not tell.

Then, they were alone. Kaimana turned and could not see any land behind her. The Atoll had disappeared. She looked to the front again, searching for the tips of peaks, or gulls flying overhead, or anything that would give her the clue of islands close by. Nothing. They were alone in a world of blue. Kaimana felt dizzy, and gripped the moss on Rakau's back.

"I trust you," she whispered to the monster. He grunted in response.

Midday came and went, and still no sign of land could be seen. Kaimana did what she could to doze on Rakau's back as he carried them onward, but part of her brain would not allow herself to fall asleep completely, and she kept waking in small jumps and starts, never fully getting the rest she needed.

It was during one of these waking moments that Kaimana realised Rakau was no longer moving. Her eyes narrowed and scanned the horizon on all sides, but she could see nothing.

"What is it?" she asked. "Why've we stopped?"

The taniwha remained silent, but kept moving his head from side to side, scanning the water ahead of them.

Kaimana felt her friend's doubt. "I'm sure it is out there, the island. Leinani had no reason to lie to us, we just have to trust her word a little bit longer."

Rakau gave a grunt. No, Kaimana had not touched upon the real reason for them stopping. Rakau was not concerned that land had not appeared yet. Something else was the matter.

"Is... is there something out there?"

Rakau grunted again. Yes.

Kaimana held her breath and sat up, pulse quickening. She was not used to looking into waters as dark as these. Normally on the Atoll she was able to pick out creatures moving underwater long before they were close to her, but she realised that catching movements out here on the open sea was going to be a lot more difficult. She felt blind, trapped.

There.

A large ripple broke through the waves just north of where Rakau was paddling, and indeed that was where the taniwha's attention was now fully focussed. Kaimana was not certain, but she may also have seen a fin dipping back under the surface.

"Sharks?" she whispered.

Another grunt. No.

"...another taniwha?"

Rakau did not respond. Despite the heat of the sun above them, Kaimana shivered, a dread chill running through her.

Then it attacked, thrusting up out of the water in front of them.

Kaimana had almost been correct in her initial question about sharks. The creature diving towards them - a creature just as colossal as Rakau - did indeed have a shark's fin, as well as the fish's grey skin and large teeth. However, the taniwha that dove out of the sea in front of them also had two shark-grey human arms on the front of its body, and pointed these towards Rakau and Kaimana, outstretched and grabbing.

Rakau was only able to save them by throwing himself to the side, barrelling both him and Kaimana under the water. Not expecting the sudden impact, and her reactions deadened by the shock of the attack, Kaimana had no chance of holding on to her friend. Suddenly, she found herself rushing about under the water, sunlight glinting in all directions, with no idea about which way she should swim to get to the surface. A large body, or possibly two of them, shoved into her, battering her further, causing Kaimana to lose all control of her senses. She opened her mouth to scream and sea water flooded her lungs.

As she choked in panic, Kaimana found herself looking down, her eyes pointed in the direction of the depths below her. Even here, under the surface, looking downward without the distraction of the sunlight and ripples of the waves, Kaimana could not find the seabed. Presented with this bottomless drop before her, her lungs filling with water, Kaimana's eyes began to roll and darkness threatened.

Before she lost consciousness, she was jolted wide awake by a tremendous blow to her leg. Kaimana was thrown above the surface of the water, expelling the liquid in her lungs violently as she coughed in desperation to breathe air again. She smacked back down into the water with a crash, coughing, spluttering, flapping her arms and legs to stay above the surface. Of Rakau and the other taniwha there was no sign, and Kaimana did not dare look down again for fear of her vertigo returning.

It was Rakau who returned to the surface first. Kaimana could tell her friend had been wounded, one of his eyes closed due to a new half-circle of teeth marks on his face. There was no sign of the other creature. Rakau did not move as confidently as before, suggesting there might be more unseen injuries, and he slowly made his way back to Kaimana and nudged her onto his back.

"Did you get it?" she asked, weakly.

Rakau made a noise that suggested he was not sure. Nevertheless, their attacker did not return, telling Kaimana that once again Rakau had saved her life.

The taniwha continued to paddle east, casting his head about warily, looking for further dangers. Kaimana gripped him tight, doing what she could to stop shaking.

That was almost it. I was so close to death, that time. He saved me again, but Rakau is hurt again. How many times is this going to happen to us? He needs somewhere safe to live.

But is somewhere safe for him going to be safe for me? Why do I feel that the other taniwha wouldn't have attacked Rakau if he had been by himself...?

Then, finally, land broke the horizon. A large island came into view. Kaimana reckoned it was about three times the size of

Nakoa's home, based on what she could see at the moment, with a trio of large mountain peaks. The rest of the island appeared to be thick forest, so different from the Broken Island all those days ago. At sight of it, Rakau's pace quickened.

Kaimana grinned. "You remember this place, don't you?" she said, rubbing Rakau's side.

They landed on an empty beach not long afterwards. When Rakau emerged from the water, pulling her canoe well away from the surf, Kaimana was able to see the damage the shark taniwha had caused - thick, angry teeth marks littered Rakau's body, further marring the beautiful design on his hide.

Aware of his injuries, and probably concerned about future attacks, Rakau became wary once again, smelling the air and taking a few steps at a time onto the beach.

He's scared. I should be too.

Rakau plodded forward, sniffing the air warily.

To the depths with being scared, Kaimana thought. *This is the opportunity of a lifetime for a storyteller like me. I knew I'd be staring death in the face at least once on this trip - what story is worth telling if you don't? I've survived this far already. Let's see what a taniwha island can throw at me.*

She ran to a large series of boulders on the beach, and leapt onto them to climb to the top, to get a look at the surrounding beach and forest for any sign of threats. As soon as Kaimana put a foot onto the largest rock, she jumped off it again. The rock had moved.

Scrambling in the sand, Kaimana sped back to Rakau, who was now tensed, ready to pounce. Kaimana got to her friend and hid behind him.

The rock continued to move, shifting in the sand. It was covered in dry seaweed, but the dead plant started to fall off as the rock stood up. As Kaimana had by now guessed, this was indeed another taniwha. The rock stood tall, the creature's head poking out from beneath it. This monster seemed to resemble a turtle, but most of it was hidden by its seaweed-covered rock shell. The turtle taniwha shook its head, eyes obscured by a mop of seaweed.

Kaimana could feel Rakau's tension, but her friend did not otherwise move or make a sound. He was waiting for the creature to attack.

Then the turtle taniwha turned and walked into the forest, either oblivious to the intruders standing right in front of it, or just not caring.

After a few tense seconds, Kaimana exhaled with a laugh. "Well, there you go then. Taniwha Island, home to the weirdest creatures you could hope to meet. And best of all? Not all of them are interested in killing us on sight."

Rakau grunted a laugh, but Kaimana could tell he was interested in pressing on. She allowed her friend to guide her, and together they made their way off the beach and into the jungle surrounding it.

In the hours that passed as they explored the island, Kaimana saw many more taniwha. Most of them bore a passing resemblance to animals that Kaimana knew from her life on the Atoll - cats, dogs, rats, birds - but with unusual features that made them unique. At one point, a spider the size of a dog scuttled past them, and Kaimana fancied that it had black, hairy human toes on the end of its eight legs. They disturbed a clutch of three-winged parrots, each roughly Kaimana's size, and the animals caused Rakau to bark in shock as they took off into the treetops, their unusual wings causing the birds to whirl around like spinning tops as they rose from the ground.

Other taniwha, like Rakau himself, were more unusual. They passed a waterfall that was singing to them, the water within it clearly alive. A grove of purple-leaved trees bent their branches to stroke Rakau and Kaimana as they walked past, enquiring as to who they were and what their purpose was on the island.

Then Kaimana and Rakau came across logs that walked.

Kaimana had heard of *rakau tipua* - enchanted logs - before, which is why she had not been completely shocked by Rakau's appearance when she had first seen him. What had made him more acceptable to comprehend was probably the fact that Rakau bore a passing resemblance to a large, green-haired dog or otter. The same could not be said of the first *rakau tipua* that they came across on the island. It was when the jungle ended, when the trees gave way to wider plains just at the foot of one of the island's mountains. Kaimana and Rakau were greeted by the sight of numerous taniwha living peacefully on this wide landscape. Giant birds soared through the sky, drifting on the breeze. In the distance, a herd of cats the size of horses grazed on some red flowers. But there, closest to them, as if by fate, were some more *rakau tipua*. These were not as animal-like as Rakau, not as well formed. Most of them were exactly how their name described them - logs with legs, and a vague collection of the right bumps and grooves for a face. However, there was no doubt that Rakau was among his own kind here. Some even bore the swirling engravings that he had on his skin, although theirs were not as intricate as Rakau's.

Rakau relaxed, his shoulders losing their tension, and from his panting breaths Kaimana could tell her friend was excited.

"Is this somewhere you think you'll be safe?" she asked.

Rakau turned to look at her, and she found herself catching her own breath as she looked into his green eyes.

I'm about to lose you, aren't I? You're going to be safe here, safe from Nakoa, and soon I'll have to leave you.

Her taniwha turned away from her and started to run towards the other *rakau tipua*.

Kaimana sat on a fallen tree and watched her friend. Rakau reached the herd with some speed, but then slowed down upon approach, his ears drooping. He walked slowly up to them and raised his chin. Kaimana was surprised to hear a low howl come from her friend's throat, a noise she had not heard from him before. She realised this noise echoed how she felt inside - a sadness was forming that she had not allowed herself to anticipate.

Rakau's howling attracted the attention of the herd and the other taniwha moved closer to investigate the newcomer. The largest of the monsters moved directly in front of Rakau, and Rakau bowed his head. The larger creature raised one of its legs - little more than tree stumps that had been taught how to walk - and it placed the leg on top of Rakau's head.

For one fearful moment, Kaimana thought Rakau was not going to be accepted, that the other taniwha would turn on him and attack. Kaimana was not certain if her friend could survive an onslaught from so many. Luckily, this was not to be - soon Rakau was mingling with others of his kind, rubbing up against them and communicating with growls and barks.

They seem so familiar already, she thought jealously. *Perhaps they already knew each other, from when he was here before. If he was here before.*

He's forgotten me so quickly.

Kaimana's eyes wandered towards the edges of the plains that the taniwha were meeting each other on. There, she spied movement in the long grasses, but thought nothing unusual about it. More taniwha, she assumed, and certainly nothing that appeared to alarm any of the inhabitants of the island. If she, an invading human, had been able to spot the movement, then the monsters below would also be aware of it.

Still, there was something unusual about the shapes that she could just about make out in those long grasses. There was more than one creature there, that much she could tell by the shadows she could spot behind the foliage. When Kaimana first caught a glimpse of the creatures, she could not help but gasp.

For a start, the animal that these smaller taniwha most resembled was a fish, even though Kaimana had spotted no major bodies of water nearby. These fish taniwha were small for their kind - about the height of Kaimana - but numerous. They were a bright blue, which explained why Kaimana had been able to spot them so easily behind the green grass. When they started to peek out from behind the blades, Kaimana was able to spy how the creatures were moving around despite their heritage - they had long feelers, not unlike those of an ant or beetle, that they were using as legs, supporting their thick bodies on those tall, spindly stalks. What Kaimana also noticed were the sharp teeth in the creatures' mouths, glinting in the midday sun.

Kaimana jumped when she heard a rustling in the jungle behind her. She turned to look, suddenly very conscious of how far away Rakau was at this moment. She studied the dark greenery behind, and then spotted a shock of bright blue. More flashes of blue were visible along the length of the jungle, connecting the monster behind her to those that she had spied in the distance. This was all Kaimana required to will her legs to run.

"Rakau!" she shouted, bursting into full speed. As she dashed over a large boulder, she turned to look behind her. Sure enough, the fish taniwha were giving chase. At least five had emerged from the nearby jungle, their thin feeler-legs moving them silently across the grass, their teeth-filled mouths opening and closing as if gulping for air. They were fast. Kaimana had no chance of outrunning them.

"Rakau! Help me!"

The *rakau tipua* below - all of them - had already begun to move. Rakau was speeding towards Kaimana, accompanied by two of his new friends. The rest of the herd were manoeuvring themselves into a protective circle. Dimly, Kaimana realised they were circling the smallest of their kind, protecting the weak, or possibly even their offspring. Rakau had not forgotten her, but

Kaimana was certain he would be far too late to save her.

She eyed some more of the fish monsters dashing towards her from her left, where the tall grasses lay. If not for the menace that they posed to her right now, the sight would be almost comical. Instead, Kaimana became more aware of how many of them there were, and began to imagine how sharp those rows of teeth would feel.

Realising she had no hope of outrunning them, Kaimana immediately changed the direction of her run, twisting off to the left, heading directly towards the closest fish. She hoped this sudden movement would confuse her attackers, giving them a few moments pause, allowing Rakau to catch to her. Instead, the fish responded quickly, almost seeming to increase their pace as they realised their prey was making things easier for them.

Inside, Kaimana's spark dimmed again, but she did not feel the blind panic from it that she had in the past. Instead, it was cautiously curious. It wanted to see what would happen next, to see if these dangers would add to its song.

Kaimana reached the first fish within seconds. The animals moved with speed across the plains, but other than their long feelers and sharp teeth they had nothing to grab a hold of her with. She leapt at the monster with her feet first, aiming for its thin legs. She was rewarded with a dry snap, like the breaking of small twigs, and the creature fell to the ground unsupported, flopping about like a regular fish, gasping for air.

Not giving herself time to savour the victory, Kaimana swivelled to face where she judged the next attack to come from. This second monster was almost on her, giving her no time to prepare another kick to its legs. This time, she ducked to the side, moving her face away from the reaching teeth and stabbing with her fingers at the large, bulbous eye on the side of the fish's head. As she had hoped, the thin flesh of the eye gave way, causing the juice inside to burst out.

Unfortunately, the taniwha did not appear to suffer any pain from this mauling, and instead batted her away with the flat of its face, stunning her with the shock of the attack. Worse still was the stabbing pain from her shoulder - the taniwha that had been chasing her from behind had caught up with her.

With horror, Kaimana felt needles digging into her skin, followed by an excruciatingly painful ripping sensation as the taniwha tried to rip her flesh from her body. Panicked, she tried to swat at the monster, but found her blows to be ineffectual. A similar stabbing on her leg told her that another monster found its mark, although in the pain and confusion she could not gain sight of it. And then she was on the ground, battered by multiple impacts from around her. The rest of the monsters, the hunting party, had arrived, breaking upon their brethren who were already feeding on her. Kaimana fell to the grass floor, finding herself being pressed under the weight of the gang of taniwha, their mouths searching for her skin, desperate to find their own place to grab hold and rip some of her free.

A roar told Kaimana that Rakau had arrived. She screamed as the monster latched to her shoulder was ripped away, taking a chunk of flesh with it. The rest of the beasts scattered as Rakau and his companions bit and snapped at them. Another of the *rakau tipua* killed the fish monster that was attached to Kaimana's leg, causing its grip on her limb to loosen. From the edges of her vision, Kaimana could see her attackers doing their best to attach themselves to the larger taniwha, with little success. Within minutes the fish were nowhere to be found, except for the carcasses that the two *rakau tipua* were dragging back to their herd.

Rakau found her. He was breathing heavily from his exertions, and had a look of concern on his face.

"I'll be fine," she said, looking gingerly at her shoulder. In truth, she was not too certain about that statement. The teeth had cut deep, and from what she could tell a lot of flesh had been taken by the bite. "I need to dress this, though."

Following what she could remember from the healing that Rawiri did for the troupe, Kaimana searched the smaller shrubs that grew where the jungle met the plains, and found the appropriate roots for dressing her wound. She ripped some cloth from her dress to make a bandage, and thanked Laka and numerous other gods that the bleeding seemed to stop quickly once it was bound.

"There," she smiled weakly to her friend, once the job was complete. "Good as new."

Rakau grunted, and then looked back to the herd of *rakau tipua*. Since the attack he had spent all of his time with Kaimana, and now the herd was moving away from them, making their way across the plains.

"We'd better go and get them, hadn't we?"

Rakau tilted his head while looking at the retreating monsters, and then turned back to Kaimana. Instead of following the other taniwha, he assumed the curled up sleeping position that he had been so used to adopting, motioning with his head for Kaimana to curl up beside him. So much had happened today, Kaimana had not noticed that the sun was close to setting.

She was confused. "But, we might lose them. Can't we catch up and rest with them?"

Rakau seemed not to notice her words, and settled himself down.

Kaimana was, in truth, thankful for the rest. The other taniwha were far away already, and continuing to journey with her injuries did not appeal to her.

Still, she thought, *the timing of that attack had been terrible. This was what we had come here for. Rakau had found his own kind, somewhere he could call home. Those fish might have taken that away from him.*

No. It's not the fish monsters' fault, not really. It's in their nature to attack smaller prey, to feed themselves. They were bound to attack me when I was by myself.

This is all my fault. This is an island of monsters, and to most of them I'm a wandering morsel. The fish weren't interested in the log taniwha. Just me, the human.

Rakau rescued me, and thank the goddess this time he wasn't hurt. Those monsters were small, and couldn't pierce his hide.

But, what will attack me next time?

Kaimana stroked Rakau's hide, now rising up and down gently as he slept. She was safe here with him, she knew, but he would never be free to find his own kind as long as she was around.

Kaimana had not spent much time considering what her plan would be once Rakau had found safety. Now that they were here, however, it was obvious she had to leave, both for her own safety, and to give Rakau a chance to call this place home.

Kaimana did not sleep much that night, and ignored the quiet mewling of her spark to spend time with it, to finish their song. Instead, she spent the time tracing her friend's decorative markings with her fingers, her heart breaking.

In the morning, she rose and stretched, looking out to the grassy plains. The *rakau tipua* had vanished, but she was sure Rakau would be able to find them once she gave him the time.

"Well," she said, "I feel much better now." This was a lie. Her shoulder ached more than any pain she had ever known, but she was confident it would mend in time, although would leave an unsightly scar. "It's time I left, then."

Rakau, who until this moment had been lazily shifting on the ground in the morning sunlight, sat up, looking at her questioningly.

"Well," she answered, "you didn't expect me to stick around forever, did you? You saw what happened yesterday - it isn't safe for me here. I have a life I need to get back to, my music. Looks like you might have a life here too."

Rakau looked briefly over the long plains, but then looked back at Kaimana, longing in his eyes. The fact that Rakau did not want to give Kaimana up made her spark sing joyfully. However, Kaimana kept her face rigid. She did not want her own emotions to cloud Rakau's judgement.

She shook her head. "I know, I'll miss you too. But this is for the best, I think. Guess Leinani was right. Taniwha and humans can't ever be friends. She got the reason wrong, though. We're fine together, it's the rest of the world that has a problem with us."

She gathered herself, rolled her shoulder, and looked up with determination.

"I know you have to find them again, but it's not safe on this island for me. Will you see me back to the canoe, back to the beach?"

The journey was uneventful, other than Kaimana's continued surprise at the variety of monsters they encountered. What made this trip less pleasurable, however, was the air of sadness between the two friends. When they had travelled through the jungle yesterday they had not spoken much, but their body language together had been full of playfulness, of Rakau's bright eyes when Kaimana had exclaimed at each new sight. Now both were quiet, plodding along past each creature that they met.

When they arrived back at the canoe, Kaimana gave a silent prayer to Laka that their parting would go smoothly.

"Well, goodbye then," she muttered, and gave the monstrous taniwha a big hug. Kaimana walked away from Rakau and began to push her canoe into the water. Rakau waded into the water with her.

She turned to look at the taniwha accusingly.

"No, you stay here. That was the whole point of this trip, to get you somewhere safe. You've found other taniwha like you, now. This is where you belong."

Rakau walked up to Kaimana and nudged her with his large muzzle, and started plodding further into the sea. As he did so, Kaimana caught sight of his ruined hide again. When she had first met him, Rakau had been perfect - unblemished by any previous encounters that he might have had. In the short time they had been together this had changed, through encounters with Nakoa and his men, the Birdmen of Broken Island, and the various taniwha attacks. What had once been art on his skin was now destroyed, and Kaimana realised that if he continued to travel with her, back on the Atoll, things would only be worse.

"No," she shouted, as angry as she could make her voice sound. "You have to stay. You stay, and I go."

Rakau completely ignored her now, moving forwards into the waves. At the same time, Kaimana was both happy that she meant so much to him, but also furious at what he was forcing her to do.

"I don't want you to come back with me. This is it for me. We had fun, I got my spark and my song, but I don't want to see you anymore."

Rakau stopped and turned back to look at her. There was clear pain in his eyes. She felt herself relenting, wanting to apologise for her harsh words. Then Kaimana realised that if she relented now, he would never agree to stay on the island.

Also, a big part of what Kaimana had said was true, or at least it had been in the beginning. The only reason she had started travelling with Rakau was to find her spark again. She had been selfish, encouraging him to adventure with her to feed her storyteller's curiosity.

He has to believe that's still the truth, so he can stay on this island and be safe.

Kaimana made her face grow cold. "Why would I want to be around you anymore? I had a good life before you were in it. I was part of a troupe, I could play my music. Since we've met I've been attacked almost every day. More crazy people and creatures have tried to kill me than I can count.

"Just look at my bloody shoulder. Who wants a life with fish monsters trying to snack on you? You are bad for me, taniwha. Just like the volcano god tried to tell me, we can't be friends."

Rakau fully turned around now, the sorrow plain in his eyes. He moved towards Kaimana, whining, pleading with her.

Now was time for the final blow.

"Stop making that noise, you stupid animal. Gods, I cannot wait to have an actual conversation with someone. Now I have my song, I can stop wasting my time with you."

At that moment, Kaimana realised she might have pushed Rakau too far.

Rakau's eyes changed, narrowed, and grew angry. He roared at Kaimana, and for the first time in weeks, Kaimana looked into her friend's face and she knew fear, her spark shrinking back from the taniwha's rage. Rakau reared up on his hind legs, and for a moment she thought he would come crashing down on top of her, crushing her for her insolence.

Rakau's feet impacted just in front of her, sending a wave of water crashing over Kaimana and her canoe, knocking her under the surf.

Is this what Leinani meant? she thought as she struggled to find purchase under the water. *Is Rakau going to let me go without killing me?*

When Kaimana surfaced and cleared her eyes, it was just in time to see her closest friend running across the beach, disappearing into the jungle and out of her life.

She had saved Rakau from a life of being hunted and attacked, at the cost of never having him as a friend again.

Inside, her spark gave out a low, keening wail, urging her to go after Rakau.

Instead, eyes obscured by tears, Kaimana pulled the canoe into the ocean and began the long journey of travelling back to the Atoll by herself.

THE
DISOBEDIENT DAUGHTER

A tale from the Crescent Atoll

This is the story of a young girl called Mereana, and of how she met her end by not listening to the advice of her elders.

Mereana lived on a large island that was home to three villages. In the centre of the island was a watering hole, and in this watering hole lay a taniwha.

This beast's lair was well known to the people of the island. In ages past, the men of the island had struck a deal with the taniwha. They would not bother it, and it would not bother them. They would live in harmony. A number of conditions to this agreement had been decided upon. The taniwha had promised it would not show its face close to the villages. It would not disturb nor strike fear into the hearts of the people of the island. In turn, the taniwha had demands of its own. It had originally asked that none of the people of the island came close to the water hole it had claimed for its home. The men and women of the villages had disagreed mightily against this request, as the water hole was a favourite place for the people of the island to bathe in. The taniwha eventually relented on this part of the bargain, but declared that nobody should bathe there at night, as that was when the taniwha was awake. The taniwha also asked that none of the villagers disturb or eat the bright red flowers of the raka tree that grew near the water hole, as this was the taniwha's favourite food.

The agreement was made, and so taniwha and man lived together peacefully for many years.

One day, a thirteen year old girl named Mereana travelled to the water hole to bathe. Her mother and grandmother had protested against her leaving. They knew Mereana was a wilful girl, and would often get herself into trouble. They did not, however, fear the taniwha of the water hole. Indeed, many of the villagers did not believe the taniwha existed, or thought that it had long ago left the island. The taniwha had kept so well to its agreement that none had seen its face since the night the promise had first been given.

Mereana travelled by herself to the water hole, stripped bare and dipped into the water. She cleaned herself and, sure that none were there to watch her, she lay naked on a large rock, basking in the sun, enjoying the quiet of the day.

It was then that Mereana's eyes fell upon the red flowers that hung high over the water hole. She licked her lips at the sight of the blossoms, and of the promise of the nectar they held within them. Mereana had, like all of the children on the island, been brought up knowing the story of these red flowers, but as Mereana had never seen nor heard any evidence that the story of the taniwha was true, she paid it little attention.

Hand by hand, foot by foot, Mereana climbed to the top of the raka tree. There, she plucked the first red flower and poured its sweet nectar onto her tongue. It was the most beautiful thing she had ever tasted, and she was pleased with herself for finding this secret treat. She spent the entire day up in that tree, picking flowers and sucking the nectar from them, letting the drained blossoms fall onto the deep water hole below her.

If Mereana had been an observant girl, she might have noticed a disturbance in the water below. The surface rippled, and small bubbles rose in steady bursts, as if some unseen creature was angry, but unwilling to surface.

This unwillingness to appear changed, however, when night fell on the island, and greedy Mereana still remained in the raka tree, sipping the nectar from the final red flower.

Mereana first became aware that something was wrong when the water beneath began to glow red. She was rooted with fear when she saw the taniwha emerge from its cave, the angry glow from its eyes illuminating the watering hole. This taniwha most resembled a giant cat, but instead of fur the beast was covered in fish scales. It eyed the young girl who had stolen all of its flowers, and began to purr.

"Do you know who I am, little girl?"

Mereana nodded, her bottom lip quivering. She knew the price she was going to have to pay.

"Do you know why you must be punished?"

Mereana nodded again.

"I will make this quick, and then balance will be restored to the island."

Mereana closed her eyes and the taniwha gently lowered its jaws onto her neck.

The girl's body was never found, but when her family went to look for her the following day they saw the taniwha's pool with the drained red flowers floating upon it, and they knew what their little girl had done.

⇌ CHAPTER ⇌
NINE

She should have been scared by the trip she was making. Only a day ago, Kaimana had been terrified by the idea of travelling the Outer Sea on the back of Rakau. Now, rowing herself slowly across the waves, she was not thinking of the potential dangers she was braving on this journey.

She was alone, now. She had lost Rakau, the closest friend she had ever had. Everyone else in her life had had some kind of expectations for her - her parents and sister pushing her to develop a Knack that she was not interested in having, her troupe and *kahuna* wanting her to play her best, or in Eloni's case just wanting her to get out of her way. With Rakau it had been different. He had enjoyed being around her, and she had enjoyed being with him. He had expected nothing of her, except to share time together travelling the Atoll.

When Kaimana had begun this journey, her main aim had been to find herself a song worth playing, to allow herself to rise in the ranks of the storytellers of the Atoll. She had her song now. Her spark - unusually silent and mourning - was almost finished, but as her heart was quietly breaking, Kaimana could care less about tales of potato gods and fish monsters.

The first peak in the distance was that of Leinani's volcano.

Kaimana had hoped she had been travelling in the correct direction to get back home, and despite her grief, she was pleased at the familiar sight.

It was during this stage of brief relief that the monster attacked.

She should have realised the possibility of this happening. It was the same taniwha that had attacked them before, the shark, but on the journey to the island Rakau had seen it off. Now Kaimana was alone, and had no chance.

Luckily for Kaimana, the first blow to the canoe did not break it or topple it. She was able to look over the side to see the tip of the taniwha's massive fin dipping back under the water. Despite the darkness of the open sea, it was clear to Kaimana that a massive creature was now submerged beneath her. She looked about, desperately. There was nothing out there to save her. Without her taniwha, without any land nearby she could hope to escape to, Kaimana was doomed.

The attacks continued for the next three hours. Kaimana was terrified, but she was also tired.

When the monster had first let itself be known, she had assumed that death would be quick. However, unlike the fish monsters that had attacked her on the island, this creature appeared to have more of an active mind, and Kaimana quickly found that mind to be cruel. Instead of splitting open her vessel and eating her, this creature seemed to be enjoying toying with her, knocking her canoe and frightening her before eventually killing her. A glimpse of the creature's red eyes under the water accompanied by its wide, white grin sealed Kaimana's theory - the taniwha was enjoying prolonging her death.

It had grown dark now, the waters being only illuminated by moon and star light. This made it much more difficult for Kaimana to see the beast under the water, allowing each eventual impact to rock her that much more. The times between each nudge increased greatly, and Kaimana realised the creature was wanting her to feel that it had lost interest, to give her the ghost of the hope that today was not her day to die. She hated the screams that she gave every time the canoe rocked and she fell from her seat, but she also suspected the joy of hearing these screams was all that kept the shark from finishing her off, and so she did nothing to quell them. Her sole consolation was the change in her spark's attitude to danger. It was clearly still afraid, and had been noticeably quieter since the taniwha's attacks began, yet its light continued to burn strong. There was no hint of it fleeing, yet.

Because of the darkness, Kaimana also found it much more difficult to tell how far from the Atoll she was. If she had been travelling at her normal rowing speed she would have reached its borders by now, but the attacks had slowed her movement considerably. Still, if she had reached Atoll waters by now the moonlight would have been enough for her to see the seabed. The waters of the Outer Sea remained black beneath her.

Kaimana was thrown to her feet by another nudge, this one more violent than any before. Indeed, Kaimana fell onto the side of the canoe, and felt her vessel tipping. With horror she realised she was slipping into the water, and reached out desperately to grab on to something to stop herself from falling into those dark depths.

Her effort was in vain, the entire canoe tipped over, and Kaimana found herself under the water.

Panicked, caught under the canoe, Kaimana opened her eyes, doing what she could to avoid looking directly beneath her, knowing she would suffer from vertigo yet again. In the distance she was able to spot a massive fin moving away from her at speed. The monster, toying with her even now when she was under the water.

Kaimana rushed to the surface and grabbed onto the ropes that were wrapped around the canoe. Holding her breath, straining herself, Kaimana pulled on the cords, trying to use her weight to tumble the canoe upright so she could climb back on board. However, her strength failed her. The hardships of the day and the exhaustion she felt through fear had stolen all strength from her arms.

Her next plan was to pull herself out of the water, to at least perch on top of the canoe's overturned hull. She sobbed tears of frustration as she hauled herself up, but could not drag herself far enough. Her muscles gave out and she slid back down, being able to do little more than pull her shoulders above the water line.

With the sudden feeling she was being watched, Kaimana turned around to look at the dark waters beneath her.

The shark taniwha was there, within an arm's distance. If she wanted to, she could reach out and touch its nose. It would be easy now for the creature to finish her, to swallow her as she had seen Rakau do all those weeks ago with the cannibals, but this taniwha was much more cruel than her Rakau. It swam there, inches from her, red eyes gleaming in the dark, taking pleasure in the fear that threatened to overcome her. Kaimana froze, gripping the canoe ropes, holding her breath.

In those moments before her death, Kaimana's thoughts returned to Rakau, to the closest thing she had in the world to a friend, a friend who now hates her. The shame and anger of how they had parted stoked a fire in Kaimana's belly, and she directed that hate towards the predator in the water.

She could not hope to defeat this taniwha, but she could make it remember her until the end of its days.

She felt to her belt for the Owl Queen's needle-thin dagger. Looking at the creature in front of her, arms shaking at the thought of the violence she was plotting, Kaimana slid the blade from her belt.

The taniwha must have realised something was amiss. In the second before Kaimana made her move, she fancied that the confidence in the creature's eyes faded as it realised she no longer looked afraid.

Kaimana thrust out the dagger and pierced the taniwha's nose. The water in front of her erupted in a foam of blood and anger. In its pain, the shark thrashed its head. Its nose made contact with Kaimana, ripping her free from the canoe's ropes, sending her flying through the air. She hit the water with an impact that drove all breath from her lungs. The creature was clearly enraged by her attack, and the water below her churned with the massive creature's throes. Thankfully, the taniwha did not appear to be able to properly focus on Kaimana, but she could not tell if this was due to the injury that she had caused it or just how angry it was. Flashes of white below her told Kaimana the shark was gnashing with its teeth, blindly, and it would only be seconds before its jaws found her.

At least I've marked it before it got me, she thought, a grim grin on her face. *One last note to play before the end of my tale.* Her spark buzzed proudly in agreement. Despite the imminent end, it did not seem to be preparing to run.

A shout from the darkness alerted her to the fact that she was not alone. This was a human voice, a man's voice.

"There!"

A whistling in the air warned Kaimana of the spear's flight seconds before it impacted the water in front of her. The spear did not find its mark, but half a dozen more followed, and the crimson that flowed from the taniwha told Kaimana at least one had hit it.

Shocked, she looked up, squinting to try to make out who else was on these dangerous seas. The moon unveiled a sight that Kaimana was thankful for - canoes. Then her heart sank. These canoes bore the markings of Nakoa. They had found her.

What is going to be the price for this rescue?

She could make out three of the vessels. Although all the sea faring boats of the Atoll were called canoes, these contraptions bore more resemblance to the large home boat Kaimana's troupe had shared than the small two-person canoe she had spent so much time travelling the Atoll in recently.

Each of the canoes could hold about twenty men, and the glints of bone in the moonlight suggested to Kaimana they were currently loaded with warriors, weapons ready for battle. From what she could see, the canoes were ornately carved, marked in honour of the war god, bearing the images of his tusks and his *Kiribati*. On the nearest canoe she made out a massive warrior balanced on its bow, a large stone-tipped spear in his hand.

"Before it goes under - loose!"

Another hail of spears pierced the water. Then there was cursing from the boats. The taniwha was gone.

"He will not forget," Kaimana shouted to them, alerting the men to her presence in the water. "Beware - it will attack again."

The large man looked at her, shock briefly registering on his face, but then nodded and quickly barked orders to those in his own vessel and across the waves to the other canoes. The sides of the boats became quickly populated with more warriors, spears in hand, all staring into the depths of the Outer Sea below them.

There was silence, and Kaimana braved the sight of the waters below. She did not believe the taniwha would remain focussed on her now that other attackers were present, but she was aware of how vulnerable a position she was in. Not for the first time, she was reminded of the sight of Rakau devouring the small canoe of cannibals in a single bite.

The taniwha's attack came at the furthest canoe from Kaimana, and was heralded by a number of cries from the warriors. The men on the attacked canoe jumped into the water, dropping their spears but also avoiding the taniwha's teeth, which instead turned their vessel into splinters. However, the crew of the other boats were ready, and peppered the taniwha's underbelly with their weapons, many of which found their mark. The taniwha landed with a splash, sending shock waves of seawater out to rock Kaimana. As she struggled to keep her head afloat, she saw the warriors that were now in the water moving towards their enemy, drawing blades from their sheaths. The taniwha roared in pain, both from the spears that now decorated its hide, but also from the number of knives that were cutting into it.

The monster was not interested in attacking the other canoes now. It seemed to realise it was in a fight for its life.

"It will dive," came another shout from the large man. "One last chance before we lose it."

A final volley of spears found their marks. Still the taniwha struggled, and dove back under the water with a splash.

Kaimana submerged her head to see the beast disappear into the darkness below. To her shock, the faint shine of moonlight showed her that at least half a dozen of Nakoa's men remained attached to the beast, continuing to hack at it with their blades as it dragged them under. Knowing the strength of the taniwha and the speed at which it could travel, Kaimana knew that continuing to hold onto their enemy was a death sentence for the warriors. Still, she could only marvel at their bravery, their dedication to remove this deadly enemy from the Atoll.

At this thought, she sniffed. *They're probably more interested in carving their own legends than actually protecting people.*

The waters below were silent. Kaimana raised her head again to see that the nearest canoe had moved towards her, the large man on it standing with a hand outstretched. His face was not kind.

Kaimana realised she did not have much choice in what happened next. There was no outrunning Nakoa now.

Kaimana reached out to take the warrior's hand. He grabbed her roughly by the wrist and pulled her aboard.

"You are the taniwha girl," he said. It was not a question. "Hohepa will want to see you."

So, Nakoa isn't here, then. This Hohepa must be some sort of high priest, leading this portion of the hunt.

Looking about on the canoe, Kaimana saw it was considerably larger than the troupe's canoe. This vessel actually had a covered hut in the centre of it, which was bizarre for Kaimana to look at, so used was she to sleeping out in the open or with a blanket or tarp covering her when at sea. The warriors were busy fishing their companions out of the water, doing what they could to rescue the survivors of the destroyed canoe.

Then a great cheer went up. All on the canoe rushed to the port side in time to see a small explosion of water from below and Kaimana found herself being dragged along. The taniwha was back, but it was not moving. Kaimana realised it had been killed, either from the many spears embedded into it, or by the final blows given to it by the warriors it had dragged below. Of these brave, stupid men Kaimana saw no sign, although a number of deep knife cuts could be seen on the taniwha's body.

"It is gone, now," the large man who held her wrist said, a hint of satisfaction in his voice. "Your taniwha is gone."

Kaimana could not help her mouth opening in shock. *They think this is Rakau.*

Of course they would, unless they had had a good look at Rakau earlier. What are the odds I'd get close to two great beasts in such a short time?

Hope welled up inside Kaimana. She did not know what her prospects were now she had been caught, but if all of the war party believed their prey had been caught and killed, then Rakau could well live on his island in peace.

"Come," the warrior grumbled, pulling Kaimana roughly by the wrist, leading her to the hut in the centre of the canoe. Others on the boat had spotted Kaimana by now and were laughing or leering at her. A sudden chill ran down her spine.

She was pulled roughly inside the hut and thrown to the floor. The interior was filled with incense and candlelight, which felt alien to Kaimana's senses after being so long at sea. The wooden floor was unadorned, but much of the rest of the cabin was decorated in fine cloths with intricate designs, many of which were based on the symbols of Nakoa's worshippers - a pig's head, a *Kiribati* sword, a whale shark.

Other uninteresting furniture littered the walls of the room - a desk, some basic chairs - but Kaimana's attention was immediately drawn to the bed in the centre of the room. It was occupied.

Kaimana's panic at the implications of being brought towards an occupied bed quickly subsided when she realised the other person in the room was female. She was also fully dressed in fine, dark cloths, with a black veil pulled across her face, reclining on top of the bed, propped up on the copious cushions that also lay there.

"So, the pupil returns to her *kahuna*."

Kaimana paused only briefly. "Eloni?"

Eloni - for it was indeed her - sat up and detached the veil from the side of her face. Kaimana's blood chilled at the look that her former teacher gave her. Eloni was smiling, and it was not a kind smile.

"I had hoped I'd be seeing you again soon. As you can see, my position has changed somewhat since you left me."

It hasn't been that long since I left the troupe. What's she doing in this get up?

"You're here with the warriors, with Hohepa?"

A brief wrinkle disturbed Eloni's smug grin, which told Kaimana she had guessed correctly, denying her former *kahuna* the privilege of relaying her tale.

"Yes," the older woman answered, "the High Priest has taken me to his bed. You caused quite a commotion when you disturbed his taniwha hunt, and after you left so suddenly, the warriors found themselves under considerable strain. Even a great man like Hohepa needs to turn to someone to comfort him when times are hard."

"And you were there to play that part..." Kaimana finished.

"Oh, he had noticed me already. As soon as I made it clear I would accept him, he made me his."

Kaimana turned her lip up at this, despite herself. *Made me his.*

"Now I've a tale to rival anything I've heard our troupe play before. Those smaller passions that I wove into my songs are nothing compared to the love of a man whose very step shakes the Atoll ring. You should hear it, young pupil, the song I am preparing now. It will make my name when it is done, and all shall beg me to play it for them. It will be a song for the ages."

"I'm sorry, let me get this straight. You think that jumping into bed with someone *again* will make you spark *again*? Eloni, I don't need to hear the tune, I've heard it already. You've played it for me time and time again, when it was about all your other conquests. It doesn't matter who they are, how powerful your lover is. Your songs are about a woman being used and cast aside. You've got no story here, still no spark, save for the one you've invented in your head. Just like the last times. Eloni, your song will be forgotten just as easily as Hohepa will forget you when he is done with you."

Eloni sat up straight, her eyes cold.

I've touched a nerve. That was probably a very bad idea, given my predicament, but I couldn't help myself. She doesn't understand. She needs a teacher.

"What about you, little ocarina player, what of your spark? All of this trouble, defying the gods, fleeing with a monster - has it given you what you wanted?"

Kaimana lowered her eyes. *What a question. Has it given me what I wanted, this adventure? When I first left with Rakau, I wanted a story, I wanted my spark to reignite. I wanted a song that would make my name, buy me more prestige in my own troupe, or possibly make other, more prestigious troupes, interested in me.*

And I found it. I've seen sights I thought I never would, and I've done things... I'm lucky to be alive, after everything I've done. Do I have a song worth playing, now? I know I do, a god told me so.

But...

"No," Kaimana said, finally. "No, I do not have what I want."

She lowered her face to the deck of the boat, allowing images of Rakau - of the moonlit sea bed and of curling up on an abandoned island around a small fire together - to dance through her mind.

"I didn't think so," was Eloni's smug reply.

At that moment, Nakoa's high priest entered. The proud man glanced at Eloni briefly, and Kaimana fancied she could see a look of annoyance cross his face. Then he turned to address Kaimana directly.

"That beast is not the taniwha from my master's island."

Kaimana's heart sank. She knew she should try to hide her emotions, that it would be best for Rakau if she try to cover for him, but she could not do so. Her face showed her despair.

The priest nodded, not requiring Kaimana to speak her answer. "So where is it then, your *rakau tipua*? Where is the beast that has besmirched Lord Nakoa's honour?"

"He's gone," Kaimana said, not giving up any more information.

The priest walked across the room and hit her across the face, sending her to the floor. Blood spilt from a burst lip. Eloni's grin grew a little wider.

"You have been on the Outer Sea. Is he somewhere out there? Is he close?"

Kaimana was in shock at the violent act. She had been attacked many times in the past weeks, but now she felt most vulnerable, in front of this woman who hated her and this man who had total command over all of the people on board the canoes.

"He's gone," Kaimana repeated, dreading the response.

She was right to do so. The high priest kicked her in the stomach, winding her.

"I'm enjoying this, my love. This girl has done much to earn my anger over the years. If she is to be killed, may I be the one to do so?"

Eloni had draped her arm over her lover now, allowing her fingers to play across his bare chest. The high priest grabbed her hand by the wrist and pulled it off him.

"No, you may not. To kill is a warrior's art, and you are no warrior. That pleasure is for us alone." He stopped for a moment to think, and allowed a thin smile to grace his face. "Warriors and taniwha. We are the killers, we are the ones who take lives on the Atoll. This is not an act for little girls."

Eloni's face soured at the insult, but she said nothing.

Kaimana remained gasping on the floor, having finally found her breath again. She felt so hopeless, unable to stand up to the man's strength, despite her urge to do so.

The priest knelt beside her, grabbed her hair and raised her head to look him in the face.

"My lord is not happy. This quest takes too long, and he is eager for vengeance. You understand I will do anything it takes to get the information I need from you, do you not?"

Kaimana looked the man in the eye and nodded, silently. She would not give him the satisfaction of seeing any hint of the fear that crawled in her belly at this moment.

"Good. Well then, I ask you one last time. Where is your taniwha?"

Kaimana opened her mouth to speak.

"My lord, we have it!" The speaker was another of Nakoa's warriors, bursting into the hut with his news.

The high priest dropped Kaimana's head to the deck with a thunk. "What do you speak of?"

"The taniwha, my lord, the one from the island. The other

hunting party came across it in the water. We have it."

No.

Panic rising in her, Kaimana rushed to her feet, barrelling past the high priest, Eloni and the messenger in her attempt to get outside of the hut to see what they were talking about. The other occupants of the structure were so intent on their own conversation that they paid her little heed.

On making it outside, Kaimana saw the sun was rising over the Atoll, painting the black waters of the Outer Sea a deep red. There, within a spear's throw of the high priest's canoe were three new boats.

Bile rose in Kaimana's stomach when she realised what was being dragged behind the boats. Under countless strands of rope and netting - great cords binding its limbs, being dragged through the water by all three of the canoes at the same time - was a taniwha. Its mossy, scarred hide was unmistakable. It was Rakau.

Cheering rose from the two remaining canoes of the priest's hunting party. These cheers were mirrored by the sobs of despair Kaimana gave at the sight of her friend.

Is he dead? How did they catch him?

Rakau rolled in the water, struggling but clearly weak, unable to break any of the bonds that held him. Tiny streams of green blood leaked into the waters behind him, leaving a clear trail to show his passage. Rakau's head lolled to one side and he made eye contact with Kaimana. His eyes appeared to brighten slightly, but he was capable of no other movement.

He was coming to me, Kaimana realised. *Nakoa's warriors are good, but a group this small could not survive that island if they even had the nerve to travel out that far. So Rakau was coming to find me. They must have come across him in the open water...*

"We will accompany them," the high priest bellowed, ordering his men to get into position to depart. "We will aid their passage to Lord Nakoa. Let us leave, now."

"My lord, that is not possible," a nearby warrior stated. "We have many wounded, and repairs are still being made-"

The high priest cut off the other by grabbing the man's jade necklace and pulling him close to his face. "I will not allow another to arrive back with the prize, without us. We sail now, or as fast as we are able."

"Yes, my lord," the warrior said, and then ran off to shout at the others, ordering the deck to be cleared of wounded.

The high priest grabbed Kaimana and pulled her back into his hut. He threw her to the floor and paced about the room. Eloni returned with them also, a look of concern on her face.

"My love, this is great news. What a victory, to have our forces defeat not one, but two taniwha."

"No. The capture should have been mine. Now another's star will rise in Nakoa's eyes. My position could be in jeopardy."

"But look at the prize we can bring him. You have killed a beast, a shark. Surely that is much better to present Nakoa with than a walking log?"

The priest shook his head. "Normally, yes, but Nakoa wants his revenge, and I have failed to bring it to him. We must leave quickly. Watch the girl while I make preparations."

The priest stormed out of the room.

Kaimana's mind raced. *Rakau is still alive, all is not lost. What am I to do, to save him? An entire army, the sea, and a war god stand between me and my friend. Not to mention my old teacher.*

As if reading Kaimana's mind, Eloni walked over to a desk in the corner of the hut.

"I have been told I am not to be the one to kill you. I do not like being told things like that."

Alert, Kaimana turned in time to see Eloni pull a thick, jade knife from a compartment in the desk.

"Eloni," was all Kaimana had the time to say before the older woman attacked.

Eloni leapt through the air at Kaimana with a snarl of victory on her face. Shocked by the attack, Kaimana instinctively grabbed at Eloni's wrist, forcing the knife point away from her face. However, Kaimana let out a cry of pain as Eloni's other hand grabbed her mauled shoulder and gripped it hard.

"I've looked forward to this for a long time, pupil of mine. You see, in the time I have spent with my lover I have learnt where real power lies. Not with music, and being able to tell tales of old victories gone by. What do all of our stories have in common? They involve death. And the victory goes to the killers. My love says that only warriors have it in them to kill. Then I must have the heart of a warrior, my Knack be damned. I will finally teach you for trying to take my place."

Despite her enemy's probing fingers gouging into her shoulder,

Kaimana realised that letting go of Eloni's knife hand now would mean her death, and so continued to grip it tight. Nevertheless, the jade blade continued to move closer and closer to Kaimana's neck. She was not strong enough to stop Eloni. Her life would be over soon, and not long after Rakau would join her.

Rakau.

Kaimana thought about that last glance she was able to catch of her friend, of how forlorn he looked tethered to the warrior's boats. Rakau would not have let himself be caught in a situation like this, with his enemy bearing down on him.

As if she read Kaimana's mind, Eloni's face erupted into a mad grin, the woman's eyes fixed on the point of the blade. Eloni lowered herself closer to Kaimana, to bring her full strength to bear and to savour her victory.

Even if Rakau did find himself caught like this, he would always find a way out. He would scratch and bite with claw and-

In a moment of clear realisation Kaimana knew exactly what to do. Eloni continued to lower herself on top of Kaimana, straining her neck to get a good glimpse of the blade that was at this moment cutting into the skin of Kaimana's neck.

Still gripping Eloni's wrist, Kaimana thrust her head up, bared her teeth, and sank them into Eloni's throat.

Kaimana's former teacher gave a panicked cry, and in her own mouth Kaimana could feel Eloni's voice, the hard cartilage of the older woman's throat pushing against Kaimana's teeth.

"Get off me, you witch, off."

Kaimana continued to hold on, despite the continuing agony in her shoulder, despite the ache of her arms, despite the blood that now rushed into her mouth. Despite what should have been the horror of what she was doing to Eloni.

Kaimana felt Eloni's movements becoming more panicked, and the woman tried frantically to free herself from the small ocarina player. In response, Kaimana bit harder, feeling her teeth pierce through more flesh, feeling the wet stuff underneath Eloni's skin tear much more easily than Kaimana had thought it would.

Eloni tried to scream, but quickly stopped, realising that the act of doing so was forcing Kaimana's teeth to dig deeper into her. Instead, Eloni began to cough, and warm, wet liquid sprayed from the woman's mouth onto Kaimana's head and face.

The knife dropped to the floor and both of Eloni's hands

pulled at Kaimana's hair, but weakly now, as the blood-filled coughs continued.

"Please," the woman said, "I'm sorry. I made a mistake. Please, release me."

I'm not a murderer. I'm only doing this because she's stopping me from freeing my friend. I take no pleasure in this.

Eloni went limp, and Kaimana immediately let go. She could see the woman was still breathing, but did not want to waste any more time checking on her - Rakau would already be far ahead of them by this point.

Taking only a few seconds to check that there was nobody standing guard, Kaimana ducked outside.

They were at sail now, and Hohepa's canoe was further behind the others, but was towing the body of the large shark taniwha behind them, a prize to present to Nakoa. Kaimana rushed to the edge of the canoe and looked down. She was relieved to see the moonlight illuminating the seabed of the Atoll beneath her again, and thanked Laka that this part of her world was back to normal.

Suddenly, she heard a shout. Kaimana turned her head to spot three of Nakoa's warriors staring at her. She was surprised to see fear on their faces, and she turned around to look at whatever monstrosity behind her had made them react that way.

There was nothing there.

Kaimana could not help the smile that crossed her face when she realised it was her own blood-soaked appearance that had given them cause to start. She turned her head slowly back to them, allowing the white of her teeth to stand out from the dark red blood that was staining her face, and then Kaimana jumped over the side of the canoe into the water, to her freedom.

THE BROTHERS
AND THE
SEA

A tale from the Crescent Atoll

This is the story of twin brothers. Both were born under the same new moon, both were given the same love from their parents. However, one of these boys grew up to be kind, hardworking and gentle, whereas his sibling was selfish, lazy and cruel.

When they were young men, their father died, taken by one of Leinani's wrathful fits. Their mother had a talent only for cookery and could not support herself with her Knack alone.

"Do not come begging at my door," the selfish son said to his aging mother. "I have so little to feed myself with, I cannot add any more labour to my day by having to think of you as well." To ensure that she would not return, the selfish son then slapped his mother's face. She left, in tears.

When the kind son heard of this, he approached his mother, finding her crying under a coconut tree.

"Do not worry, mother of mine," he said, drying away her tears. "I have food and shelter for us both. You took care of me when I was young and weak, and now it is my turn to care for you."

The mother looked at her son with thankful eyes, knowing full well the burden she was placing on him. "Tangaloa bless you, my son, and may he give you plenty. May your mana grow more bountiful with every kind act."

Years passed, and the kind son continued to look after his mother until she faded away. After her death, both brothers decided it was time to marry, and unfortunately both set their sights on the same maiden from the village, the chieftain's daughter.

The kind brother knew the chieftain's daughter was tired of being pursued by suitors who only wanted her hand to get closer to her father's position of power. Instead of approaching her father first, the kind brother decided to take his time to woo the girl, bringing her flowers and pearls that he fished from the sea. The chief was happy to watch this courtship quietly blossom, and eventually the chief's daughter fell in love with the kind brother, and she agreed to marry him.

"You are a good man, to win my heart in such a way instead of forcing me into a life with someone I do not love," the daughter whispered to her intended on the eve of their wedding. "You must have strong mana to have faith in such a course of action."

The kind brother smiled and thought of his mother. "My kindness is the source of my mana, and it is strong."

Unfortunately, the other brother had a strong source of mana as well. His mana was born from violence, and cruelty was his gift. As the chieftain's daughter spoke with her intended under the stars, the selfish brother and his men crept into the chief's hut and gutted and butchered everyone they found there. When the kind brother and his wife-to-be returned, they were both taken captive. The selfish brother took the chief's daughter as his own wife, and exiled his brother from the island forever.

The kind brother spent many years travelling the islands in misery. Eventually, he found solace in Tangaloa's priesthood, the god of the sea, and as an old man he was given the responsibility of watching the eastern passages across the Atoll ring, watching and recording signs of large sea creatures moving to and from the Inner Sea. It was a peaceful existence, and after a lifetime of serving his god, the brother thought only rarely of the island that had once been his home.

One day, the goddess Leinani became angry, and the waves rose high and the sky blackened. The kind priest found himself marooned for weeks on his small island outpost. His food and water stores quickly ran low, and the sea was too rough for him to travel back to his temple.

Two weeks after the storm began, the priest found a young man washed up on his beach, the survivor of a large canoe destroyed by the storm. The priest nursed this man back to health. He was shocked to find, however, that this young man was his nephew - his brother's son with the chief's daughter. When the priest found out about the young man's parents, he was in a state of shock. He experienced emotions of anger and regret that he had thought were long buried, and for a brief, horrible moment he considered murdering the young man in his sleep.

However, the priest's wisdom prevailed and he caused his nephew no harm. He tried to hide his revelation from his nephew, but the young man could tell the priest was in some distress and eventually pried the information from him. For a long time after that the priest's nephew was silent.

The storm began to die down, and food was running low, so both men faced a problem. They could not afford to wait much longer for a rescue from their remote island, as there was only a day's worth of food left between them. The priest's canoe remained, but it would hold only one of them, and both knew that the priest's aged muscles would not be able to fight with the still-angry waves that assaulted the Atoll.

"I will rescue you," the priest's nephew said. "I am strong enough to row your canoe to the nearest island. Let me go for help. I will be back within a day with friends, and will bring you to safety."

Could this boy be trusted? His father certainly was not worthy of trust, but the priest decided he should not judge this boy by his father's sins.

"My mother told me I had an uncle," the boy said as the priest agreed that his nephew should take the canoe. "She also told me that he had great mana, born from his endless kindness. I can see now what she meant."

With a weak smile, the priest handed the boy over the rest of the food, most of the water, and watched the boy paddle over the distant horizon.

No rescue came.

It was by the third day, when the priest had been without fresh water for too long, that he allowed himself to admit he would never see the boy again. Moreover, although it was very possible his nephew had been overcome by the high waves of the raging seas, the priest knew in his heart of hearts that the boy had made it to safety, but had broken his promise.

That night, water-starved and heart-weary, the priest died. He died sitting upright on the beach, staring at the moonlight reflected onto the now-calm Atoll waters.

In that magical moment as the spirit readies itself to leave a dead body, Tangaloa came to visit the priest.

The sea god took the form of some seaweed, washed up on the beach in front of the dead priest. The seaweed took the shape of a man's face, with tangled hair and crab-infested beard, and moved as Tangaloa spoke to his servant.

"Rarely has one come into my arms with such plentiful mana, and having travelled such a difficult road to gather and keep such a bounty. Kind One, I take you willingly into my kingdom, and because of your kindness and your service in my priesthood, I offer you a boon. You may name one thing of me, and I will grant it to you as best I can."

The priest's spirit thought for a short while, and then spoke to his god. "Great Tangaloa, you must know that I have a brother. You must know he has taken much from me - my island and my love. His wife once loved me, but now lives happily with him and their son. And this son, he lied to me, and his lies have resulted in my death."

"Yes, all of this I know."

"My request has to do with them."

Tangaloa said nothing, waiting for more.

"I want you to kill them. I want you to wipe them from the face of the Atoll, and let none who share their bloodline survive to cheat, lie and forget their loved ones ever again."

Tangaloa's mouth opened in a grin to show white cowry shells, glinting like sharp teeth in the moonlight.

"You are indeed kind, to request such a thing from me. You must know I will find great pleasure in this task. Come into my kingdom, Kind One, and watch as your request is fulfilled."

The sea god's waves reached out for the dead priest and carried his body to Tangaloa's kingdom. Within the hour, the Atoll waters had become violent again, and giant waves began to wage havoc upon the islands.

One island in particular, the island that the priest had been born on, did not survive the storm. When visitors attempted to find it days later, when the waters had abated, it was nowhere to be found.

Some claim to have seen a giant wave crashing down over the island, a wave mounted by Tangaloa himself, with a grinning old man in priest's robes sitting on his right shoulder.

However, this story cannot be true, for nobody who saw the waves break upon the island survived that night to tell the tale.

≋CHAPTER≋
TEN

As soon as she was under the water, Kaimana acted quickly. She had to jump off the canoe to escape further capture, but she could not let them get away from her - Rakau would have precious little time left after he arrived in front of Nakoa, and the high priest's boat was already much further behind the captive taniwha.

Blinking as the salt water stung her eyes, Kaimana made straight for the dead monster trailing behind Hohepa's canoe. From under the water, Kaimana could see the attention the dead monster was attracting from the local wildlife. The entire underbelly of the monster was swarming with small fish, nibbling on the dead taniwha's flesh. There were also more than a few Atoll sharks lurking nearby, darting in for a quick bite, but otherwise keeping their distance.

As the corpse was dragged past her, Kaimana reached out to grab one of the ropes the taniwha was being towed with. She underestimated the power with which it was being pulled, and nearly lost her grip straight away, which would have left her stranded in Atoll waters with no chance of keeping up with her friend.

Rung by rung she pulled herself along the netting on the underside of the monster's belly, her lungs burning with lack of air.

She knew, however, she could not surface now - the warriors were alerted to her escape, and would be scouring the waters behind the canoe for her. Kaimana waited until she was hidden from sight by the dead taniwha before allowing herself a breath.

Now what? We have at least a day's travel before we reach Nakoa's island, and I can't imagine they'll stop before we get there. Am I just to hang on here until we arrive?

She eyed the dead creature she was clinging to. There was no feasible way she could climb on top of it, especially without the warriors on the boat looking.

At least we're still travelling forward. They can't be that concerned about where I got to, or else they'd have stopped to find me.

She shook her leg to fend off some of the curious bottom feeders who were investigating the new arrival. They went back to chewing on the taniwha's underside.

I wonder if they've found Eloni yet? I didn't want to hurt her, but isn't it strange that I don't feel bad about it either? It's exactly what Rakau would've done for me. He didn't hesitate to hurt others to save me, whether I was under threat from taniwha or humans. Still, it would please me to think she survived. Survived, and learnt to shut up a bit more.

The next day went slowly for the musician. She clung on tight to the dead taniwha, arms looped around the ropes, never allowing herself to rest or sleep, too focussed on making sure she did not slip off or was not bothered by any more sharks. On that long journey her spark left her alone, as if it realised that Kaimana's attention needed to be on staying alive, on holding tight to the ropes around the dead taniwha. As Kaimana hung there, she prayed to Laka for her guidance. Only once did her mind stray to the other god in her life, to round-bellied Yam, and the image of him made her smile.

Wherever you are, great Yam, I hope you're in a better situation than me.

The sound of horns blowing in the distance warned Kaimana when they arrived at Nakoa's island.

Knowing she would have no chance of concealing herself from the warriors if she stayed with the taniwha corpse until it was dragged ashore, as soon as Kaimana could see the island, she slipped away from the carcass, treading water and watching the canoes pull the dead body away from her, around to the other side of the island. Not travelling all of the way with them meant her trip would take more time, but she hoped it would allow her to travel with little fear of discovery.

Steeling herself, hoping her friend still lived, Kaimana began the long swim to the distant beach.

Night had fallen by the time Kaimana reached the war god's temple. The trek through the dense jungle surrounding the temple had been tougher than expected, particularly because every movement in the trees had made her freeze in fear at the thought of being discovered.

Her plan had been to scout the temple from the undergrowth to find the best way to gain entry. All of that left her mind, however, when she arrived up there. Her former performing troupe was still camped outside of the temple.

Why're they still here? I thought they'd have been kicked out in disgrace after I left, or maybe even disbanded after Eloni eloped with the priest.

All of the troupe seemed to be present. Old Rawiri was sitting in a circle with the dancing girls, heads bowed and eyes closed. Kaimana was not close enough to hear anything, but she suspected they were in prayer to Laka. Mahina the chanting boy sat unusually close to them, not part of the group, but he appeared to be listening in. Poli and Tokoni sat by the camp fire, and Kaimana gave a half smile to see Tokoni run his hand softly down the turtle-faced girl's back. Aka sat at the fire also, alone and staring into the flames.

She watched them for a while, becoming more aware of how downbeat the group was.

I can't imagine life on Nakoa's island could have been that pleasant for them. I wonder why they've been kept here?

She had a sneaking suspicion it had something to do with her.

Kaimana was also aware of the loud noises coming from the temple courtyard. It sounded as if all of Nakoa's warriors were there, chanting.

Rakau must already be inside.

At that moment, Aka got up and made his way into the forest, probably to relieve himself. Kaimana darted through the bushes and crept up behind her former troupe leader, covering his mouth with her hand.

Aka started to struggle, trying to shout. Kaimana knew she would not be able to use strength to keep him quiet for long.

"Aka, it's me, Kaimana. Don't let them know I'm here."

He turned around to eye her, the shock clear on his face. Kaimana slowly moved her hand from his mouth, waiting to see what he would do.

After a pause, his eyes darting from Kaimana's weathered face to her wounded shoulder, Aka spoke. "What're you doing here?"

The chanting from the temple grew louder.

"I've come back for him, Aka, the taniwha. Is he in there?"

Kaimana was taken aback by the anger on Aka's face, making her remember the slap he had given her when removing her from the troupe.

"You've come back for the taniwha?" His mouth was open, aghast. He looked towards the temple, then back at Kaimana. For a moment he could not speak, but gesticulated towards his chest with both hands. "What about us, Kaimana? You never thought about coming back for us, your friends, the people who took you in for years?"

Friends? Friends don't slap you across the face and then leave you to fend for yourself. "I didn't know you were still here, thought you'd be long gone. Rakau - the taniwha, my friend - needs me now, if he's still alive.

"You're kidding me! Don't worry about the actual people you have lived with, but you've got no problem getting yourself killed for the sake of a murdering monster? And yes, it's still alive, but I don't reckon it'll be that way for much longer. There was blood in the eyes of the warriors who dragged him in there, and so there should be. Let him be killed, end this so we may be sent on our way."

Kaimana was surprised to find she was now crying. "How could you, Aka? I always thought you were kind, that you had a good heart. Yet here you are wishing the death of the creature - the person - that means more to me than…" Kaimana's spark erupted, tears of amber flowing from her as she realised that, unless she did something, Rakau's final moments were upon him. Inside, her song was singing, complete. It was ready for the world to hear. All Kaimana had to do now was play it, to let it live forever it in history.

Later, she chided the jealous song. *First we save Rakau, then everyone will hear you.*

For his part, Aka was confused at the grief his former ocarina player was experiencing.

Kaimana could see his resolve wavering, and grabbed Aka's shoulders. "He is good, Aka. He saved my life, more than once. He is kind, and gentle, and unique. He doesn't deserve to die this way, gutted like livestock."

Aka studied her once more, then turned away.

"We have to play for them, to perform when the sacrifice is done. We've been setting up all morning, our equipment is in there. All of us have been coming and going through the north doorway, and the guards are too drunk to really pay attention. Act like you're one of us and they won't spare you a second glance. That'll get you inside, but after that you're on your own. I won't endanger the others for your monster, and I've no idea how you could possibly help him with all those warriors crawling over him."

Kaimana nodded, taking all of the information in. Then, she leaned forward and planted a gentle kiss on Aka's shoulder.

"Thank you, Aka. For my part, I'm sorry. Sorry you've had to suffer because of all this."

Then Kaimana left, not waiting for him to reply.

At the north door to the temple, events transpired almost as Aka had described. Both guards were so drunk, it seemed as though neither of them were going to even look in Kaimana's direction. However, as she passed them, head lowered out of respect and genuine fear, one of them took the opportunity to slap her on the bottom, eliciting chortles from his companion.

Kaimana was surprised by the sneer that bloomed on her face in response, but she kept this hidden and walked back towards the stage she had played on weeks ago.

The sight of the temple courtyard was horrible.

Last time she had been here, the warriors had been organised but rowdy, giving all of the performers the notion that these were not safe men to be around, but they were kept in check by their masters.

Tonight, things were different. The warriors were riotous, consumed by drink and bloodlust, milling and tousling with each other around the courtyard, full-scale brawls running continuously in many pockets of this sea of flesh. The men were shouting and screaming, the content of which was mostly incoherent, but many of them were loudly praising their lord's name.

Nakoa sat there, overlooking them all. The raised podium for his driftwood throne had been repaired, but the broken wall behind him had not yet been touched. A shiver ran up Kaimana's back when she realised that Nakoa too was intoxicated, a barrel-sized cup in his hand continuing the job. The god was shouting along with the rest of the warriors, one hand balancing his drink on the edge of the throne, the other whirling his *Kiribati* around his head every time he sighted a display of bravery and strength that pleased him. The war god was laughing, and for all purposes he sounded to Kaimana like a fat pig who had just gained access to a farmer's field.

Behind Nakoa, standing silently, were a number of others Kaimana recognised. Her eyes quickly went to Eloni. Kaimana was relieved to see she had not killed her former teacher. Eloni's throat was wrapped and bound, and the woman's hollowed expression suggested she would rather be recovering in bed than celebrating tonight, but she was alive. Eloni stood behind Hohepa, whose eyes were full of thunder, constantly fixed on the young warrior who stood to Nakoa's right. This young man Kaimana did not recognise, but she suspected he was the one responsible for Rakau's capture, and was now benefiting from increased status because of his success.

Rakau was there too. It took a few moments for Kaimana to spot him, because of all the people standing or sitting on him. Rakau was bound in the centre of the courtyard, but the courtyard was so tightly packed with men, they had taken to using the taniwha as part of the floor. Ropes as thick as Kaimana's arms held the taniwha firmly to the ground. Kaimana fancied that Rakau would still be able to break free if he wanted to, but he did not appear to be moving, despite the constant abuse his body was now receiving. For a moment, she feared he was already dead, but then she spotted a loud warrior whipping out a knife and slicing a nick from Rakau's skin. The warrior proceeded to lick at the taniwha's blood, drinking it with resulting shouts of encouragement and disgust from his peers, but Kaimana's heart was gladdened to see her friend shudder at the knife's touch, briefly opening his green eyes and letting out a growl of pain.

Quickly, Kaimana threw a *tapa* shawl over her head and pushed her way into the crowd. Her spark inside her, now ready to sing, began to panic as Kaimana was jostled and bumped by the celebrating warriors.

We'll be fine, we'll be fine, she chided the spark, *they're so drunk and consumed by themselves, they don't have time for me.*

Oh Rakau, what've they done to you? I'll try to free you from your bonds, but you're going to have to fight your way out yourself.

Despite her thoughts of encouragement, Kaimana was aware that she and Eloni were the only women present at these festivities. The idea of sneaking around undetected underneath the throng of warriors would have had a lot more merit if Kaimana could have blended in better.

Still, she was able to reach the first rope without her presence causing any commotion. Rakau's bonds were tied to thick wooden stakes that had been driven into the courtyard's earth, and it took only a few seconds of cutting with the Owl Queen's knife for the rope to break. As the binding went limp, Kaimana's head snapped up, fearful the men around her would finally notice what she was doing. Thankfully, they were all too busy and inebriated to notice.

As Kaimana moved to the next stake, she let her fingers run over the taniwha's hide.

I'm here, now. Be ready.

As the chord at the second stake broke, Kaimana heard a shout from behind. She could not make out exactly what had been said, but its meaning was very clear - she had been spotted. She pushed into the crowd of warriors blocking her way to the next rope, but the growing noise of unrest from behind her told Kaimana her time of anonymity was up, and word of her rescue attempt was spreading.

As she emerged from the bodies at the third stake, she cut at the rope desperately, aware that most of the shouts in the courtyard had turned from the noise of celebration to that of outrage. A rough hand grabbed her wrist just as the third rope severed, crushing her muscles, causing her to drop the knife in pain. Kaimana looked up to see the tattooed face of an older warrior, excitement building on his face as he realised the prestige he was about to receive before his god.

Remembering how she had dealt with Eloni on the canoe, Kaimana sank her teeth into the older man's fingers, drawing blood. He had clearly not been expecting any reprisal from her, and his grip slackened in shock. This was all the opportunity Kaimana needed to pull away from him, disappearing into the crowd once again, making for the final stake in the ground.

The going was not easy now, all in the temple were aware that something was wrong. Hands grabbed out for her, but she wormed her way between the men's bodies as quickly as she was able. A warrior grabbed her shawl, pulling it off her as she continued to push past. Another grabbed Kaimana by the hair, and for a brief moment, she thought it was all over, that she would not be able to escape this attack. However, she pulled with all of her might, and after a painful ripping sensation, she left a clump of hair in the man's hand, but continued, free.

She reached the final stake, knifeless. Desperate, Kaimana grabbed the stake and began to pull on it. Inside, her spark was screaming at her, knowing how close it was to being lost forever.

I can't do this, this is too much for me. I must have loosened him enough by now.

Angry hands found Kaimana. They grabbed at her, trying to pull her away from the stake. Instead, she gripped tight, no longer trying to pull it from the ground, but just holding onto it to stop herself from being moved.

She moved her head around to try to catch a glimpse of the taniwha.

"Rakau! I've done all I can," she shouted. "Pull free, pull free now. Get out of here, run while you can."

The taniwha did not move.

Behind her came a laugh, and Kaimana cried out in pain as a foot made contact with her gut, winding her, causing her to finally let go of the stake. Her hair was pulled, throwing her head back, letting her look into the satisfied eyes of her captor, Hohepa.

"My thanks to you for this opportunity," he sneered quietly at Kaimana, before bringing his forehead down on her face with a crack.

The breaking of Kaimana's nose was accompanied by an explosion of sound from the surrounding crowd, the multitude of warriors congratulating their high priest on his success. Her head ringing from the noise and the pain, blood flowing freely from her crumpled nose, Kaimana felt Hohepa lift her roughly above his head, carrying her to his lord and master. Inside, her spark was whimpering, a flower which had been ready to bloom, but was now preparing itself to be chopped at the stalk.

All Kaimana could think of was Rakau. *Why didn't you try?*

As if sensing her thoughts, one of Rakau's eyes opened, weakly looking at her in shame. He was forced to close it when one of Nakoa's men took the occasion to kick the taniwha's eye. Kaimana let out a long breath as she realised all was lost, and she felt empty, like a hollow shell. Once more, her spark dimmed, preparing to flee.

She was thrown roughly to the floor.

"It is already beaten."

The speaker was Nakoa. Kaimana found herself once again at the mercy of the war god. As she lifted her head to look at the pig, all of the cuts and bruises she had suffered when struggling through the crowd began to protest, and she groaned in pain. Nakoa was looking at her, grinning with menace, his long-toothed overbite dripping beer-soaked drool onto Kaimana's face.

"The taniwha knows it is beaten. It has tried to escape, and I have beaten it back."

The war god tipped back his head, emptying the remnants of his cup into his open mouth, allowing a good amount of it to splash down onto Kaimana's face. Then, Nakoa threw his cup at Kaimana, sending her head crashing back into the dirt and opening up a large gash on her forehead.

"Send for the performers! The time has come to rid the Atoll of the beast."

Kaimana could feel herself slipping into unconsciousness, but she fought it back.

If I can't save him, I'll be with Rakau now, at the end.

She lifted herself off of the ground, gritting her teeth against the pain of the throbbing inside her skull. Dimly, she was aware of Aka and her former troupe - except for Eloni - being escorted onto the performer's podium.

Then Nakoa knelt down beside Kaimana, the odour of his fermented breath causing her stomach to clench.

"But first, let us show the people of the Atoll what happens to those who deny a god his due."

More pain as Kaimana was hauled to her feet again, this time grabbed by an oversized hand on the back of her neck. Nakoa held Kaimana just above the dirt floor of the temple courtyard, holding her high enough for her desperately searching toes to taste the solid ground but find no proper footing on it.

Her spark screamed. However, unlike all of the other times Kaimana's life had been threatened, her spark was not screaming out of fear. It was angry. Through her pain, through her sadness at the thought of Rakau leaving this world, Kaimana could sense her unborn song screaming in anger at Nakoa, cursing him for denying it its chance at life, cursing him for forcing a tragic end to its tune. In response to these screams, the amber sparks of Kaimana's Knack flowed from her eyes like never before, settling on the war god's hand and arm like small, flickering flames. Unfortunately, these flames quickly faded, and appeared to cause no discomfort to the god.

"This girl has wronged me," Nakoa growled to his audience, and his men nodded solemnly. "We were attacked - I was attacked - and she helped the attacker to escape."

Through her tears of pain, Kaimana could see her former troupe staring at her. To a person they seemed to be in shock, unable to fully believe what they were seeing.

Nakoa threw Kaimana to the dirt again, and stood over her. She did not need to look behind to know that the god's *Kiribati* was now raised, ready to deliver his sentence. She allowed her spark's anger to overcome her own fear, and kept her face hard, staring back at her troupe in grim resolution as she waited for the end. She knew the spark would not leave her now, she knew it wanted to see her story to the end, whatever the cost. The otherworldly creature's bravery was enough to inspire her own.

"Let this be a lesson to all who think to cross me," the war god said.

In her final moments, Kaimana's amber eyes met Rakau's green, and she smiled at him.

At least we are together. We will go to the next life together.

A hush settled over the courtyard.

The killing blow did not come.

After a few seconds, Kaimana dared herself to turn to look at Nakoa in confusion, wondering why he had paused. The war god remained standing above her, his weapon raised high above his head, but Nakoa was no longer looking at her. Instead, his eyes were looking across the temple floor, well beyond Rakau's prone body or the hapless troupe. Kaimana followed his gaze to where every single person in the courtyard was looking.

In the main entranceway to the courtyard stood a black figure.

For a moment, Kaimana thought that it was a person, a woman, but she quickly realised there was no way this could be the case. The figure's body was not solid, but almost seemed to be made up of woven black fabrics, pieced together to give the impression of the shape of a lady wearing a fine black dress, but the weaving of the fabric had left gaps, like the windows in a spider's web, and through these holes Kaimana could glimpse the starlight of the night sky. The figure's face was impossibly white, and after a second Kaimana realised it was painted that way, and the features of a woman's face - black eyes, dots for the nose, red lips - were painted onto what seemed to be some sort of polished clay.

"You may not touch her," the figure said, indicating Kaimana. It sounded almost as if the words were sung, somehow accompanied by an invisible choir, hiding somewhere in the distance. "That girl belongs to me."

Kaimana's eyes widened as she realised the identity of the newcomer, but it was Eloni who first croaked the goddess' name.

"Laka."

The goddess of performance drifted across the courtyard towards them. Nakoa's men, now seeming oddly sober, clutched their weapons, trying to show their master that they did not fear the presence of another deity. Kaimana briefly took at glance at the troupe, and was pleased to see a look of relief on Aka's face, and genuine glee on the faces of all the dancers.

Behind Laka, doing his best to lurk in the shadows, was a smaller figure who was instantly recognisable to Kaimana.

Yam! Kaimana grinned at the sight of the harvest god. *They heard me. They heard my prayers.*

Yam's eyes met hers, and he gave a weak grin in response, but then diverted his attention back to his siblings. Help had arrived, but if the gods came to blows over Kaimana, no mortals on the island – possibly on the entire Atoll – would be safe.

Kaimana's spark glowed brightly inside, reaching out to Laka with open arms, recognising its master.

"Sister," Nakoa eventually greeted the goddess when she reached him. "You overextend yourself. I claim this girl as a trophy of war."

"You may not," Laka sang to her fellow god, and she lowered her clay face down to Kaimana to look at her.

Kaimana was surprised at how unnerved she was by the

goddess' attention. The unmoving features of Laka's face highlighted how inhuman she was, and one of Laka's black folds of fabric ran down Kaimana's cheek. Kaimana shuddered as she realised that this was as close as the goddess could come to touching her.

"You heard my prayer," was all Kaimana could say to her goddess.

Laka drew her face back and cocked her head. She was confused.

Yam coughed and stepped forward, sheepishly. "You see, it's been a while since any mortals reached out to me for anything that didn't concern earth, water or sun. Or shit, I guess. They pray a lot to me about the best shit to put on their crops. Anyway, what's important is that your voice stood out like a rooster crow. Thought my sister might be interested, and turns out she was."

Kaimana gave Yam a smile of thanks, causing the small god to blush, then roll his eyes and turn to inspect the crowds behind him.

Laka, almost as if she was growing bored of the exchange, turned back to Nakoa. "I have given this girl a gift, something dear to me. You cannot take that from me. I will not let you."

"And if I refuse?" Nakoa growled, his sword now lowered but his stance still speaking aggression. "If I take this girl's life now, take what is due to me, should I fear you?"

Laka raised herself until she was face to face with Nakoa again. For a moment, there was silence as the two gods regarded each other.

"You should fear me, Nakoa the *kupua*. And you should also fear my sister, Leinani, who for some reason also seems to have a vested interest in the song this girl carries inside her."

At the mention of the volcano goddess' name, Nakoa's eyebrows furrowed and he bared his teeth.

"Nobody thinks to mention me as a threat? Nope? Just asking..." Yam grumbled, but neither of his siblings paid him heed.

After another few heartbeats, Nakoa grunted, "Fine. She is yours, then."

Kaimana stiffened. *Really? That's it? We're free?* She sat up, then stood and could not help the grin that spread across her face. Then, however, she glanced at Yam. He was looking at her grimly. Something was wrong.

Laka, standing beside her, allowed several strips of fabric to lie across Kaimana's shoulder. "The song inside this girl will last forever, for longer than any mountain or beach created by our sister." At these words, Kaimana could feel her spark urging Kaimana to start singing. She could not help her fingers making their way to her ocarina hanging from her belt, thankfully unharmed by the recent violence. She did not care that they were in the war god's temple, that she had just escaped death - she wanted to play to please Laka, and she wanted to do so now.

"The taniwha, of course, will die," Nakoa said, moving towards Rakau.

"Of course," Laka answered, stepping aside to allow her brother past. "I have no claim on him, and his end will close this story. I above all appreciate the need to finish these things."

Kaimana's mouth opened, and she looked at Yam again. *He knew. That was why he was so serious.*

Kaimana threw herself at her goddess' feet. "Wait, what? Laka - no."

Again, the goddess lowered her clay mask to gaze at Kaimana with her lifeless eyes. Laka's strips of fabric wove themselves gently around Kaimana's shoulders. "It must be this way, child of mine. The taniwha belongs to the war god by way of conquest. Indeed, he is correct - even if I did want to save the beast, it would not be within my power to do so, and no others out there - certainly not my older sister - would protest Nakoa's claim over this creature."

Tears began to form in Kaimana's eyes, and she looked over to Rakau, lying with his eyes closed, the war god standing beside him now. Slits of green opened to look at Kaimana, and from beneath his heavy bindings, Rakau gave a weak smile. She knew he would be happy now that she was safe, but that gave Kaimana little consolation. If Rakau died now, she would carry this pain for the rest of her life.

Her spark began to rumble. This was different from the buzzing it had done before to attract her attention, it was more urgent. Kaimana had no more practising to do. Their song was ready, her spark was anxious to let the rest of the world hear it.

Yet, for some reason, the spark was no longer thinking about the song. It was reaching out to Rakau, vibrating in anger, filling with rage at the sense of betrayal that it shared with Kaimana.

"Child, I know this causes you pain," Laka sang. "Do not think I am immune to your feelings. As artists, this pain is our lifeblood.

Think of how that song within you has been shaped by your trials over the past weeks. This moment - the death of your friend and your failure to save him - is crucial for you. This final end to your story will seal the memory of your song. Kaimana - all in the Atoll will know your name. Forever. Now, take your ocarina and prepare to play."

Shaking, Kaimana took her instrument from her belt and brought it to her lips. A few steps away, Nakoa raised his toothed blade and grinned at the helpless taniwha beneath him. Inside her, Kaimana felt the spark straining, willing her into action.

It took a few seconds for Kaimana to realise that her spark was not asking her to play any music.

Save him, it said to Kaimana, in a voice as clear as if the spark was standing next to her.

"Now I shall have my vengeance," Nakoa said, unaware of the conflict within the young woman standing behind him.

Save Rakau, the spark said again. *Save our friend.*

You will die, Kaimana thought. *We both will. We cannot hope to defeat a god.*

I know, her spark sang back, and Kaimana could hear the self-pity in that lost tune, her own heart filling with pride at the bravery the spark was finally showing. *But I do not want him to die without trying. He means too much to me now.*

Kaimana felt Laka's black fingers thread around her, squeezing her shoulders, willing her to begin to play, willing her to let the world hear the gift that the goddess had given her.

She brought her ocarina to her lips and took a deep breath. For the final time, her spark flared up, and the amber in her eyes flowed down her face, mixed with her instrument and her fingers, causing them to glow with the fire of creation.

Nakoa bellowed in triumph as he swung his *Kiribati* down to sever the taniwha's neck.

And then Kaimana was there in front of him, holding her simple clay ocarina above her head, using it to intercept the war god's blow.

The ocarina shattered as the blade hit it, and there was an explosion of amber light and a child-like scream heard by all as Kaimana's song died.

All in the courtyard took a second to blink the bright light from their eyes, stunned into silence. A curious scene greeted them when they regained their sight. The war god stood puzzled, his *Kiribati* now only a pommel and a hilt. The blade of his weapon mingled with the clay of the ocarina on the floor, both broken into tiny pieces. Kaimana remained standing, with her head bowed and empty hands still outstretched to intercept Nakoa's blow. All around them, small orange wisps of flame floated in the air, the remnants of Kaimana's dead song.

"What have you done?" both Laka and Nakoa said at the same time, and the young ocarina player raised her head to look at them both with grave determination, eyes wet at the loss of her spark.

Then, a rope snapped.

The amber flames of Kaimana's dead song settled onto the skin of the wounded taniwha, and they glowed brightly for a moment before disappearing, fading into Rakau's body.

Another rope snapped, and Rakau raised his head. A low rumble began from his throat as he fixed the war god with a hunter's glare.

The taniwha rose to all fours, the rest of his bindings snapping effortlessly. Heart swelling, fit to burst, Kaimana grinned to see her friend back and ran to him, letting her hand rest on his side.

Then she looked at the war god. "Go get him," she told her taniwha.

With a roar, Rakau leapt at Nakoa.

Kaimana should have been worried for her friend. She knew that Nakoa was much more powerful than a single taniwha. But, Nakoa was weaponless, he was surprised, and the death cry of Kaimana's song had given them both strength through courage.

We will win this. We will be free.

Rakau's teeth aimed for Nakoa's head, and he would have swallowed him entirely in his first bite if the war god had not grabbed the taniwha's jaws with both hands, forcing them wide open, wrestling Rakau down to the floor. A splintering of wood sounded from Rakau as he strained against the god's strength, and he roared in frustration and defiance at his would-be executioner.

At that moment, Kaimana caught sight of Laka, lurking in the shadows behind Nakoa's throne, and her excitement disappeared.

There is more than one god here. I can't imagine Laka is all that pleased about the loss of the song.

Laka's black ribbons rippled, as if she was about to intervene, but then a shock of green wrapped itself around the goddess of performance, causing her to stop and look at it in confusion. The green shoot continued to grow, becoming thicker and wrapping itself around Laka, binding her to the spot. Kaimana cheered when she spotted Yam, fingers kneading the dirt close by, a nervous grin focussing on his sister.

"I imagine Mother might have a thing or two to say about this, don't you?"

A similar wall of green began to erupt at the feet of Nakoa's followers, pulling back the multitudes who stepped forward with knives and clubs towards Rakau and Nakoa, hoping to intervene on behalf of their god. Yam did not allow them to pass, cocooning them in greenery, using the front line of warriors as a barrier against those behind.

In the middle of this wall, combat between god and taniwha continued. Nakoa threw Rakau back and stood crouched with fists clenched, waiting for the monster to strike again. Rakau pounced, and Nakoa leapt too, faster than the taniwha and he intercepted the monster above the temple floor, his fist impacting on Rakau's side with a thunderclap, sending Rakau flying across the temple, demolishing Yam's wall of warriors.

A streak of pain across her cheek jolted Kaimana away from the combat. She turned just in time to dodge another knife thrust, but lost her footing doing so, landing on her bottom in the dirt. Above her, eyes wild and hungry, stood Eloni, her knife-hand outstretched and shaking.

"I have you now, bitch," Eloni spat, her now-gravelly voice betraying the damage Kaimana's teeth had done to her throat.

In response, heart thumping, Kaimana kicked at her *kahuna's* legs, sending the flute player tumbling to the ground in a string of curses. Kaimana turned, got up and ran from Eloni, raising her eyes just in time to see Nakoa marching towards Yam.

Rakau seemingly forgotten, the war god now had a sword in his hand, and had it raised to strike at his smaller brother. Sweat was pouring from Yam's face, his eyes locked on his brother, but his fingers continued to knead the spell that kept Laka and the remaining warriors bound in green roots.

"I never liked you," Yam addressed Nakoa, voice noticeably shaking. "Couldn't keep your hands off my sister. How would you like it if I found a nice piggy and-"

Nakoa silenced the small god by slicing him across the chest, opening him up. Yam crumpled as Kaimana's head began to spin, the exhaustion and trials of the last few days threatening to overcome her.

"No!" she shouted at the sight of the harvest god lying in his own blood.

All around, Yam's shoots began to unravel, releasing those he had imprisoned, rushing instead to cradle Yam himself, doing what they could to close his wound. Cries of relief and indignation arose from the released warriors, but Kaimana was more concerned about how angry Laka was going to be now that she was free.

A snarl of fury warned Kaimana that Eloni had recovered, and was approaching her again with her knife, swinging it wildly. Despite this immediate danger, Kaimana wheeled around to find Laka, to see where the goddess of performance was, and to see what form her vengeance would take.

Kaimana's eyes narrowed when she realised Laka was not looking at her, nor at Rakau and Nakoa grappling with each other in the middle of the courtyard. The goddess was staring at the performance troupe on the stage.

With Eloni almost upon her, Kaimana turned around to look at the troupe, and gasped.

They were all sparking. Every single one of them.

Eyes wide with wonder, Kaimana looked at her former companions. Aka stood there, dumbstruck, holding his palms close to his face, trying to catch more glimpses of the bursts of orange. The dancing girls were in a circle together, arms locked on each other's shoulders, screaming with delight each time an amber spark burst from their faces. Poli and Tokoni stared into each other's eyes, and then kissed when they both sparked together. Old Rawiri had sat down on the stage, crying, with young Mahina close by. It was the first time Kaimana had seen the little boy smile.

A cry from behind warned Kaimana that Eloni was in striking distance, and she turned to face her teacher. Eloni was on her knees in front of Kaimana, her hands clutched to her face, sparks forcing their way through her fingers.

Kaimana turned back to look at Laka, but the goddess had vanished.

Kaimana smiled.

It is us. It is me - they're sparking because of me. How could they not be inspired, witnessing all of this? Three gods, one monster, a girl giving up her dream to save her friend.

She put her hand on Eloni's shoulder. Her former teacher looked up at her with eyes on fire, mouth hanging open in shock, tears of joy flowing freely down her face.

"Enjoy this gift," Kaimana whispered sincerely to Eloni. "Play songs of me."

Eloni moaned, and Kaimana could not tell if it was a sound of joy, or of despair.

I will go down in history, they will remember me on the Atoll, but not because of the songs I play and sing. They will sing about me. About me, and my friend the monster.

Kaimana turned and inhaled deeply, fixing her attention on Rakau and Nakoa, readying herself to move.

They were struggling on the dirt in front of her, and by now Nakoa's men had learnt to give the combatants a wide berth. A few bodies of warriors lay trampled underneath the warring titans, all that remained of the men who were too stupid or too brave to know that such a combat is not meant for mortals to intervene in.

Despite his size, common sense dictated that Rakau could not win this fight. The power of a god outweighs the power of a taniwha ten times over. But Rakau's normally green eyes flared amber now, inspired by the dead spark, and that gave Kaimana hope.

Finish this, Rakau. Let's leave together.

The taniwha batted at Nakoa, but the war god caught Rakau's paw effortlessly, gripping it with both hands. The god grinned and started to pry Rakau's paw apart, the sound of ripping timber reverberating throughout the courtyard. Rakau howled in pain and batted at the god with his free limb, bloodying Nakoa's face, but not loosening his ruining grip.

The tearing of wood continued, growing louder.

Rakau's beats upon Nakoa's face became more frantic, full of rage and pain. Kaimana knew her friend was losing himself, that Nakoa's torture was stopping him from thinking about what he was doing, was forcing him to act like a wounded animal.

She felt the fingertips of despair creep up her spine, threatening to take her by the throat. Not letting herself be overcome, Kaimana looked around and spotted Eloni's jade knife, now forgotten on the courtyard floor beside her.

Kaimana looked again at the war god just steps away, taking glee at the pain he was inflicting upon her friend.

Bad things come to mortals who interfere in the affairs of the gods.

Kaimana paused only for a moment. *Let the bad things come. I've got a taniwha to help see them off.*

She ran forward, knife held above her head, and threw herself at Nakoa's leg, driving the blade as hard as she could into his flesh.

It was a shallow cut, and the war god kicked back against her, throwing Kaimana hard to the ground once again. The god turned to look at her, nostrils flared, lips curled in anger.

"You dare?" he bellowed at her.

Kaimana's blood rushed around her body, her breath quickened. She was excited. Elated.

"Yes, we dare."

Rakau's jaws clamped down onto Nakoa's shoulder, causing the god to scream in pain. The taniwha shook the war god briefly, then threw him to the dirt. Nakoa's shoulder was red now, the blood from his wound seeping into and staining his woven armour. The god tried to lift himself up, but found that his arm would not move anymore, and collapsed back down. Rakau lowered his head and growled at Nakoa, readying himself for the kill. Kaimana noticed the multitude of nearby warriors drawing their blades.

She ran to her friend's lowered head, and jumped up onto him, sitting on his neck.

"Rakau, we're done here. Let's go."

The taniwha stopped growling and turned his head to the hole in the temple wall he had caused some weeks ago. With a run and a bound, the taniwha and the ocarina player disappeared into the night.

THE
TANIWHA GIRL

A tale from the Crescent Atoll

Nyree had gone to the beach to kill herself.

She had stolen a black potion from the medicine woman's hut, and knew it would do the job. Her death would have been quick and quiet, if not for the young woman Nyree spied when she reached the beach.

The girl was a stranger, that much was clear. She looked wilder than other women from the island, with hair that needed combing, a crooked nose that seemed to have been broken and then set badly, and a bare shoulder on which Nyree could see puckered and scarred skin. The woman was resting against a fallen tree that had been washed up onto the beach, and was playing music on a small, unadorned ocarina.

The music the stranger was playing was beautiful, haunting, and somehow incomplete.

Nyree could not help herself - she walked up to the stranger, and the woman stopped playing at her approach.

"That was beautiful," Nyree said, still wary of this new face.

The stranger smiled, somewhat sadly. "Thanks."

"Does playing always make you sad?" Nyree asked.

The stranger looked surprised for a second, then gave a laugh. "It depends what I'm playing. What about you? Does hearing music always make you sad?"

Nyree could not help herself. At that question, she burst into tears. The ocarina player quickly rose to her feet and comforted the islander.

"What's wrong?" the stranger asked.

Nyree shook her head, unable to speak through her sobs. The ocarina player led her to sit on the sand with her back against the giant log. Nyree noted how much the log had been chipped at and marked by the elements, but had no more time to think of this because of the new face that arrived on the beach from the village.

"Nyree! Do not do it!"

It was Heeni, Nyree's best friend. At the sight of the pretty girl, Nyree's grieving face turned into a sneer.

"It's her. She's the one who broke my heart."

Heeni reached her friend, quickly nodded her head to acknowledge the stranger on the beach, and then fell on her knees, begging. "Please, do not kill yourself, Nyree."

The ocarina player was surprised. "Is this true? You came here to die?"

"Yes," Nyree spat, angry eyes still locked on Heeni. "She has taken everything from me, I have nothing left to live for."

The ocarina player's eyes narrowed. "What's happened?"

"My betrothed," Nyree said. "The man I have loved since I was a little girl, we were to be married. She seduced him and stole him away from me."

It was now Heeni's turn to cry. "Please forgive me, Nyree. It was he who seduced me, and I was too weak to resist. I did not want to drive you to this."

The ocarina player rolled her eyes and shook her head. "You really were planning on killing yourself because of a man?"

Nyree said nothing, but continued to lock her hateful gaze on her former friend.

"You two were friends once, right?" the stranger asked.

Heeni nodded. "Best friends, yes. That's why I would never want to hurt her."

The ocarina player grinned. "Best friends." She stroked the side of the fallen tree. "Listen, I don't know much about men, but I've been learning a lot about friends." She stood up, putting her unpainted ocarina into a pouch at her waist.

"The friendship you have, it is worth everything."

The woman pointed at Heeni. "You hurt your friend. You did something really stupid. That was bad, and you should have warned her when you knew something was wrong, but now you're asking for forgiveness."

She turned to Nyree. "That silly man isn't worth your life. He certainly isn't worth losing her, either. Listen to your friend. I know she hurt you, but listen to her, remember all the good things about having her in your life, and never let that go again."

Nyree stood up, angry now. "How dare you. What makes you think you know my pain? What gives you the right to talk to me in this way?"

The ocarina player gave a thin grin. "I've been around, seen a thing or two. Learnt some lessons. Stick with your friend, no matter what. Keep her close and all your other troubles will wash away with the tide. You'll make each other happy."

The stranger slapped the side of the fallen log. "I think it's time we were leaving."

The log began to shake. Nyree and Heeni both gave screams, instinctively held each other's hands and backed away from the vibrations.

The log pulled itself out of the sand, and turned to look at the two girls with its green eyes. Then it turned to the ocarina player and smiled.

Together, the ocarina player and the taniwha waded into the sea, and Nyree and Heeni watched as the young woman got onto the monster's back.

"You know who that is?" Nyree whispered to her friend, otherwise rigid with fear. "That's Kaimana, the Taniwha Girl."

"I know," Heeni whispered back. She squeezed her friend's hand, and Nyree squeezed it back. "Thank Leinani, we're lucky to be alive."

They watched Kaimana ride her taniwha towards the horizon.

On her friend's back, the young woman was smiling, content, looking forward to whatever came next.

A WORD FROM THE AUTHOR

The seeds for *Where the Waters Turn Black* were sown when I was a much younger man. In my student days I spent a summer in New Zealand, and it was as I made my way around Wellington's Te Papa museum that my eyes were opened to a rich mythological culture that was nothing like any stories I had read before, with bickering gods and outlandish imagery. During the same trip, the image of Kaimana and her monster began to form in my mind. She didn't have a name yet (in fact, she began life as a very young girl, not unlike the toddler we met at the opening of the story), and Rakau was simply a menacing, formless shadow lurking in the waves beneath her, but I've been nursing the image of a girl and her huge, horrifying friend travelling around Polynesian islands for over a decade. The Yarnsworld seemed like a perfect home for her.

Much like the folktales in *They Mostly Come Out At Night*, the stories in this book are a mix between retellings of real traditional tales, and my own work doing its best to ape their style. Much like in the previous book, the more unusual stories tend to be the real ones, such as *The Disobedient Daughter*, which is actually a straight-up retelling of a New Zealand newspaper report from the 1870s. A newspaper report, not a fairytale book. The concept of taniwha protecting the land remains important for many Maori today.

I'll make individual thankyous elsewhere, but I just want to offer up a heartfelt 'cheers' to all of the support I've received from readers of *They Mostly Come Out At Night*. Writing can be a lonely pursuit, and it is extremely gratifying when readers get in touch to let me know they've enjoyed my work. When my first book was released, I felt like one man sitting in a dark room, clicking a publish button and hoping. This time around, there feels like a bit more weight surrounding this release. Fellow authors wishing me well, some amazing bloggers eager to get a peek, and - unexpectedly, but most, most welcome – some actual, real life readers who want to find out where the Yarnsworld stories go next.

As before, the best way to stay in touch with me is to sign up for my newsletter. I send messages once or twice a month with updates on my writing and bits and pieces from the wider world of fantasy fandom. Newsletter readers also have access to a number of exclusive Yarnsworld tales, including *The Further Adventures of Yam*, which continues Yam's story after the events in *Where the Waters Turn Black*.

Head to www.benedictpatrick.com to get your free stories and to stay in touch.

Take care, and I'll see you in 2017 for the next Yarnsworld novel, *Those Brave, Foolish Souls from the City of Swords*.

Benedict

The standalone fantasy book that readers are calling a delightfully weird, dark fairytale.

The villagers of the forest seal themselves in their cellars at night, whispering folktales to each other about the monsters that prey on them in the dark. Only the Magpie King, their shadowy, unseen protector, can keep them safe.

However, when an outcast called Lonan begins to dream of the Magpie King's defeat at the hands of inhuman invaders, this young man must do what he can to protect his village. He is the only person who can keep his loved ones from being stolen away after dark, and to do so he will have to convince them to trust him again.

They Mostly Come Out At Night is the first novel from Benedict Patrick's Yarnsworld series. Straddling the line between fantasy and folklore, this book is perfect for fans of the darker Brothers Grimm stories.

Start reading today to discover this epic tale of dreams, fables and monsters!

Made in the USA
Columbia, SC
14 April 2021